To my amazing wife, Mary – sometimes we need someone else to believe in us before we really believe in ourselves. None of this would have happened without your unfailing belief and support.

THE SCARECROW

THE NOLAN CORMAC FILES

P.F. FORD

PROLOGUE

March 22nd, 2024 13:00

Forty-four years old, six feet tall, and of medium build, the man with blue eyes and greying brown hair blended into the background as he approached the restaurant—a fact he welcomed. As soon as he pushed open the door, he spotted his contact, sitting alone at a table, working his way through an unappetising-looking salad. Nolan Cormac walked up to the table, pulled out a chair, and sat down opposite him.

The man at the table glanced up, scanned the rest of the restaurant, and then returned to his salad. Cormac was impressed. Superintendent Barry Eagan was one of the youngest officers to reach the rank of superintendent and had a reputation for using other officers as the rungs in his rapid ascent up the ladder, but he was obviously a cool customer who wasn't easily ruffled.

Eagan stared at Cormac. 'I'm sorry. Do I know you?'

'My name's Nolan Cormac. I've been trying to speak to you for weeks, but you won't take my calls, and you seem to have blocked my emails. I've written three letters, the last of which was two weeks ago, but you haven't replied to them either, so I thought I'd come and find you.'

Eagan pondered as he chewed his salad, then swallowed. He reminded Cormac of a lizard.

'Ah, yes, Cormac. I remember. You've become my stalker now, have you?'

Cormac gave the comment the contempt he thought it deserved. Eagan acknowledged the look.

'You're right,' he said. 'You've done nothing to deserve that comment. Actually, I did read your first letter. You're from the Midlands drug squad, and you're asking me to grant you a transfer into my team even though you're suspended from duty and under investigation by Professional Standards.'

'That's right, I did say that,' said Cormac.

'Suspensions are unusual,' said Eagan.

'If you've read my letter, you'll know the whole situation is unusual.'

'The thing is, Cormac, if I haven't replied to your letter, and I won't take your calls, that should tell you all you need to know. Surely you can see you're a poisoned chalice. Why would you expect me to take a risk like that?'

Eagan shovelled another forkful of salad into his mouth.

'My situation has changed since I wrote the first letter,' said Cormac. 'That's why I've not given up trying to contact you.'

Eagan stared impassively at Cormac as he chewed his food. This time, he washed it down with a mouthful of water before he spoke.

'Changed in what way?'

'I've been cleared of all charges.'

Eagan couldn't hide his surprise.

'The investigation was over a colleague who was wounded in a shoot-out, is that right?'

'I'd hardly call it a shoot-out,' said Cormac. 'They had guns; all we had was piss-poor intelligence that assured us there wouldn't be any. It's a miracle no one was killed.'

'I thought it was assumed drugs and guns almost always go together these days,' said Eagan.

'Yes, exactly,' said Cormac. 'The whole thing was highly irregular, but we were told it would be two small-time local dealers, and there would be no weapons. Turns out it was organised crime armed to the teeth with automatic weapons.'

'And the bad intelligence? Where did that come from?'

'Not from anyone on my team,' said Cormac. 'We were just following orders from above. I got the blame as lead officer on the raid, but the incompetence was a couple of levels above me, not that anyone there wants to hear about it.'

'If you've been cleared, why not stay in your old job?'

'And be set up as target practice again? I don't think so, do you?'

'You think you were set up?'

'I think it's a distinct possibility,' said Cormac.

'That's a serious accusation to make, unless you have proof.'

'I'm not accusing anyone. I admit I have my suspicions but, unfortunately, I don't have proof. But if, as I suspect, I do have a target on my back, I'm better off out of it.'

Eagan managed a half-hearted smile. 'Look, I can understand why you might want a change of scenery, but I don't run the drug squad locally, and as far as I know, they're not looking for anyone.'

He shovelled another forkful of salad into his mouth and began chewing again.

'But I don't want to join the drug squad,' said Cormac. 'I'm trying to get away from all that. I want to make a clean start.'

Eagan swallowed and grimaced. 'But is it really necessary to move after the investigation cleared you? Can't you get a transfer out of the drug squad where you are?'

'Professional Standards in the Midlands don't like to be proven wrong. Once they get their teeth into something, even if they can't make it stick, they're reluctant to let go.'

'And yet they haven't found anything?' asked Eagan.

'Of course not. There's nothing to find,' said Cormac. 'I admit I've sailed close to the wind once or twice, but I'm sure you didn't get where you are by playing nice all the time.'

Eagan stared impassively at Cormac as he chewed more salad and washed it down with another mouthful of water.

'Look, I've got nothing against people wanting a transfer, but I'm a busy man without enough hours in the day. That means I don't have the time to personally do background checks so I can decide if I should bring someone into my team.'

'The word is you've been brought in to clean the place up,' said Cormac.

Eagan's expression remained impassive, but for a split second, his eyes said otherwise. It was enough to tell Cormac his information was correct.

'I don't know where you heard that,' said Eagan. 'The truth is I was just in the right place at the right time to hear about the position. I applied, and I was accepted.'

'You were fast-tracked from university ten years ago, and you've made a name for yourself as you've zoomed up the ladder,' said Cormac. 'You were headhunted for this job specifically because you have a thick skin and ice in your veins.'

For the first time, Eagan allowed a genuine smile to flit across his face, as though Cormac had paid him a huge compliment.

'That's very flattering, but don't you think I'd be a bit young for such a job?'

'Being young means you're less likely to have bad habits of your own and, despite your youth, you already have a reputation for being ruthless,' said Cormac. 'The word is Windover needs cleaning up, and they brought in an outsider for obvious reasons.'

Eagan considered as he chewed the last mouthful of salad. Then he set his knife and fork neatly on his plate and pushed it away.

'Even if what you said was correct,' he replied, 'what business is it of yours?'

'The thing is, I can help you with that. I hate bent coppers, and I want to join your team,' said Cormac.

'Yes, and, as I said, I—'

'You don't have time to check people out because you're too busy catching bent coppers,' finished Cormac. 'And yet I get the feeling you know a lot more about me than you're letting on.'

'I'll admit I had someone take a look at your record.'

'So, what did they find?' asked Cormac.

Eagan motioned to Cormac to be quiet while the waiter collected his empty plate. He waited until the waiter had gone before he spoke again.

'You worked in this area until seven years ago, and then you left to become a private investigator. Five years ago, you applied to rejoin in the Midlands, where you joined the drug squad. While you were here, you had a favourable conviction rate—'

'Which you'll see I've maintained if you check my record in the Midlands.'

Eagan nodded to acknowledge Cormac's information. 'Yes, you have. However, this latest suspension isn't your first. There was a previous case in which you were found guilty of punching a colleague. Assaulting colleagues is not a habit I like my officers to have.'

'It's not a habit; it was a one-off that happened a long time ago when I was relatively new, and there were mitigating circumstances. There was a queue of people wanting to punch the guy; I just happened to be the first one to do it. And, as you will also know, I spent six months back in uniform because of that incident. I learnt my lesson, and I've never done anything like it since.'

Eagan's expression indicated he was also aware of these facts.

'Didn't you also have a personal issue around the time you moved away?'

'I had a long-term girlfriend who left me. I took it badly.'

'I'm sorry about that, but I don't see how—'

'We were on holiday in Thailand. We were even talking about getting married while we were there, but after a couple of days, she suddenly disappeared.'

'What do you mean, she disappeared?'

'The Thai police say she ran away with someone.'

Eagan considered for a moment. 'Did she pack a bag?'

'Well, yeah, she did, but—'

'What about her ID, credit cards, etc.?'

'Yes, they disappeared too, but—'

'Was there any evidence to suggest she was abducted?'

'Not according to the Thai police.'

'And was there any?'

Cormac sighed. 'No, not if I'm being honest,' he said reluctantly.

'Then you can hardly blame the Thai police for reaching their conclusion, can you? I'm sorry, but this sort of thing happens. The fact that she didn't tell you she was going to run off with someone else is hardly a surprise, and it certainly doesn't make it a major conspiracy.'

Cormac stared intently into Eagan's eyes.

'Yes, I know all that, and in the end, I did accept that she had left me,' he said testily. 'But the thing is, while I was still in Thailand, I started asking my own questions. Within 48 hours, some wonk from the British Embassy arranged for me to be deported.'

'You were deported from Thailand?'

'That's not what they called it officially, of course. They said it was compassionate repatriation, or some such crap, but I believe the reality is I was making waves and someone wanted me out of the way...'

Eagan's eyes seemed to light up as he became more interested in the story.

'So, you're saying someone had you removed from the country because you were asking too many questions?'

'That's precisely what I'm saying,' said Cormac. 'Now, I'm no expert, but that's not something you or I could arrange at a moment's notice, is it?'

'It's certainly way above my pay grade,' said Eagan.

'Exactly,' said Cormac.

Eagan took another sip of water and considered for a few moments. 'It's an interesting theory to bring to the table, but it sounds a bit vague and pie-in-the-sky to me. And I'm not sure we need anyone here working to a personal agenda.'

Cormac said nothing. Although Eagan sounded nega-
tive, he sensed that he was also tempted by the conspiracy
idea.

For his part, Eagan suspected Cormac could prove to be
a liability but, on the other hand, if there was any truth in
what he was saying, then he could prove to be really useful
to a man with ambition. 'So, hypothetically, you want me to
green-light your transfer to my team, and in return, you're
going to help catch bent coppers and perhaps land a big fish,
too. Is that right?'

'I'm not promising anything, but that's the gist of it,
yeah.'

'But why come back to Windover?'

'I moved away from here because I needed a new challenge to help me get over my girlfriend leaving. And it
worked; I'm well over her. But after everything that has
happened in the Midlands, it seems like the right time to
come back.'

'So, why would you do this for me?'

'You'll accept my transfer, then?'

'I used the word "hypothetically" for a good reason,'
emphasised Eagan.

'I wouldn't be doing it for you,' said Cormac. 'I want a
change of scenery, and you want to reach the top of the
ladder. Quid pro quo, right?'

Eagan studied Cormac's face as he tried to determine if
the risk would be worth it.

'What rank are you?' he asked.

'I was a Detective Inspector, but after the shooting
fiasco, I've been demoted to DS.'

'That seems odd if you've been cleared of all charges—'

Eagan held up his hand again as the waiter brought over

his dessert, nodding for Cormac to continue once the waiter had moved away to attend to another table.

'During the investigation, Professional Standards couldn't find anything they could use against me. They didn't have grounds to fire me, but to justify their existence, they had to do something, so they decided the way the raid went down suggests I'm reckless. Demotion was deemed an appropriate punishment to teach me a lesson.

'I'm not quite sure how that can be right when I was just following orders, but during the inquiry, I revealed a few home truths that seem to have made one or two people feel uncomfortable. I'm sure you can draw your own conclusions as to the real reason I was demoted.'

Eagan made a face that suggested he didn't exactly disagree. 'And how do you feel about that?' he asked.

'As I did nothing wrong, how do you think I feel? I want my rank back.'

'I'm not sure I'd be able to do anything about that straight away,' said Eagan.

'Yes, I understand that, but you can see why I want a transfer out of there so badly,' said Cormac. 'The question is, will you help me?'

'I'll think about it,' said Eagan. 'I need to check your record before I commit to anything.'

'Didn't you say you already had someone check me out?' said Cormac. 'Surely, if you have enough trust in this person to look into it, you must trust their opinion.'

Eagan managed a hint of a smile. "Touché,' he said. He pulled a small notebook from his jacket pocket and wrote 'DS/DI Nolan Cormac' in neat handwriting, followed by the word 'check,' which he underlined twice. He then stared expectantly at Cormac, who completely missed the hint.

'I've allowed you to interrupt my lunch,' said Eagan. 'But now, if you don't mind, I'd like to eat my dessert in peace.'

'Oh, right, sorry,' Cormac replied.

'I'll be in touch if I decide to recommend your transfer.'

'Do you want my number?'

'That won't be necessary,' Eagan said, raising a spoonful of dessert to his mouth. 'I seem to recall it was in the last letter.'

He filled his mouth and began to chew, ignoring Cormac as he walked away.

CHAPTER 1

Detective Sergeant Nolan Cormac gripped his mobile phone tightly and groaned. It was just after 10 p.m. and he was looking forward to his dinner.

'A car on fire?' he repeated. 'On the old gasworks site? Isn't that a job for uniforms?'

'Yes,' came the weary reply. 'Normally, it would be, but they're all dealing with a massive brawl going on in the town centre, so unless you want to swap places with one of them, you're all I've got spare right now.'

'What about the Fire Service?'

'They're on their way but have requested we attend as well.'

'Oh, come on, Rob,' Cormac appealed to the harassed voice. 'I've just collected my dinner from the takeaway.'

'My name is Sergeant Gleeson,' snapped the voice. 'And you can count yourself bloody lucky you have time to visit the takeaway. Didn't you volunteer to work nights this week?'

'Well, yes, but I—'

'If you volunteered, I don't understand why you're complaining. I'm told Superintendent Eagan believes we should be one big happy team. He also says there's no I in team, yet all I can hear from you is I, I, I. So how about, just to please Eagan, you get your arse in gear, stop complaining, become one of the team, and do your bloody job!'

The line went dead, and, not for the first time since he had moved to Windover, Cormac was left wondering why on earth he'd bothered. And how did Gleeson's surly attitude fit in with Eagan's idea of 'one big happy team'? Just because his wife had left him, there was no need to take it out on everyone else, was there?

Cormac was annoyed that Superintendent Eagan had finally granted his transfer request and then lumbered him with a temporary appointment as bagman to Detective Chief Inspector Driver, as Driver's usual assistant, DS Michaels, was sick. This, in itself, wasn't a problem, but Driver didn't seem to trust Cormac to do his job, which was both irritating and disconcerting.

On his good days, Driver could be a joy, but so far, for the most part, Cormac had found himself sorting files, which he considered a trivial, time-wasting job. Nevertheless, he gritted his teeth and refused to be put off. He had transferred to Windover for a reason, and nothing was going to deflect him from that. Despite his best efforts, all Driver had accomplished so far was to delay him, making him even more determined.

Cormac got in his car and pulled away, swearing and grumbling his way to the roundabout, all the way around it, and then back in the opposite direction towards the scene of the reported fire. There was no doubt his dinner was going to be cold before he could eat it, and if it was just because of some stupid kids having a laugh, he would be seriously unimpressed.

But as he drove, his irritation subsided, and Cormac admitted to himself that there was no denying this particular cloud did, at least, have a silver lining. Driver considered working nights beneath his dignity, so volunteering to fill in for a sick colleague on the night shift provided Cormac with much-needed relief from his new boss.

The old gasworks site was on the edge of town, beyond an industrial area littered with disused and derelict buildings that had clearly seen better days. He was surprised to see flashing blue lights beyond the trading estate, and as he pulled up to the scene, he could see the fire crew had the fire under control.

Under the fire crew's floodlights, the charred wreckage released steam and black smoke that spiralled lazily skywards. Looking at the damage to the vehicle, Cormac guessed that the fire had started in the engine compartment and spread to the back.

As he pulled up and wound down his window, a white-helmeted crew manager approached. 'I must ask you to keep back while we deal with the fire.'

'DS Cormac,' he said, emerging from the car and showing his warrant card.

'We rarely get detectives first on scene.'

'Yeah, tell me about it,' said Cormac. 'Everyone else is attending a massive punch-up in town. I was passing nearby and got handed the short straw. Is there anything for me to do?'

'It's a bit early to tell, but usually when we attend a burning car on a site like this, it's been started deliberately, often by kids. So far, there's no reason to think this one will be any different.'

'In that case, if it's all right with you, I'm going to sit in my car and eat my takeaway before it gets cold,' said Cormac.

'You carry on, mate. We've got it under control and it's more or less out. We'll give it another ten minutes for dampening down, and with any luck, we'll be on the way back for our own dinners.'

Cormac got back in his car and rubbed his hands together. He hadn't had a Chinese takeaway in ages, and he was really looking forward to it. Just the thought of sweet and sour chicken was making his mouth water. He reached for the takeaway bag on the passenger seat, lifted it across to his lap, and peered inside.

Just as he reached in for the first carton, he heard an exclamation from the direction of the burnt car. Turning his head to the right, he saw that the fire crew had stepped back from the car, and the crew manager was shouting at him. At first, Cormac couldn't make out all the words, but there was something frantic about the way they were waving at him.

'Un-bloody-believable,' muttered Cormac as he put the dinner bag back on the passenger seat. 'What's all the bloody fuss about now? How is a guy supposed to eat his dinner with all this going on?'

He climbed out of the car and began walking, then caught a faint whiff of a smell he recognised, and now he knew what all the fuss was about. His years of training kicked in, and all thoughts of dinner vanished as he rushed towards the charred car. The crew were gathered together, looking into the open boot of the car.

'What's going on?' asked Cormac.

The crew manager pointed into the boot. One of the firefighters shone a massive torch into the boot of the car, and in the fierce glare of the light, Cormac could see a charred figure curled into a foetal position. He made to move towards the body.

'No need to check, mate,' said a voice. 'The poor bugger's well dead.'

'Oh, bollocks,' muttered Cormac. Automatically, he reached for his mobile phone and began organising the processes that would launch a murder investigation.

The last call he made was to DCI Driver, whose phone rang for so long that Cormac thought it would never be answered. Just as he was about to give up, a voice snapped, 'Yes?'

'Ah, sir. Sorry to disturb you. It's Cormac.'

'You do know what time it is, Cormac?'

'Yes, sir, I do.'

'And that it's Sunday night?'

'Yes, sir, I'm aware of that, too.'

'Then this had better be important,' said Driver.

'You mentioned the other day how much you'd like a nice, fresh murder case.'

'That's right, I did say that, and I would like that.'

'Then you're in luck, sir.'

Cormac could hear the immediate change in Driver's tone. 'I take it you've got everything under control?'

'I set the wheels in motion before I called,' said Cormac. 'The doctor, pathologist, and forensics are all on their way.'

'Very good,' said Driver. 'In that case, you'd better tell me where you are.'

* * *

* * *

The area had been cordoned off and was being guarded by two uniformed officers who had been summoned from the pitched battle in the middle of town. In the centre of the plot, the charred wreckage of the vehicle was now under the cover of a hastily erected forensic tent. The immediate scene and surrounding area were lit up by powerful floodlights as white-suited technicians busied themselves photographing the scene and gathering evidence.

Cormac met Driver as he stepped from his car.

'What have we got?' asked Driver as they walked across the site to the car.

'The Fire Service said the fire was started deliberately. There are no number plates on the car, but they think they can recover the Vehicle Identification Number. A charred body was found hidden in the boot, curled in the foetal position. I didn't want to poke around, so I couldn't get a look at the face, but I doubt it will be recognisable.'

'I find it's best not to get too involved with bodies at this stage,' said Driver. 'Leave that stuff to the doctor and pathologist. It's what they get paid for.'

They stopped far enough away from the car not to crowd the pathologist as she examined the body in the boot.

'This is our pathologist, Dr Martha McGowan,' Driver told Cormac. 'Martha, this is DS Cormac. He's the newest addition to our team.'

The pathologist looked up at Cormac and gave a little wave. The white 'one size fits all' forensic suit looked several sizes too large for her, and a face mask hid the lower half of her face, but her eyes smiled beneath the surgical cap covering her head. He smiled back and returned the wave.

'Have you found any ID, Martha?' asked Driver optimistically.

The pathologist pulled the face mask away from her

mouth. 'Not so far. You might be lucky, and there may be something underneath when we move him, but I wouldn't hold your breath.'

'Can you tell us anything to be going on with?' asked Driver.

The pathologist smiled grimly. 'I can tell you he's dead.'

Driver offered a sardonic smile of his own. 'So you're on the same page as the doctor. That's good to know. Although, to be honest, it would be more helpful if you were both mistaken and the victim could tell us who put him in the boot and set the car on fire.'

'Ah, yes, but then you'd have no detecting to do,' said McGowan. 'Everyone knows you love a good murder.'

'I can't deny murders are more interesting than most crimes,' said Driver. 'But you're digressing. Can you tell us anything else here?'

'The part of the victim you can see is char-grilled, but underneath, he's not too bad.'

'So that means he didn't burn for too long,' said Driver. 'Am I right?'

'The fire service guys reckon they were lucky,' said Cormac. 'He would have been burnt to a crisp if they had arrived a few minutes later.'

'I'm sure that will be a great consolation to him now,' said Driver.

'That black stuff under his head,' said Cormac. 'Is it dried blood?'

'Good guess,' said McGowan. 'And because of that, I can also tell you he couldn't speak if he was alive. His tongue's been cut out.'

'Bloody hell,' said Cormac.

Driver grimaced. 'That seems both extreme and somewhat unnecessary. It's not as if he was going to tell us anything once he'd been roasted alive.'

'I don't suppose you can hazard a guess as to whether he was alive when the fire started?' Cormac asked the pathologist.

She sniffed haughtily.

'You guys don't want much, do you? And you're correct to not suppose; there's no chance I'm going to take a guess at something like that. I won't know for sure until I examine his lungs. In fact, I don't think I can be much help to you until I get him back home, where I can examine him properly.'

Cormac turned a quizzical face to Driver. 'Home?' he asked quietly.

'Martha's lab,' explained Driver loudly. 'She has a coffin in the crypt where she sleeps by day. That's why she looks wide awake now, while the rest of us look like the knackered wrecks that we are.'

McGowan flashed a glare in Driver's direction. 'As you well know, DCI Driver, I keep the coffin in the crypt, not the basement,' she said. 'And unless you have any objections, I'd like to take this one back to my lair sooner rather than later. I can't afford to be out here when the sun comes up, or I'll turn to dust.'

'No objection here,' said Driver. 'You carry on and move him.'

She gave a signal to the two technicians who were waiting nearby, and as they moved in to recover the body, she stepped away from the car.

'Post-mortem at 9 a.m.,' she told Driver.

'We'll be there,' he said.

As the pathologist walked away, the two detectives watched as the two-man recovery team moved in. They removed the body from the boot of the car and, after a brief struggle with the awkwardly shaped body, managed to fit it into a body bag, zipped the bag up, and lifted it onto a trolley. Before they wheeled it away, one man called out, beckoning a forensic technician over and pointed into the boot.

The technician lifted a small object from the boot and slipped it into a clear evidence pouch. Then she walked across to show the pouch to Driver and Cormac.

'A mobile phone,' said Cormac. 'Now that's a bit of luck.'

'Make sure that gets to the tech department as soon as possible,' Driver told the technician.

'Yes, sir, no worries,' she said.

As the technician moved away, Driver turned to Cormac. 'You asked if the victim was dead before the fire; what are you thinking?'

'Well, if you wanted to make sure his body burned enough to make it unrecognisable, you'd sit him in the front and douse everything in petrol, wouldn't you?'

'Do you think we were supposed to find him before he burned?'

'Removing a tongue isn't the sort of thing your run-of-the-mill murderer does, is it? So, I'm thinking this has to be a message.'

'That seems a reasonable assumption,' agreed Driver.

'But what would be the point if the body got burned so badly that we couldn't tell the tongue was cut out?'

'Okay, so I agree, it's a message,' said Driver. 'But who is it for? Us?'

'I'm not saying it's necessarily for us. I just think the message only works if it's obvious and clearly recognised, no matter who it's meant for.'

Driver thought for a moment. 'But if we were supposed

to find his body intact, why set the car on fire at all? And why dump it right out here where there's a risk it might burn out before anyone even noticed?'

'Come to think of it, the fire station must be twenty minutes from here,' said Cormac.

'Right,' said Driver. 'Does that car look as though it was burning for more than twenty minutes before the fire brigade got here? No, it doesn't.'

'Good point,' said Cormac. 'And no one in their right mind is going to be accidentally passing this dump at ten-thirty on a Sunday night.'

'And even if someone was passing by and called nine, nine, nine—'

'It would have burned through long before a fire engine could get here,' finished Cormac.

'Right,' agreed Driver. 'So, the question is, how did the Fire Service know, and who told them?'

'For them to get here in time to save the car, it must have been an early warning,' said Cormac. 'And whoever made the call must have known how long it would take the Fire Service to get here.'

'It's a risky strategy, though,' said Driver. 'What if there had been a big fire on the other side of town and there was no engine to come out here?'

'Perhaps they were watching the fire station, or they might even have a radio scanner,' said Cormac. 'I'll check if there was such a call and what time it was received.'

Driver looked at his wristwatch. 'It's 2 a.m.' He scanned the surroundings. 'It's all about forensics finding us some evidence now, so there's not much point in us hanging around; we'll just be in the way. I'm going back home to my bed. I'll be back in at 8 a.m., and I expect to find a cup of tea waiting for me when I get there.'

'What do you want me to do?' asked Cormac.

'Find out everything you can about that car. I want to know who owns it, where it came from, and how it ended up being torched in this shithole. Then get hold of the control centre and ask when the emergency call was made and who made it... you know what to do.'

'But I'm supposed to be working the night shift.'

'Not any more,' said Driver. 'You may only be a temporary appointment, but you're my bagman at the moment, and we have a murder on our hands, so that's your priority. Don't worry; I'll square it with that miserable git, Gleeson.'

CHAPTER 2

Monday 30th April 08:00

True to his word, Driver was back right on time.

'Any progress?' he asked.

'The emergency call was made at 21:45. I've asked for a recording to be sent over. It'll probably be a waste of time, but you never know. I also spoke to the fire crew. They think the fire was started with an accelerant, probably petrol, and that the car had been burning for less than ten minutes when they arrived on the scene.'

'So you were right; it was an early warning,' said Driver.

'Looks that way,' said Cormac.

'Any luck with the car?'

'Registered to a Nigel Densley. Reported stolen two days ago in Birmingham. Densley had left the keys in the ignition outside his kebab shop.'

'Brilliant,' said Driver. 'And people wonder why crime figures keep rising. Is it a genuine report?'

'Not sure, but it looks that way. I've asked them to send us a copy.'

'So what do we think? Stolen to order?' asked Driver.

'I reckon so,' said Cormac.

'So, basically, we're waiting on forensics and the pathologist before we can get started.'

'That just about sums it up,' said Cormac.

'In that case, Cormac, I believe we've got time to stop for breakfast on the way to Martha's.'

'That sounds like a plan I can work with, sir.'

* * *

Following Driver's directions, Cormac was soon parked outside a small greasy spoon café. He followed Driver as he pushed through the door into the busy, fuggy warmth of the interior. Cormac would be the first to admit he had no clue about décor, but he felt this place would best be described as nineteen-sixties industrial chic, if that was even a thing.

'Don't be put off by the décor,' Driver assured him. 'This is the best breakfast for miles.'

They placed their orders at the counter, collected a mug of tea each, paid, and then settled at an empty table. Their breakfasts arrived within minutes and they eagerly tucked in.

'So, tell me about Nolan Cormac,' said Driver.

'There's not much to tell.'

Driver chuckled. 'Now, come on,' he said. 'How can a man who was a police detective, left to become a private detective, and then come back to work in the drug squad, not have much to tell?'

'What do you want to know?'

'Why did you leave in the first place?'

'It started when I was overlooked for promotion, not once, but twice, and then ended up working with a DI who had been brought in from outside. She turned out to be a raging psychopath, and from that point on, I felt as if I was cursed. Everything just seemed to go pear-shaped, and I felt like I was living on the edge, you know?

'Then my dad died and left me some money. I was fed up with the job, so I quit, and I set up on my own. The trouble is, there's not much demand for private detectives in a small town. I had a couple of cases, but it was never going to be enough. And the thing is, I found I missed being a proper detective, solving crimes, you know?'

'I know I'd miss it,' said Driver.

'And that's why I rejoined.'

'So why not rejoin where you were before?'

'When I was working as a PI, I met this woman, Heather Collins. You might know her. She was a DI in the drug squad.'

'The name doesn't ring a bell,' said Driver. 'But then drug squad people aren't my sort of people. Most of them seem to think they're something special, above the rest of us.'

Cormac looked suitably offended.

'Present company excepted,' added Driver hastily. 'You must be all right, or you wouldn't have come back to join us normal people.'

Cormac managed a half-hearted smile. 'Anyway, Heather had been attacked while doing surveillance on a drug dealer, and when I first met her, she was signed off with PTSD. She came back and did a bit of desk duty, but eventually, she was never fit enough to return to active duty and decided to leave.'

'You were in a relationship with her?'

'Yeah, I'll say. I loved her, and I thought she loved me. We even talked about getting married.'

'Ah,' said Driver. 'So she was the one you took to Thailand, right?'

'You've done your homework, haven't you?' said Cormac. 'Are you sure you need me to tell you all this?'

Driver shrugged. 'I only know what you told Eagan. He passed it on to me.'

'So it was you who checked me out?'

'Someone had to do it. If it had been left to Eagan, you'd still be waiting for something to happen.'

'So you knew about my suspension before I came here?'

'For something that wasn't your fault? Yes, but I won't hold it against you. We've all been there. Professional Standards are a bunch of bastards. They would have nothing to do most of the time if they only went after the truly bent coppers. I swear they persecute people like you and me to justify their existence.'

'They left me feeling like I had a target on my back,' said Cormac.

'Oh, yes, they're good at that sort of thing,' replied Driver.

They had both finished eating now.

'Was I right about the breakfast?' asked Driver.

'Best I've had in a long time,' said Cormac. 'I can see myself coming here a lot.'

'Then you'll probably bump into me on occasion,' said Driver.

'You're not going to interrogate me every time, are you?'

'Aw, come on, it's not that bad, is it?' said Driver. 'I just like to know what makes my colleagues tick, that's all.' He looked at his watch. 'Anyway, we'd better get moving. We don't want to be late.'

As they opened the car doors and stepped inside, Driver muttered something that Cormac didn't catch.

'Sorry, what was that, sir?' asked Cormac as he started the car and set off for the mortuary.

'I said I would also like to know why you've come to Windover.'

'You've seen my application.'

'Yes, but I'd like you to refresh my memory.'

'First of all, it's a convenient place to work because I own a house not far from here.'

'So why are you living in a motel?'

'Yeah, well, it's a bit complicated. I've had an agent letting my house while I was away, and there's a tenant living in it.'

'That must be annoying.'

'Just a tad,' said Cormac sarcastically. 'And second, I wanted to escape the Midlands because I felt like a marked man. I needed a change, and it felt like the right time to come back home. You should already know all this. I told Superintendent Eagan. Didn't he tell you?'

'Yes, he did tell me,' said Driver as Cormac pulled into the mortuary car park and stopped the car. 'But the thing with Eagan is that he only thinks about himself and maintaining the upward trajectory of his career. He tends not to see anything beyond that.'

'I'm not sure I understand your meaning, sir.'

'What I mean is, when you buttonholed him in that restaurant, he only had eyes for what might be in it for him. You dangled a big, juicy carrot that you knew he wouldn't be able to resist.'

'Carrot, sir?'

'Don't play innocent with me, Cormac. You offered him the chance to catch corruption much higher up the food chain than he can usually reach.'

'I admit I may have mentioned something like that, but I'd never met him before,' said Cormac. 'How would I know he liked carrots?'

'Look, you might be able to pull the wool over the eyes of some young go-getter like Eagan, but that won't work on an old hand like me because I'm not interested in carrots.'

Cormac shook his head. 'I don't follow. What are you saying?'

'I think what you told Eagan about coming back here is mostly bollocks, and I'm curious to know the real reason you've come here.'

'Trust me, there is no other reason, sir,' said Cormac as he opened his car door. 'And we'd better not keep Martha waiting.'

Driver looked at his watch. 'Yes, you're right there. She is a stickler for timekeeping.'

Cormac thought Dr McGowan looked quite different without the white forensic suit and face mask. He wasn't sure if it was the skinny blue jeans, white T-shirt, and slip-on clogs she was wearing, or the fact he could now clearly see her pale face framed by long dark hair. In fact, with the goth makeup she had applied, he could almost believe she did sleep in a coffin.

She showed them into her lab, tied back her hair, slipped on a lab coat, head-covering and face mask, then took them over to the dissection table where the body was laid out beneath a white sheet. She took hold of the sheet, then stopped.

'I should warn you he's going to look a bit weird because of the swelling where his tongue was removed.'

'Was he alive or dead when the tongue was removed?' asked Driver.

'You saw the blood in the boot of the car. Dead bodies don't bleed like that.'

'Bloody hell,' said Cormac. 'Does that mean he was alive in the boot of the car when they took it?'

'Either that, or it was done immediately before he was put in the boot.'

'Christ,' said Driver. 'Who does something like that?'

'I'm afraid that's not my field,' said McGowan. 'But I would suggest it can't be anyone normal, can it?'

She pulled the sheet down to reveal a face distorted by the damage done to his mouth.

'Is this him?' asked Driver. 'I was expecting a piece of charcoal.'

'If I turn him over, that's what you'll see,' said McGowan. 'With his body curled into a foetal position, the fire scorched his back but didn't reach the front.'

As he took in the man's face, Cormac shifted, his jaw tightening.

Driver caught the movement and turned to him. 'Are you okay?'

'I think I recognise him.'

'Really?' Driver took another look at the face. 'How do you know him? He's not a local villain I've come across.'

'His name is Marcus Whitmore, known on the street as Marky. Back when I worked in the Midlands, I nicked him a couple of times.'

'Are you sure?' asked Driver.

Cormac took a closer look. 'He had a tongue last time I saw him, and he hadn't been beaten up and burned, but yeah, that's him.'

'He was a junkie?'

'Small-time dealer with a habit,' said Cormac. 'I did him for possession with intent to supply.'

McGowan slowly pulled the sheet away, exposing a body marked with cuts and bruises.

'And, as you can see, he had a severe beating,' she said. 'We've got all sorts here; kicks, punches, blunt instruments, you name it. He's got several broken ribs and a fracture to the left forearm. I'm pretty sure when I open him up, I'll find his internal organs will be smashed to pulp.'

Over the next hour, Cormac and Driver stood back and watched as Dr McGowan dissected the body, all the time muttering into a small headset microphone. Cormac couldn't stop thinking about Marky. Why would he turn up here in Windover, over two hundred miles from home? Of course, it could be a coincidence, but Cormac didn't think it likely.

He was still lost in thought when Dr McGowan wrapped up her post-mortem.

'Well, that's it,' she said, leaving her assistant to finish cleaning up. 'I'll send the full report across later.'

'What, no time for coffee and biscuits?' asked Driver.

'I'm sorry, I'd love to pass the time of day with you, but I have a funeral to attend, and I'm running late as it is.'

'Oh, right,' said Driver. 'In that case, we'll get out of your way.'

'What now?' asked Cormac as they walked towards their car. 'Back to the station?'

'I'd like another look at the crime scene,' said Driver. 'Perhaps we'll see something we missed last night.'

* * *

Standing under a bleak stretch of grey sky on the outskirts of Windover, the lonely, charred hulk of the car still seemed to smoulder faintly when Cormac and Driver returned to the scene. The early morning frost had lifted a while ago, but a thin mist clung to the surrounding hedgerows.

As they climbed out of their car, the stench of charred rubber and something worse lingered in the air. Driver stopped and took a good, long look around the site.

'The nearest road is over half a mile away,' he told Cormac. 'And the access track is in such a poor state it's barely drivable. Whoever left the car here must have scouted this spot and worked out how long it would take the Fire Service to get here.'

'You're right about that,' said Cormac. 'This doesn't seem anything like a panic dump. It's more like a delivery.'

They walked across to the car. Cormac crouched beside the blackened boot, open and gaping like a ruptured wound. The forensic team had already done its work, bagging and tagging bits of cloth and ash, and fragments of body tissue. Now all that was left inside was the faint outline where the body had been curled in on itself.

They knew from the post-mortem that the victim had been dead before the flames reached him, as if that were any consolation. But it was the mobile phone that had been revealed when the body was removed that was the real intrigue.

'So, what do you think about the burner phone?' asked Driver, staring into the boot.

Cormac stood up and scanned the site, as if the landscape might offer an explanation.

'How do you mean, what do I think?' he asked. 'It looked like a basic burner phone to me, and it was under the body.'

'Yes,' said Driver. 'But did it slip out of his pocket and end up there, or was it placed deliberately for us to find.'

'You think it's some sort of further message?' asked Cormac.

'You agree we were supposed to find the car before it burnt out, right?'

'Yeah, I reckon so.'

'Okay, and we think the reason we were meant to find the car was so we would discover the body. And we believe the body is a message for someone.'

'That's how it looks, yeah,' said Cormac.

'Right. Now, we know this guy, Marky, was given a beating. My guess is someone wanted to know what he knew. Agreed?'

'With you so far,' said Cormac.

'Right, so, if you wanted to know what someone knew, or who he'd been talking to, what would you do? Say you've beaten the crap out of him, but you still think he hasn't told you everything. Wouldn't you take his phone and see what's on there?'

'Ah, right, now I see what you're getting at,' said Cormac. 'You think we were meant to find the phone.'

'Exactly,' said Driver. 'Let's hope the tech guys can tell us what's on it.'

Cormac tried his best to suppress it, but the yawn he had struggled to hold back for the last hour finally got the better of him and almost turned his head inside out.

Driver stepped back theatrically.

'You want to be careful, Cormac,' he said. 'You could easily swallow someone yawning like that.'

'I'm sorry, sir. It's just that I've been on duty since early yesterday evening, and it's catching up with me.'

'Tell you what,' said Driver. 'Why don't you head home and catch a couple of hours' sleep?'

'I'd appreciate that, if you don't mind.'

'I've got an incident room full of people back at the station. I'm sure they can manage without you for a few hours. Come back in at 5 p.m., and we'll catch up then.'

* * *

CHAPTER 3

Just as Cormac parked his car, his mobile phone beeped to warn him of an incoming text. He read the message and then wound down his window as a car pulled up close by, lowering a window next to his.

'Were you waiting for me, sir?' asked Cormac.

'Pure coincidence,' said Eagan. 'I was in my car about to go home when I saw you drive in. I thought we could have a quick catch-up.'

'Is this cloak-and-dagger stuff really necessary?'

'I don't want anyone to think I'm favouring you,' said Eagan.

'I should think that's exactly what people will think if we're seen doing this.'

'How are you getting on with Driver?' asked Eagan.

'He can be a bit of a dinosaur at times,' said Cormac.

'Yes. Tell me something I don't know,' said Eagan. 'But that's not what I mean.'

'I'm not sure he believes I'm capable of standing in for DS Michaels.'

'Yes, I'm sorry about that,' said Eagan. 'They've been working together for a long time.'

'Yeah, well, because he doesn't trust me, he tends to keep me at arm's length. We've got this murder case now, but I've spent the first two weeks sorting the bloody filing.'

'Actually, the filing was my idea,' said Eagan. 'We've been waiting for someone efficient to sort out that mess, and apparently, you are that someone.'

'It was your idea? Well, thanks for that, sir, but I didn't come here to sort filing. I'm a detective, not a filing clerk.'

'I wanted to break you in gently,' said Eagan.

'That wasn't part of the deal,' said Cormac. 'I made you an offer.'

'I'd say it was a bit vague to be called an offer,' said Eagan. 'But whatever, quid pro quo. You want me to scratch your itch; you have to scratch mine. That's how it works. Or are you saying you didn't understand how quid pro quo works?'

'Of course I understand how it works, but you didn't say anything about me being a clerk, and it turns out I hate being one.'

'But you're still here,' said Eagan.

'Are you saying it was a test?'

'Don't forget I'm the one taking a risk here,' said Eagan. 'So if I feel I need to test your patience, then I bloody well will.'

'Okay, fine,' said Cormac. 'But sorting your filing is not why I came here.'

Cormac wasn't convinced Eagan had any intention of keeping his side of the bargain, but he also knew he had no leverage to force his hand. And anyway, right now, there was a more pressing matter.

'Look, I'd love to sit and catch the breeze with you, but DCI Driver is expecting me.'

'Funny enough, DCI Driver and I had a chat about you earlier. You may think he doesn't trust you, but he told me he quite likes you.'

'This chat, is that why he wants to see me?'

Eagan looked surprised.

'Has he told you he wants to see you?'

'Yes, he has.'

'Oh, well, if he's arranged a meeting with you, I have no desire to get in the way and delay you.'

With that, Eagan put his car in gear and headed for home.

* * *

At around the same time Cormac was making his way into the building to meet DCI Driver, ten miles away, just outside a village called Templeton, Detective Constable Charlotte (Charlie) Aconna was easing her car off the road into a lay-by and pulling up behind a battered Land Rover that had clearly seen better days.

Aconna had only been working at Windover CID for a week. So far, the job had been nothing like she had expected. DCI Driver didn't seem to think she was capable of anything more than filing and tea-making, so she hadn't done a stroke of detective work until today, when she had been asked to go out and check an alibi.

Now, on the way back, she had been asked to meet a retired farmer who seemed to have a problem with a scarecrow. She had been told it would likely be a waste of time, but as far as Aconna was concerned, anything would be better than filing, so she was happy to meet anyone.

A tall, gnarled-looking man in his late sixties with the tanned, ruddy complexion of a farmer was standing by the vehicle, looking up and down the road. He was obviously waiting for someone and kept looking at his watch.

Aconna could see the surprise on his face when she climbed from her car, smiled brightly, and walked towards him.

'Mr Madeley?'

'Who are you?' he asked.

She produced her warrant card.

'Detective Constable Aconna, from Windover police.'

'I was expecting a proper police officer, in a uniform.'

'Yes, normally a uniformed officer would be the first response, but we're pretty busy today, and I was passing, so rather than keep you waiting for hours, control asked me to stop by.'

'You look a bit young to be a police officer.'

Her green eyes twinkled as she forced a smile. 'And yet here I am, showing you my warrant card.'

The old man was clearly unimpressed.

'I promise you it's a genuine warrant card, and I am a real police detective. You can phone the station and check if you like.'

'But you're a woman.'

'Not much gets past you, does it?' said Aconna with patient good humour.

'I was expecting someone older and a bit more detective-like,' he said.

'Yes, you've made that quite clear, Mr Madeley, but I believe what you really mean is that you would prefer it if I were a man.'

'Well, yes, I suppose I do.' The old farmer looked the

slim woman up and down again. 'The thing is, this is urgent.'

Aconna shrugged. 'Well, I'm sorry, Mr Madeley, but I'm afraid all the men are busy doing important man stuff, so you'll just have to make do with me. And trust me, I can do urgent if it's necessary.'

Madeley still looked doubtful.

'I can go away if you like,' said Aconna, 'but if I do, you might be waiting hours, or even days, before anyone else comes out, and even then, I can't guarantee it will be a man. It might even be me again, and that would double your disappointment.'

The old farmer grunted, then grudgingly turned and pointed towards the hill opposite where a scarecrow could just about be made out a short distance from the top.

'I drive along this road nearly every day, and I never noticed there was a scarecrow up there before.'

'I'm not surprised you didn't notice it,' said Aconna. 'Not many people would.'

'But I've been farming all my life. It's the sort of thing a farmer notices.'

'Okay. So, you noticed it. What makes it so urgent you needed to call the police?'

'The birds.'

Aconna squinted at the distant scarecrow. She could just about make out what looked like a swarm of dark specs around its head.

'What about the birds?' she asked.

'They're crows.'

Aconna heaved a weary sigh. No-one likes a time-waster, and this afternoon, when she would quite like to get finished and get off home, definitely wasn't the best time to be confronted by one.

'You mean the scarecrow doesn't work.'

'Of course it doesn't work. They never work. They're clever birds, crows. They soon figure out there's no danger from a few old clothes stuffed with straw.'

'Have you called me out here just to show me a scarecrow that doesn't work?'

'The thing is, I asked myself why would anyone put a scarecrow in a place like that?'

'I'm not with you?'

'There are no crops growing up there. So why bother?'

'I don't know, Mr Madeley, and frankly, I'm not sure I care. Perhaps whoever farms the land wanted to conduct an experiment to prove scarecrows don't work.'

'But that's what I'm saying. No one does farm that land.'

'Local kids then.'

'Huh! You know as well as I do that kids these days wouldn't be able to tear themselves away from their smartphones long enough to climb that hill. And as for making a scarecrow, well, I don't think so, do you?'

Aconna sighed. 'So you're saying you think there's a mystery scarecrow builder in Templeton. Now, I'm not saying you're wrong, but I don't believe there's an actual law against it, and even if there was one, I've really got better things to do. And I should point out, there is a crime called wasting police time.'

The old farmer grunted. 'So you think I'm wasting your time, do you?'

He reached through the Land Rover window and grabbed a pair of binoculars. 'Crows don't usually eat scarecrows, do they?' he asked as he handed the binoculars to her.

'I'm not sure I'm qualified to answer that,' said Aconna. 'The behaviour of crows isn't my specialist subject.'

'Take it from me, young lady, they do not.'

'Okay. I believe you,' said Aconna. 'But I don't see what you're getting at.'

The old man nodded towards the distant scarecrow.

'Take a look through the bins, DC Aconna, and maybe then you'll understand.'

Aconna took the binoculars and raised them to her eyes. It took almost a full minute, but she finally located the scarecrow. It was all a bit blurry, but she thought she could make out several crows that appeared to be squabbling over the head.

'What's the head made of? Is it a pumpkin, or something?'

'Wrong time of year for pumpkins,' said Madeley. 'Besides, I farmed vegetables for over forty years, and I can assure you there isn't a pumpkin, or any other vegetable, anywhere in the world, that looks like that.'

'What is it then?' she asked.

Madeley tutted loudly. 'Take a closer look. Perhaps if you adjust the focus...'

Aconna's patience was wearing thin to the point of being threadbare but, to humour the old man, she carefully re-adjusted the focus until it was pin sharp, and as she did so, took a sharp intake of breath.

'Jesus!' she muttered as she lowered the binoculars. 'That's not a bloody pumpkin.'

'Aye,' said the old farmer. 'And that's not a bloody scarecrow. I bet you don't think I'm wasting your time now, do you?'

Aconna rushed over to her car and grabbed her radio.

'Hello, control? This is DC Aconna. I need help. I've stumbled across a body and I'm not sure what to do.'

'A body where?' asked the calm voice on the radio.

'It's up on Barley Brow Hill, just outside Templeton. The thing is, I think the body's been staged.'

'Staged how?'

Aconna hesitated. 'Er, it's sort of tied up, as if it was crucified and made to look like a scarecrow.'

'Right,' said the steady, reassuring voice in her ear. 'You stay where you are, take some deep breaths and calm down. I'll get everything moving from this end, but while I do that, I want you to call DCI Driver as he's your boss. You can tell him I'm organising everything from here, but you should tell him what you've found. Okay?'

'Yes, right. Call DCI Driver. Yes, I can do that,' stammered Aconna.

CHAPTER 4

Cormac sat in Driver's office, the creak of the old leather chair beneath him offering no comfort. Driver was brooding silently, reading from the tablet in his hand, one eyebrow raised as he scrolled. Finally, he put the tablet down, steepled his fingers together, and stared at Cormac.

'So, remind me, Cormac, why exactly did you come to Windover?'

'I thought we had this conversation this morning, sir.'

'Yes, we did,' said Driver. 'Just humour me, will you?'

Cormac sighed. 'I came here because I needed a change of scenery.'

'Yes, but you could have got that anywhere in the UK. Why here in particular?'

'Sir?'

'There were other places you could have gone.'

'Yes, but Windover was suggested, and I own a house not that far from here, so I applied.'

'Except that's not exactly how it happened, is it?' said Driver. 'Superintendent Eagan told me you didn't just apply for a transfer and wait to hear from him; you actively pursued him, even to the point of joining him for lunch, uninvited.'

'I admit I was keen.'

Driver guffawed. 'You call stalking a senior officer at lunchtime, keen? I think even you would agree that's an understatement.'

'He wouldn't take my calls,' said Cormac. 'I had to reach him somehow.'

'I understand you were in the Midlands drug squad?'

'That's right.'

'So why not transfer to our drug squad?'

'As I said, I wanted a change, and Superintendent Eagan was willing to take me on.'

Driver rolled his eyes. 'I'm not sure I believe it's as simple as that, Cormac.'

'Sir?'

Driver observed Cormac for a good minute. Cormac knew the tactic. He, too, had used it on many occasions; if you leave a long enough silence, the suspect almost always feels compelled to say something. But he wasn't a suspect. Or was he?

'Have I done something wrong, sir?'

'I don't know,' said Driver. 'That's what I'm trying to find out.'

'I know you've been working with DS Michaels for years, but I thought you were reasonably happy with my work standing in for him.'

'Yes, I suppose I was, but things change, don't they?'

'I'm afraid you'll have to give me a clue, sir,' said Cormac.

'When you were in the Midlands, you were suspended from duty—'

'Yes, but the subsequent inquiry cleared me of all responsibility,' interrupted Cormac.

'And yet, they still demoted you,' said Driver.

'Yes, well, as you said yourself, Professional Standards think they have to punish people to justify their existence.'

'When we were in the post-mortem, you said you only knew the victim because you had nicked him for possession.'

'Who, Marky? Yeah, that's right. The first time he got a slap on the wrist. The second time he got six months.'

'And that's it? You never kept in touch?'

'Kept in touch? Now, why would I keep in touch with someone like that?'

'I'm going to ask you once more: did you keep in touch with him after you nicked him?'

Cormac studied Driver's face. He didn't know what was going on here, but it looked as though lying wouldn't be a good idea.

'No, sir. As he was into drugs and I was working for the drug squad, I naturally saw him around occasionally, but I didn't speak to him unless I had to.'

'All right, so when did you last see him?'

'I'm not sure. Probably about a year ago, around the time everything went pear-shaped for me. I've neither seen nor heard from him since.'

'So, he's not a police informant, then?'

Cormac frowned. 'No way. I would have registered him if he was a snout.'

'That's a pity,' said Driver. 'It would have explained it.'

'Explained what?'

Driver ignored Cormac's question, instead asking one of his own. 'So, what's he doing down in this neck of the woods?'

'How would I know?'

'You have to admit, it's a bit of a coincidence, isn't it?' said Driver. 'I mean, you transfer here to Windover, over a hundred and fifty miles from the Midlands, and who should show up in the same town just a couple of weeks later in a torched car with his tongue cut out? Your old friend Marky.'

'I know nothing about that,' said Cormac. 'And, as I said, he wasn't a friend. Last time I nicked him, he was a small-time drug dealer who fancied himself as the big I am. Maybe he tried mixing it with some real big boys and came unstuck.'

'So why is his body here in Windover?'

'How am I supposed to know? Perhaps he was getting too well known up there and wanted to try to make a name for himself in a new area.'

Driver sat back in his chair and placed his hands on the desk. 'D'you know, I could almost believe that. In fact, I want to believe it,' he said. 'But unfortunately, it's not that simple.'

'Why not?'

'Remember the mobile phone that was under the body?'

'What about it?'

'As we thought, it's an unregistered burner phone,' said Driver. 'Of course, we all know there's nothing remarkable about some low-life like that having a burner. But what is remarkable about this particular burner is that there's only one number stored in the contact list.'

Driver studied Cormac's face, waiting for a response.

'I'm not following,' said Cormac.

Driver sighed wearily. 'Then let me get straight to the point. Why is your mobile number the only one stored on the burner phone found with the victim?'

Cormac's mouth dropped open. 'My number? What do you mean it's my number?'

Driver slid a notepad across the desk. 'Is this your number? I can dial it right now if you're not sure.'

Cormac looked at the number scrawled across the notepad and then gaped up at Driver.

'Honest to God, sir, I have no idea why he's got my number. Surely you can't believe this has anything to do with me. I mean, Marky! Come on, he's a bloody nobody.'

'He certainly is now,' said Driver.

'I don't know what I can say or do to convince you,' said Cormac. 'I suppose you're going to report me.'

'Don't think that hasn't crossed my mind,' said Driver.

'You mean you haven't?'

'No, I haven't.'

'But I heard you'd been speaking with Eagan about me. I assumed—'

'How do you know about that?'

'I just bumped into him. He said you'd been discussing me.'

'Yes, well, you can relax on that score. I didn't mention the mobile phone.'

'Why not?'

'Because the Eagans of this world work on the assumption that we're all bent, and all he has to do is wait for one of us to make a mistake and then, bish, bosh, bash, he's gained another inch or two up that greasy pole. On that basis, how long do you think it would take him to have a Professional Standards investigation team on the premises if he knew about that phone? And trust me, no one in this building wants those bastards poking around.'

'But you could be concealing vital evidence,' said Cormac.

'But I'm not, because it isn't,' said Driver. 'The tech boys believe the number was on the SIM card when it was loaded into the phone. And it appears the phone itself has never been turned on, so there's no location data or anything. As evidence goes, it proves nothing.'

'Yeah, but it will be in the chain of evidence, so we can't pretend the phone doesn't exist.'

'I didn't say we should pretend it doesn't exist. We just don't need to draw attention to it.'

'I don't get it,' said Cormac. 'Why would you put your own career at risk for me?'

'Funny enough, I've been asking myself that question ever since I saw the report from the tech guys.'

'Yeah, and?'

'I think whoever killed Marky planted that phone to implicate you.'

'What makes you say that?'

'Because there are no fingerprints. It's been wiped clean. So I asked myself, why would Marky wipe his own phone clean before he was turned into a kebab? And, of course, he wouldn't, would he? What would be the point? No, it only makes sense to me if someone else put the phone there.'

'So you just asked all those questions when you already knew...'

'I couldn't ignore the possibility, could I?' said Driver. 'What would you have done?'

Cormac shrugged. 'The same as you I suppose.'

'Right, so there's no need to be quite so indignant, is there?'

Cormac nodded. 'No, I guess not. But why would anyone want to implicate me?'

'That's what I want to know,' said Driver. 'And I was rather hoping you could enlighten me on that score. I mean, you did five years on the drug squad. You must have pissed off one or two people in that time.'

Cormac managed a wry smile. 'I'm sure I could write you a long list, but I can't think of anyone who has used a car as a barbecue before.'

'This all goes back to what I was asking you about before, doesn't it?' asked Driver.

'Sorry?'

'Why are you here?'

'I told you before, sir; there is no hidden reason.'

'I'm trying to help you here, Cormac, but I can't do that if you won't tell me what's going on.'

'There is nothing to tell,' insisted Cormac.

Driver studied Cormac's face. 'Am I making a mistake looking out for you?'

'No, sir, you're not, but I will understand if you feel you need to inform Superintendent Eagan.'

'I'm hoping and praying it won't come to that,' said Driver. 'Anyway, whatever you're up to doesn't matter because I've found something for you to do that will keep you out of the way.'

'What does that mean?'

'I've got someone I want you to babysit.'

'Babysit?'

'The name is DC O'Connor.'

'Do I know him?'

'It's a her, not a him,' said Driver.

'Is she new?' asked Cormac. 'I don't think I've come across her.'

'Yes, she is new, but no, you wouldn't have come across her,' said Driver. 'Up until the end of last week, I had her sorting the filing on the first floor.'

Cormac's mouth kicked in before his brain could stop it. 'What did she do to deserve that?'

'What's that supposed to mean?'

'Well, I realise that I was given the filing on the second floor because you didn't trust me to fill in for Michaels, but now I'm just wondering what O'Connor must have done wrong.'

'She's new on the job and everyone needs to learn their way around the filing,' said Driver.

'You don't like me, do you?' asked Cormac.

Driver pursed his lips and considered for a moment. 'Do you seriously think, for even one moment, that I would be sitting on evidence in a murder case if I didn't like you? Just remember, if I wanted to, I could sink you any time I like. But I haven't.'

'Sorry, sir,' said Cormac, chastened. 'I don't know why I said that. This mobile phone business has come as a bit of a shock, and—'

'I admit I don't like to think we're taking people in just so Eagan can tick another box.' Driver's lip curled at the mention of Eagan's name. 'You see, as far as I'm concerned, if you couldn't handle the job where you were before, we're just wasting our time expecting a different outcome here. The definition of stupidity is to keep on doing the same thing and expecting a different outcome.'

'It wasn't a question of not being able to handle the job; it was—'

'Yes, I know, it was a disciplinary issue,' said Driver.

Cormac didn't feel he owed Driver another explanation. 'If you have an issue with me—'

'I don't have an issue with you personally; I have an issue with your particular situation.'

'And yet, you're going to trust me to train a new detective.'

A tiny smile briefly drifted across the driver's face. 'Actually, it's Eagan's decision, not mine, but I agreed with it because, now that you've been around for a couple of weeks, I happen to think you're a very capable detective, and you're perfect for the job.'

'So what am I supposed to do with DC O'Connor? Is she joining our murder team?'

'No, she is not. I don't want a newbie under my feet while we have a murder on our hands.'

'But I thought I was going to be the one keeping an eye on her.'

'And so you will be.'

Cormac suddenly realised what Driver was suggesting.

'Wait a minute. Does this mean you're throwing me off the case? I suppose this is your revenge because you think I have a secret I won't share.'

'Don't be ridiculous, Cormac. I'm simply moving you elsewhere for your own good. Don't forget that mobile phone with your number on it; can you imagine what a defence lawyer would do if we put a case together and then they found out I had allowed you to continue as one of the investigating officers?'

Reluctantly, Cormac had to concede Driver had a point. 'Of course, you're right, sir,' he said. 'Do you have another case for us to work on then?'

'Not yet, but trust me, I'll find something for you.'

The phone on Driver's desk began to ring. He snatched it from its cradle and snapped his name into it. 'Driver.'

Cormac watched the DCI's face. His frown, as someone described something into his ear, suggested it wasn't the best connection, but he finally scribbled one or two sentences on his notepad, said, 'I'll send DS Cormac over,' and then hung up.

'It appears I don't have to find a case for you and O'Connor. She's found one for you.'

'What is it?' asked Cormac.

Driver looked down at his notepad. He was struggling to decipher his own writing. 'I'm not absolutely sure. Her signal was breaking up, but I think she said something about a scarecrow.'

'A scarecrow? What about a scarecrow?'

'I don't know, do I?' said Driver irritably. 'I just said I'm not exactly sure. She just mentioned something about a scarecrow. It's probably been stolen.'

Now Cormac couldn't decide if Driver was joking.

'A stolen scarecrow? You're joking, right?'

'Look, as I understand it, someone from Control took a call, O'Connor was passing, so they asked her to deal with it,' said Driver. 'It's her first case, so they're hardly going to send her to check out a serial killer, are they?'

'No, I suppose not. Are you going to tell me where it is?'

'It's somewhere called Barley Brow, or something like that, near some remote outpost called Templeton. Do you know where that is?'

'Yeah, I know it.'

'Oh, yes, of course you do. You used to live there, didn't you? What's Barley Brow? Is that a pub or something?'

'It's nothing special, just a hill,' said Cormac. 'I've never been up there, but I know where it is.'

'Right, so you're all set then,' said Driver.

'So, is it just me and O'Connor?'

'Well, it will be if you get your finger out and get over there.'

'All right,' said Cormac. 'Pardon me for asking!'

'Sorry,' said Driver. 'I didn't mean to snap at you like that. And, by way of an apology, and to prove how generous I am, I'll warn you now that while she was working for me, DC O'Connor was a pain in the arse with her incessant questions.'

'So that's why you want her out of the way.'

'Let's just say I'm not sorry she'll be out of my hair and out in the boondocks with you.'

'Okay then, I'll be on my way,' said Cormac, jumping to his feet.

'And remember,' said Driver, 'I still want to know what you're really up to. Understand?'

'Understood, loud and clear,' said Cormac. 'And I still say I've nothing to hide.'

* * *

As Cormac made his way down to the car park, he wondered about the mobile phone found in the car with Marky. And what the hell was Marky doing here, anyway? Before he could climb into his car, his mobile phone rang. He raised the phone to his ear.

'Is that DS Cormac?'

'Yes, speaking,' he said.

'It's DC Aconna.'

'Is it important? Only I'm in a hurry, and... Hang on, did you say DC O'Connor?'

Aconna sighed. 'Actually, it's Aconna, but I suppose that's as close as anyone there is going to get.'

Cormac missed the sarcasm entirely. 'Right, well, it's you I'm coming to find.'

'That's what I'm calling about,' said Aconna. 'I wasn't sure if you knew where to find me.'

'Just outside Templeton, I was told.'

'It's called Barley Brow. It's a big hill, just outside the village.'

'Yeah, I know it,' said Cormac. 'DCI Driver mentioned something about a stolen scarecrow.'

'Yes, well, I didn't think he was listening to me. Anyway, I think you'll find it's a little more interesting than that. The pathologist and a forensic team are on their way as we speak.'

'Wow! Really? Driver seemed to think it was your first call-out—'

'Two things,' said Aconna. 'First, the reason I'm here is that I was passing by and willing to answer a call, and second, you have to remember that men like DCI Driver assume women can't handle anything more complicated than a simple theft. And you know what they say about people who assume.'

'Okay, I'm on my way,' said Cormac. 'I'll be there in about half an hour.'

'If you're coming from Windover on the dual carriage-way, there's a lay-by on the left at the bottom of Barley Brow, about a mile outside the village. You can't miss it— one lane has been cordoned off, and there are police vehicles everywhere. What car are you driving?'

'Old, knackered VW Passat.'

'Flash your lights at the officer manning the barrier as you approach, and I'll warn him you're on the way.'

'I'll be there in half an hour.'

'I'll make sure I'm down in the lay-by waiting for you. Oh, and I hope you're feeling fit. The crime scene is at the top of the hill.'

Cormac ended the call and had just opened his car door when a voice called out to him.

'DS Cormac?'

Cormac looked round to see a man approaching with his arm outstretched.

'I'm DS Michaels,' he said. 'Pleased to meet you.'

Cormac hadn't been expecting a warm welcome from Michaels but shook the proffered hand.

'Sorry if I look surprised,' said Cormac. 'But I didn't think you were coming back to work just yet.'

'I thought I'd come in and be nosey,' said Michaels. 'I get bored being stuck at home.'

'At the moment we have a char-grilled corpse to deal with,' said Cormac. 'I'd run through it with you, but I've been diverted elsewhere. To be honest, I wouldn't be sorry if you came back tomorrow.'

'Been giving you a hard time, has he?'

'I'm not sure I could work with him all the time.'

'He's not so bad when you get to know him. Believe it or not, he and I make a pretty good team.'

'You do?'

'Look, I'm a good bagman. I'm never going to be Inspector Morse, and I'm not the quickest at putting everything together, but I'm honest, reliable, and I don't give up easily. I'm also bloody good at keeping notes in order and knowing where things are—something Driver is not so good at.'

'You're not saying Driver is Inspector Morse, are you?'

Michaels laughed. 'He's not quite that good, but show him a set of random clues, and if there's any sort of link, he usually finds it. I suppose you could say he's the yin to my yang.'

'So, why does he hate newcomers so much?'

'It's nothing personal; he's like that with anyone new.

You should consider yourself lucky. As I understand it he actually likes you.'

'Likes me?' said Cormac. 'He's got a bloody funny way of showing it.'

'Who do you think Eagan asked to check you out?'

'What, Driver? So he really did.'

'Not only did he check you out, but it was his recommendation that convinced Eagan to allow the transfer. He reckons you got crapped on from a great height.'

'He's not wrong there,' said Cormac. 'But how come you know so much if you've been away?'

'As I said, Driver keeps me up to speed. I'm like his sounding board. He likes to run things past me before he makes decisions. Mind you, I don't know why, because he never takes much notice of what I say.'

'And what about you? What do you think?'

'If you mean, what do I think of allowing you to transfer in, from what I've heard, I agree with Driver. And anyway, to be honest, I wouldn't care if you were a little green man who'd transferred in from Mars—as long as you can do the job and you don't stop me from doing mine, that's all I care about.'

'So, you're saying Eagan listens to advice from Driver? I got the impression they didn't have much time for each other.'

'Yeah, it's a weird set-up, alright,' said Michaels. 'It's as if they have this mutual respect for each other, but it's disguised because they don't want anyone to know.'

'Does Eagan know about Driver giving new people a hard time?'

'Driver has always done it, but Eagan knows and has asked him to continue doing it.'

'What do you think of Eagan? He asked me to spy on Driver; what's that all about?'

'Eagan thinks everyone's bent. And the old man knows Eagan asked you to spy on him.'

'But I wasn't spying on him,' said Cormac. 'As I mentioned, Eagan asked me to, but that's not what I'm about. I came here to be a detective, not a spy.'

'Anyway, it doesn't matter. Eagan's wasting his time with Driver,' said Michaels. 'Yes, he can be a moody bugger, and he can be a dinosaur sometimes, but he's no fool, and I guarantee he's not bent.'

Michaels was so emphatic in defence of Driver that Cormac was momentarily taken aback.

'So, what did you tell Eagan?' asked Michaels.

'What did I tell him about Driver? Much the same as you just said. Yes, he can be a bit of a throwback, but that doesn't make him bent, and I haven't seen anything that would make me think otherwise.'

Cormac watched as Michaels tried to read his face to determine if he was telling the truth. Eventually, he seemed satisfied.

'What else do you know?' asked Cormac.

'I know Driver had no choice about moving you on because there's a mobile phone with your number on it, and you've been compromised,' said Michaels. 'But Driver's not going to dob you in to Professional Standards.'

'Yeah, I know,' said Cormac. 'But I don't understand why he's looking out for me.'

'He's been shat on himself in the past, so he felt an affinity with you from the start,' said Michaels. 'And he's convinced the mobile phone was planted to point the finger at you.'

'Is there anything else?'

'Yes, Driver thinks you're on a mission of some sort.'

'Yeah, he said that, but he's wrong.'

'He doesn't think so,' said Michaels. 'Trust me, whatever your problem is, he only wants to help you.'

'Really?'

'Definitely.'

'But I don't have a problem for him to help me with,' said Cormac.

'Okay, if you say so,' said Michaels. 'But when you decide you need help, Driver's your man. My advice would be to give the guy a chance. Yes, he can be a pain in the arse sometimes, but I wouldn't want anyone else in my corner.'

Cormac looked at his watch. 'Look, I really should get going,' he said. 'I need to examine a crime scene before it gets dark.'

'Sure,' said Michaels, heading off across the car park. 'I'll see you around.'

As Cormac settled into his car and began driving, he thought about DCI Driver and how the indignity of being investigated by Professional Standards would have affected him. Being able to empathise with the old dinosaur was the last thing he had expected!

CHAPTER 5

* * *

Thirty minutes later, as he drove along the dual carriageway, Cormac could see the traffic slowing and moving to the outside lane to skirt around the closed lane up ahead. Keeping to the inside lane, he flashed his lights at the uniformed officer guarding the barrier, and just as Aconna had promised, the barrier was raised to allow him through. The officer made a note of his details and then showed him where to park.

True to her word, DC Charlotte Aconna was waiting for him. Dressed in a dark blue trouser suit and enormous-looking DMs, she was slim, almost as tall as he was, with short dark hair, piercing green eyes, and a bright smile that displayed a set of perfect, sparkling white teeth.

She had been passing the time of day with the uniformed PC who was carrying a clipboard on which he recorded all the comings and goings, but as soon as she saw his car, she left the PC, gave him a wave, and walked across to meet him.

Cormac parked in the lay-by, but then, as he pushed his car door open, his mobile phone rang. Aconna stopped and took a respectful step back so as not to intrude on Cormac's call.

'Bloody phone. Can't you see I'm busy?' muttered Cormac as he slumped back into his seat and reached for the phone. He was tempted just to cancel the call, but then he noticed the number calling. Clive Anderson was the letting agent Cormac had retained to look after his house while he had been away. It wasn't ideal timing, but Cormac had been trying to reach Anderson for days.

'Clive! Where have you been? I've been calling for weeks.'

'Whatever happened to the normal answer, such as, 'Hello Clive, how are you?" asked Anderson. 'And you know very well I've been on holiday for the last three weeks, as I sent the same email to all my clients.'

'Oh, did you? I must have missed it,' said Cormac.

'That'll explain why I've got about a dozen voicemails from you, then,' said Anderson. 'I am allowed a holiday, you know.'

'All right, Clive, you've made your point. And I'm sorry for all the voicemails.'

'It's not my fault if you don't read your emails.'

'No. You're right, Clive. It is my fault, and I apologise.'

There seemed to be a sulky silence from Anderson's end, so Cormac felt he should start again. 'So, how are you, Clive? And how was your holiday?'

'As it happens, it was terrible,' said Anderson. 'Just about everything that could go wrong did go wrong.'

'Oh dear. I'm sorry to hear that,' said Cormac. 'But if it's any consolation—'

'Is there any news?'

'I've been cleared of all charges,' said Cormac.

'Well, that's good news, then, surely,' said Anderson.

'Yeah, but I've also been demoted to DS.'

'What? How does that work if you're innocent?'

'Don't ask, Clive. Just put it down to internal politics; my face didn't fit,' said Cormac.

'What do you mean, 'your face didn't fit'? You haven't resigned, have you?'

'Not this time. Remember I said I was going to try to get a transfer back to Windover? Well, it's been approved, and I'm back. Now I just need my house back.'

'It's like I said when we spoke about this before,' said Anderson. 'Our hands are tied. There's nothing we can do.'

'Oh, come on, Clive,' said an exasperated Cormac. 'It's my bloody house!'

'Yes, it is your house, but if you recall, you came to me and asked me to let it for you while you were working away. As a letting agent, it's what I do, and I don't mind saying I'm rather good at it.'

'But I want to live in it.'

'And so you shall, once the current tenant's lease expires.'

'When's that?'

'In eleven months' time.'

'That's nearly a bloody year! I can't live in a motel for a year.'

'I'm sorry, Nolan. It's just unfortunate timing on your part.'

'Can't we evict the tenant?'

'On what grounds?'

'I don't know; isn't that where you come in? Perhaps they've done some damage. Surely you can come up with something.'

'Did I really just hear those words uttered from the mouth of a detective in the UK police service?'

'Come on, Clive, I'm desperate. You must be able to do something. As you're so keen to tell everyone, you are the expert.'

'Indeed, I am and, as the expert, I can assure you there are no grounds for eviction. In fact, I would go so far as to say you seem to be lucky enough to have the perfect tenant. May I remind you that I have a great reputation for looking after both landlords and tenants—a reputation I have no intention of damaging.'

'There must be something you can do. I'm living in a piddly motel room when I own a perfectly good house.'

'That's not my fault, nor is it your tenant's. If you had kept in touch and let me know your plans earlier, I wouldn't have set up the tenancy agreement. You only have yourself to blame.'

'Yes, but—'

'I'm sorry, Nolan, but nothing can be done. It is what it is, and you'll just have to accept it. Now, if there's nothing else, I am rather busy.'

'Bugger!' muttered Cormac as he opened the car door and slipped the phone into his pocket.

'Sorry about that,' he said as Aconna stepped forward to introduce herself and shake his hand. 'I shouldn't have answered it, but I've been trying to reach him for ages.'

Aconna had heard the muttered curse. 'Everything okay?'

'What? Oh, yeah, it's nothing. Just personal stuff.'

'If there's anything I can do...'

'Thanks, but no thanks,' said Cormac. 'No offence, but I try to keep my private life separate from work.'

Aconna smiled. 'Fair enough, I'll bear that in mind.'

'Where are we going?' he asked.

Aconna pointed to a path led through the trees and bushes that lined the back of the car park.

'That's the path to the top of the hill. It's quite steep, and it's still slippery from the rain the other night.'

'Great,' said Cormac. 'Just what we all love: an easily accessible crime scene.' He pointed to the path. 'Well, lead on, DC O'Connor—'

'Can I just stop you there, sir?'

'Sorry?'

'It's about my name. Everyone keeps calling me O'Connor, but it's actually Aconna, A.C.O.N.N.A.'

'Oh, I see,' said Cormac. 'Sorry, DCI Driver told me—'

'Yes, well, let's face it, DCI Driver's not that good with names, is he? He's been calling me O'Connor from day one. I even told him my distant relatives were Italian and not Irish, but would he listen?'

'I think you'll find he was doing that on purpose,' said Cormac. 'It was probably part of your induction test.'

'What induction test?'

'Apparently, Driver feels it's his job to test the patience of new arrivals, to make sure they've got what it takes. That's why I spent the best part of two weeks reorganising the filing on the second floor. Anyway, trust me, your surname is duly noted and corrected in my memory. In future, I shall call you DC Aconna and not O'Connor, unless you have a first name you'd like me to use?'

'It's Charlotte, but everyone calls me Charlie.'

'In that case, lead on, Charlie.'

Aconna set off up the hill, Cormac following a yard or

two behind. He had to raise his voice to speak to her, and of course, she had to call her replies over her shoulder, but he thought he might as well find out what he could.

'What's waiting for us when we get up there?'

'A body, tied to a cross.'

'Crucified?'

'Not your classic hammer-and-nails job, but sort of. It's been made to look like a scarecrow. It's been up on that hill in full view of the road.'

'Do we know how long it's been there?'

'The old farmer who reported it reckons it could only have been there for a day or two, or he would have spotted it sooner. He says he noticed it because of all the bird activity up there.'

'Bird activity?'

'Crows have been feasting on the head. They've had the eyes out and made a right mess of the face.'

'Oh, right. I see. It won't be an easy ID, then. Unless he's carrying some.'

'I doubt that,' said Aconna. 'He's not quite as naked as the day he was born, but almost. So, unless he's got it tucked away somewhere really personal...'

'Right, I think I understand what you're saying,' said Cormac.

They walked on in silence for a minute or two.

'Look,' said Aconna. 'Can I just say how much I'm looking forward to working with you? I've heard you have years of experience, and I'm really keen to learn.'

Cormac smiled. 'Driver mentioned you have a tendency to ask a lot of questions.'

'Is that going to be a problem?'

'Not for me. I'm on your side. You won't learn anything if you're not allowed to ask questions.'

'I get the feeling DCI Driver would prefer it if women didn't ask questions, or even have opinions. And better still if they were mute,' said Aconna.

Cormac thought she was probably right, but he didn't want to go down the 'let's slag off the boss' route, so he changed the subject.

'This is going to sound sexist and is probably very un-PC, but what are you like in a fight?'

'I'm sorry? Are you saying you want to fight me?'

'What I mean is, if we're going to be working together, I need to know you can handle yourself if things get a bit heavy. Now, I don't want to be rude, but I can't help but notice you're quite tall but not exactly built like a heavy-weight boxer.'

Aconna stopped, and as she spun round to face Cormac, she produced an extending baton as if from nowhere. She waved the baton at him as she spoke. 'Actually, I'd hate to look like a heavyweight boxer, but you don't need to worry about me, Sarge. I can look after myself if the need arises.'

'That's very impressive,' said Cormac, taking a step back. 'But you don't need to batter me into submission to prove your point. I'm prepared to take your word for it, so you can put the weapon away.'

Aconna looked satisfied with herself as she folded the baton and slipped it into her pocket. 'I'm quite good at judo and pretty handy with pepper spray, too!'

'Right, I get the message,' said Cormac hastily.

The sun was low in the sky by the time Cormac and Aconna reached the point where a pop-up tent had been erected and cordon tape had been stretched across the path. Fifty yards beyond the tape, Cormac could make out the limp cruciform figure. The low sun behind it cast a long, grim shadow down the slope towards them.

They could see two figures in white forensic suits taking a video of the crucified victim. Further away, another pair were pointing at something on the ground. As they watched, one figure sank to its knees and appeared to collect samples.

'Who do we think we're going to need to keep out up here?' asked Cormac, pointing at the tape.

'Actually, I insisted on putting the tape up,' said Aconna. 'As I recall, it's correct procedure, and I wanted to get it right. That's also why there's a PC here issuing forensic suits.'

'Well, that's a big tick in my book,' said Cormac. 'It's good to know at least one of us won't be cutting corners.'

As they approached, they could see the almost naked body had been bound to a rough cross made of wooden stakes. The body was bound with rope around the neck, and the waist, his feet just about touching the ground. The left arm was bound to the cross with more rope, but the right arm was cocked at an odd angle, elbow bent so the forearm pointed away from the cross, index finger extending into the distance.

As one of the white-suited figures turned towards them, Cormac recognised her as Dr. McGowan, the pathologist.

'I didn't expect to see you here, Dr. McGowan,' said Cormac. 'I thought you said you were going to a funeral.'

'I had been to the funeral and was attending the wake,' she said. 'And then my bloody phone started to ring, just as the party was getting started. I didn't even get to finish my first drink!'

'There's a lesson there,' said Cormac. 'Always switch your phone off if you don't want to be disturbed.'

'And you practise this yourself, do you?' she asked.

Cormac shrugged. 'Can't really. Not when I'm supposed to be available, 24/7.'

'Then we have a shared problem,' said McGowan. 'Much as I sometimes hate the intrusion, it goes with the territory.'

'What can you tell us about our victim?'

'Male, I'm guessing mid-forties by the look of his body, though the condition of the face makes it hard to be sure.'

'Time of death?' asked Cormac.

'My best guess at the moment is that he's been dead around forty-eight hours, but that could change when I get him to the lab.'

'You're thinking he died Saturday evening, then,' said Cormac. 'How long's he been out here?'

'Again, it's a guess, but it's been a cold, wet weekend, and he's not too ripe, so he was probably murdered and crucified the same night.'

'Can you tell us anything about the rope?' asked Cormac.

'It's coarse. Looks industrial. Maybe something from a farm or construction site.'

'What about the cross he's tied to?'

'It's made of wooden poles, some sort of softwood; I'd guess pine, untreated. The sort of thing you'd buy if you wanted cheap fence posts.'

Cormac realised Aconna was standing a few feet back, looking disturbed.

'Are you okay, Charlie?'

'I didn't get this close earlier,' she said. 'It seemed okay from a distance, but...'

'Is this your first murder?'

Aconna nodded. 'I've only been a detective for two weeks.'

'Well, we've all been where you are now. And if it's any consolation, I can promise you they're not usually as bad as this.'

'I just don't understand how anyone could do something like this,' said Charlie. 'It's as if it's been staged, like for the theatre.'

'A piece of theatre is exactly what it's meant to be, if you ask me,' said Cormac. 'I mean, this isn't an attempt to hide the body, is it? This is quite the opposite. It's all about showing it off.'

Cormac scanned the grass. Visible scuff marks showed the body had been dragged from the edge of some woods about forty yards below them.

'There are tyre impressions in the mud on the other side of the woods,' said McGowan. 'That's what they're looking at over there. I suppose it was as close as they could get by car.'

Cormac led Aconna down to the woods. There was a clear trail of muddy footprints and flattened vegetation leading through the trees to a clearing on the other side.

'I'm guessing there must be some sort of access road leading up to the woods,' said Cormac. 'How far is that through the trees, do you reckon?'

'Not far,' said Aconna. 'Ten, maybe fifteen yards.'

Cormac turned and looked back at the crime scene, imagining the effort it must have taken, and for what?

'I don't get it,' said Aconna. 'Why would anyone go to all this trouble to dispose of a body? Wouldn't it be easier to dump it by the side of the road somewhere?'

'Of course it would,' said Cormac, heading back towards the body. 'So, we have to ask ourselves why anyone would go to all this trouble, and I can only think of one reason.'

'So we could find it?' asked Aconna.

'Well, yes, but why did they want us to find it?'

Walking alongside him, Aconna could see that Cormac already knew the answer and was asking her what she thought.

'I'm afraid I don't know,' she said. 'You're streets ahead of me.'

'I think it's a message.'

'How so?'

'Well, as you just said, it's one hell of a lot of trouble for someone to drag a dead body through those trees and then across this field, which, although not that steep, is still uphill. It's bloody hard work moving a body a short distance on the flat, so it must have taken a monumental effort to drag it this far. And then, not content with doing all that, they built a cross and crucified the body on the very site where anyone with a sharp eye was bound to see it eventually.'

'So, probably more than one person involved?' asked Aconna.

'Yes, more than likely,' said Cormac.

They were walking past the body now.

'The old farmer only noticed it because of the crows,' said Aconna.

'Maybe that was part of the plan. Perhaps they used some sort of bait to attract the birds. Crows eat carrion all the time,' said Cormac.

'Carrion? That's an unusual way to describe a murder victim,' said McGowan, listening in as they passed.

'In the end, it's all rotting flesh, isn't it?' said Cormac. 'It may well be rotting human flesh, but to a hungry crow, it's just more carrion.'

'I wonder, does that make me some sort of crow, then?' asked McGowan absently.

'Only if you eat it,' said Cormac.

They were ten yards beyond the body, and now Cormac turned to look back at it.

'If you're right about it being left as a message, I think the whole thing must have been done at night,' said Aconna. 'It would have been a massive risk to do it in daylight.'

'Yes, I think we can safely assume you're right about that,' said Cormac.

'So, the next question has to be, who is the message for, doesn't it?' asked Aconna.

Cormac had a sinking feeling he might already know the answer to that but decided he would keep his own counsel for the time being. 'Now that, we don't know,' he said.

The sun had disappeared from view, and the light was fading fast as he walked back around to the other side of the crime scene, where the pathologist was still working under the glare of a powerful lighting rig.

'Excuse me, Dr McGowan.'

McGowan looked up at Cormac and smiled. 'If we're going to be working together, I think we would both feel a lot more comfortable if you dropped the formality and called me Martha. Everyone else does.'

'Martha. Okay, I can work with that,' said Cormac.

'What did you want to know?'

'His right hand; has it just fallen like that accidentally, or is it really pointing into the distance?'

'Ah, I'm glad you noticed that. It's actually been wired into that position.'

'Wired?'

'Yes, look here.' She pointed to the arm in question. 'There's stiff wire nailed to the cross behind the elbow, and then wrapped around the arm to hold it in place. They've even passed a second wire through the hand and bound it so the forefinger points like that while the rest of the fist is closed. It's actually very clever.'

In the fading light, Cormac tried to gauge the direction the finger was pointing.

'If the sun's setting behind us, that means he must be pointing more or less due east,' he said. 'So, next question: is he pointing at something specific, or is the direction he's pointing in irrelevant?'

'You mean like a red herring?' asked Aconna.

'Yes, exactly that.'

Aconna peered into the distance. 'It's getting difficult to make out what it might be now that the light's gone.'

'We'll need to come back in the morning when the light's better,' said Cormac. He turned to McGowan. 'Any idea how much longer you'll be, Martha?'

'As soon as my team gets their van up here, I'm going to take the body away.'

'Post-mortem?'

'Does 9 a.m. work for you?'

'Sounds good to me,' said Cormac. 'I'll let the DCI know.'

'What should we do now?' asked Aconna.

'Hmm? Oh, right. Well, I suppose I'd better call DCI Driver and explain that you have indeed been dealing with a scarecrow, but it's rather more complicated than the simple theft he thought it was.'

'What about me?'

Cormac looked at the weary young woman before him.

'I think you should go home, maybe have a stiff drink, and try to get some sleep.'

'But I thought the first twenty-four hours were the most important. There must be loads to do—'

'Yes, you'd think so,' said Cormac. 'And if this was a fresh murder with lots of nearby neighbours, we could do house-to-house inquiries and all sorts. But take a look around you. There are no houses with doors to knock, and there are no neighbours to question...

'The fact is, things won't really get going in this case until we have the post-mortem and forensic results. All we can do in the meantime is check missing persons and hope for a match. But, thanks to the crows, we don't know what the guy really looks like, so we might as well wait until morning. Perhaps Dr McGowan will be able to give us an idea of what he looked like before this happened.'

'Are you sure?'

'Honestly, Charlie. You're new to the job, and you've had a rough day. I think the best thing is for you to go home and rest. First thing tomorrow, you can start with that missing persons search.'

Aconna nodded reluctantly. 'Okay. I'll see you in the morning then.' She plodded off to the pop-up tent to hand back her forensic suit before heading back down the hill.

Cormac lingered near the crime scene, taking one last look at the victim, the glare of the floodlights highlighting the ragged eye sockets, the deep bruises, and the ligature marks on the neck.

This man had been restrained, beaten, strangled, and finally displayed on a cross. Cormac was becoming convinced the display was for his benefit. Was it another message to reinforce the earlier charred body in the car? Or was he just being paranoid about the whole thing?

But if it was a message, what the hell was someone trying to tell him?

* * *

CHAPTER 6

* * *

THE PHONE RANG JUST four times before Driver answered.

'What can I do for you, Cormac?'

'It's about this scarecrow, sir. It's a bit more complicated than we first thought.'

'Complicated how?'

'It's another murder, sir. A young man tied to a cross made to look like a scarecrow. His face is a mess, and he isn't carrying any ID.'

'Bloody hell,' muttered Driver. 'This is getting out of hand. Do you think the two murders are connected?'

'We definitely can't rule it out,' said Cormac.

'I'd better head out there right now—'

'There's not much point, sir. The body is being moved any minute. Forensics have photographed and videoed everything, and it's getting too dark to see. I think it's probably best if we come out first thing in the morning when we can see what we're doing. I've sent Aconna home and told her to start a missing persons search in the morning.'

'You're probably right,' said Driver. 'There's no point in blundering about in the dark. Speaking of Aconna, how is she working out? All right, is she?'

'She turned a bit green around the gills when we got close to the body, but it is her first murder and, to be fair, it wasn't a pretty sight. It even made me feel a bit queasy, if I'm honest. But, having said that, she managed to get everything up and running before I got there. I think she'll be a real asset.'

'You need to look after her, then,' said Driver.

'There is something you can do that would help, sir.'

'Oh, yes, and what's that?'

'You could try getting her name right. It's not O'Connor; it's Aconna, spelt A.C.O.N.N.A.'

'Really?'

'I think we owe it to her to get it right, don't you?'

'Come to think of it, she may have said something about her family having Italian roots...'

'Yes, that's what she told me,' said Cormac.

'Oh, well, point taken, Cormac. You're absolutely right. I'll make sure I don't get it wrong again.'

'Well, if there's nothing else, sir...'

'Actually, there is something I need to speak to you about.'

'Fire away, sir.'

'It's a bit delicate,' said Driver.

'Delicate?'

'Look, what I mean is, I don't think it's something we should discuss over the phone. I'd prefer to speak to you in person.'

'Can it wait until the morning?' asked Cormac.

'Yes, I suppose it can, but I'd rather we just focused on the murder.'

'What's it about? Can you give me a clue?'

'As I said, I'd rather speak to you in person.'

'Now you've got me worried,' said Cormac. 'Am I in trouble?'

'Not to my knowledge,' said Driver. 'I tell you what, why don't we meet somewhere?'

Cormac realised that whatever Driver wanted, he wasn't going to wait. 'You want to meet up tonight?'

'I could come over to Templeton if you like. Didn't you say you've got a house over there?'

'Ah, yes, the thing is, as I told you before, I don't actually live in the house at the moment. While I was working away, it was being rented out. I've come back earlier than I had originally planned, and there is still a tenant in the house, so until I get my house back, I'm living in the Bar Road Motel. Do you know it?'

'I know it's a den of iniquity,' said Driver. 'We've raided it God knows how many times over the years.'

'I'll grant you it's not the most salubrious,' said Cormac. 'But the way I look at it, it's cheap, and I only go there to sleep.'

'That's what half the prostitutes in Windover say,' said Driver.

'Yeah, well, they're not doing it in my room.'

'I'm glad to hear it.'

'Anyway, there's a pub a little way up the road called The Red Cow,' said Cormac. 'They do half-decent food, so I'm fast becoming a regular.'

'I know it,' said Driver. 'It's my cousin's pub. They serve a good pint there.'

'How about I head that way now and meet you in there?'

'I'm on my way,' said Driver.

* * *

'Is this a regular haunt of yours, sir?' asked Cormac as he raised his glass to Driver. 'Only you said they serve a good pint.'

'Not really. It's too far from Windover for me to be a regular,' said Driver. 'By the way, as we're off duty now, I think we can forget about rank and formality.'

'Fair enough,' said Cormac.

'The reason I know it's a good pint is because I usually sit in here and have one when we raid the motel.'

'You don't want to get your hands dirty, then?'

Driver smiled. 'Privilege of rank,' he said. 'Let's be honest, they don't really need me here for something like that. Michaels can handle it. I just come along for appearances. And a pint, of course.'

'You said it was you that checked me out,' said Cormac.

'Someone had to do it,' said Driver.

'Yeah, I get that,' Cormac replied. 'But I don't understand why you approved me and then did your best to piss me off as soon as I arrived.'

'If you mean the filing, that wasn't my idea. Eagan wanted to make sure I was right about you,' said Driver. 'He figured if you could put up with crap like that after being treated the way you were in the Midlands, then you must have your share of grit and determination. He likes that in his detectives, and I agree with him. Without it, you've got nothing.'

'Talking about being treated badly, I hear we have something in common,' said Cormac.

'You mean Professional Standards? Bunch of bastards,' sneered Driver. 'It wouldn't be so bad, but all they seemed to want to do was ruin my career. When they found they had no grounds to do that, they just walked away. I mean, if they proved it wasn't me, then it must have been someone else. But did they try to find out who? Did they bugger.'

'Yeah, tell me about it,' said Cormac. 'It was the same in my case. Once they proved it wasn't my incompetence, they didn't seem to want to take the next step and find out who was really responsible.'

'I've always said there's a conspiracy of silence once you get to the senior ranks,' said Driver.

'What d'you think it is?' asked Cormac. 'Rolled-up trousers and funny handshakes?'

Driver grinned. 'It makes you wonder, doesn't it?'

They drank in silence for a moment before Driver spoke again. 'Eagan told me about your girlfriend, and he asked me to look into it.'

'About Heather? Good. I was beginning to think he wasn't taking me seriously.'

Driver frowned.

'What?' asked Cormac. 'What's wrong?'

'Eagan told me her name was Heather Collins, she was a DI, and she retired about five years ago. Is that right?'

'Yeah, that's right.'

'And I'm guessing she was somewhere around your age.'

'four years younger,' said Cormac.

'Right. Well, the thing is, I've only been in Windover for three years, which means she would have left before I arrived. So I asked around, and no one who was here back then can remember her.'

Cormac frowned. 'That seems weird.'

'I thought so too,' said Driver. 'So I tried records. The thing is, I've now searched everywhere I can think of, and I can't find any trace of her. It appears there has never been a DI called Heather Collins working in Windover.'

Cormac's eyes widened in alarm. 'No, that can't be right.'

'Honestly, I've searched the entire database,' said Driver. 'I've even gone UK-wide. She's just not there.'

'Well, she won't be on the database now,' said Cormac. 'She took early retirement due to PTSD.'

'I've gone back ten years,' said Driver. 'I've searched current staff, leavers, deceased, early retirees... I'm sorry, but a detective by that name just doesn't exist.'

Cormac's mouth was moving, but he was struggling to find words.

'But she must... I mean, she was my girlfriend for God's sake. Are you suggesting I made her up? That I imagined her?'

'No, of course I'm not saying that,' said Driver. 'I'm—'

'What, then?'

'I know a couple of DIs in the drug squad, so I did some digging around the time you mentioned, five years ago. I discovered there was some intelligence at the time about a woman who was supposedly going around impersonating a detective. She had a fake warrant card and everything.'

'I never heard anything like that.'

'Ah, yes, but wasn't that around the time you were out of the loop?'

'Oh, yeah, of course. That was when I was trying to be a private investigator.'

'Not that you would have heard about it anyway,' said Driver. 'Even people who worked in the same bloody building weren't told about it unless they were actually part of the drug squad. They kept it to themselves because it might compromise one of their undercover investigations. Apparently, the rest of us are too damned stupid to be trusted with intelligence. The fact it might compromise every detective in the entire county didn't seem to occur to them.'

'Wait a minute. Are you saying you think Heather was manipulating me? You think I'm compromised?'

'Were you working in this area at the time?'

'Well, yes, but as I said, I wasn't in the police.'

'Then, as far as police work is concerned, you can't have been compromised, can you?'

'No, I suppose not,' said Cormac.

Driver studied Cormac's face.

'You already knew all this, didn't you?' he said.

'Of course I didn't,' replied Cormac.

'Why don't you tell me why you've really come back here?'

'As I told Eagan, I just want a fresh start.'

'Now, you see, I don't buy that,' said Driver.

'Okay, I admit I'd like to know what happened to Heather, but who wouldn't want to know why their girl-friend walked out on them?'

Driver scrutinised Cormac's face, then shook his head.

'I think you know a lot more than you're letting on,' he said. 'You see, if this had just happened and she had left you a couple of months ago, it would make sense to come back and try to find her. But after waiting five years? No, for me, that doesn't add up. I reckon you know she's somewhere in this area, and I'm beginning to think she's connected to these murders, and you know why.'

Cormac assumed a look of total innocence. 'Sorry, sir, but I have no idea what you mean.'

'If you tell me what you know, I might be able to help,' said Driver.

'As I said, there's nothing to tell,' Cormac insisted.

'And, as I said, I don't believe you,' Driver replied. 'I'll tell you something else: if you think Eagan's going to help you, you're wrong. He doesn't care about anyone except himself, whereas I'm not in it for myself. And, having been here longer, I know a lot more people than he does.'

Driver continued in the same vein for another five minutes, but Cormac remained adamant that he had no secrets. Eventually, Driver looked at his wristwatch, then drained his pint.

'Well, I must get off,' he said, getting to his feet. 'It's been nice having this little chat, but don't forget what I said. Eagan won't help you. I'm probably the only person here who can. But even I can't help if you don't tell me anything. So, my advice would be to come clean before you get in too deep and things get out of hand.'

'I'll bear that in mind,' said Cormac.

'I'll pick you up at the motel in the morning, at six-thirty,' said Driver. With that, he gave Cormac a sad little smile and headed for the door.

As Cormac watched Driver leave, he wondered if he was doing the right thing by keeping what he knew to himself. Two people were dead, possibly because of him or what he knew. No matter how he looked at it, things were already out of hand.

CHAPTER 7

* * *

A HEAVY MIST had formed in the early morning chill as Driver pulled up outside the motel. He managed a grunt in reply to Cormac's 'morning, sir,' before adding, 'You look like shit warmed up.'

'I didn't sleep very well,' said Cormac.

Apart from this solitary observation about Cormac's appearance, Driver didn't speak again, only managing occasional grunts during the brief journey to the crime scene as Cormac gave him a quick rundown of what they knew so far. By the time they reached the lay-by at the bottom of Barley Brow, they both realised that what they knew amounted to not very much at all.

The mist seemed to get even heavier as they made their way up the hill, and Cormac thought they would be hard pressed to see what they were doing at the top. However, as they reached the pop-up tent where the forensic suits had been handed out the previous evening, they suddenly found themselves through the mist and into bright sunshine.

A small team of white-suited technicians scrutinised the scene to ensure they had missed nothing. The makeshift cross now stood alone, the scarecrow victim long gone. The only thing that marked it out as a crime scene now was the blue and white tape still strung around it on temporary metal poles.

'How did they get the body up here?' asked Driver.

'Vehicle of some sort.' Cormac pointed to the small clump of trees and then followed as Driver marched over to take a look.

When they got to the trees, Cormac pointed beyond them. 'There's a track that gives access from the other side of the hill and leads up to the trees.' He pointed back towards the cross. 'Then he, or they, dragged the body through the trees and over to where they built the cross.'

'The body was definitely dragged over there?'

'It's difficult to see now, but there was a rough trail of scuff marks,' said Cormac.

Driver looked from the trees to the cross and then back. 'There must have been more than one person,' he said.

'I reckon so,' said Cormac. 'Either that, or we're dealing with a superhuman.'

They ambled back to the cross.

'You said one of his arms was arranged so it was pointing,' said Driver. 'Is that relevant?'

'I'd say yes, because it appeared to be very deliberate,' said Cormac. 'His arm and hand were actually wired into position so his index finger was pointing, more or less, due east.'

Driver turned to face the rising sun and raised a hand to shade his eyes. 'Well, there you go; that's obviously east. But good luck trying to see what's out there; it's so bright I can't see a thing!'

A large cloud crept in front of the sun, allowing them an opportunity to stare eastwards. From their vantage point, they could see that the mist, although dense around the base of the hill, seemed to become thinner further away from it. In fact, in the far distance, they could just about make out the three tower blocks that dominated the centre of Windover.

'That must be Windover,' said Cormac.

'Well, I hope that's not where the finger is pointing,' said Driver. 'Because if it is, we've got a suspect pool of about 75,000 people.'

'That's the problem, isn't it?' said Cormac. 'We have no idea how far we're supposed to look; it could be a mile, it could be a hundred miles.'

'Well, let's try to narrow it down, then,' said Driver. 'Let's assume the body was placed here so we, or at least someone, would see it and then come up here to investigate.'

'That sounds as if you're convinced it was put here for us to find,' said Cormac.

Driver turned to face Cormac and locked eyes with him. 'Yes, I'm pretty sure it was. But here's the thing I'm wondering: is it meant for all of us or just for one of us?'

Cormac shrugged, licked his lips, and swallowed hard. Then he looked away.

'Yes, well, never that mind for now,' said Driver, turning back to the view. 'We can come back to it later. But first, before I lose my train of thought, we're assuming we've been led up the hill so the scarecrow can point something out to us, right?'

'Yeah, but that's what I'm saying. How the hell do we know what we're looking at?'

'That's what I'm getting to, if you'll just stop interrupting me,' said Driver irritably. 'Now, I don't carry binoculars or a telescope around with me. Do you?'

Cormac was surprised by the question. 'I probably should have done this morning, but I didn't give it a thought.'

'Nor did I, but I'm not trying to make you feel guilty. My point is that you wouldn't normally carry anything like that, would you?'

'No, I can honestly say that's not something I normally do.'

'Right. And I'm betting whoever set this up doesn't, either. So, I reckon for this message to be clearly understood, they're not going to point to something we can't see with the naked eye. On that basis, my best guess is that we're looking for something that's not far away and is big enough to be obvious.'

Cormac allowed his eyes to trace a straight path back from Windover.

'There,' he said excitedly, pointing directly ahead. 'That big white house among the trees.'

Driver swung his gaze to where Cormac was pointing. 'Now you're talking,' said Driver. 'How far away do you think that is? I'd say it's not much more than a couple of miles.'

'It's got to be, or thereabouts,' agreed Cormac.

'This is your neck of the woods; do you know what it is?'

'Something tells me I should know it, but I can't place it right now,' said Cormac, producing his mobile phone. 'Let me give Charlie a call and get her to find it on a map.'

Driver raised an eyebrow. 'Charlie?'

'DC Aconna,' explained Cormac as he made the call. 'Her name's Charlotte, but apparently everyone calls her Charlie.'

Driver waited while Cormac spoke with Aconna before ending the call and slipping his phone back into his pocket.

'On first-name terms already, are we?' asked Driver.

'I was just trying to get her to relax a bit,' said Cormac. 'Besides, I can't be doing with that formal crap all the time.'

'I hope you don't think you're going to be calling me by my first name.'

'No way, sir. I wouldn't dream of it.'

'Good, I'm glad to hear it,' said Driver as he swept a last glance around the site. 'There's nothing more we can do out here, so we'd better get back.'

'While I remember, Dr McGowan said I should tell you the post-mortem's at nine,' said Cormac.

'I think I'll be attending that on my own. I want you to go back and get everything up and running. And I don't expect to hear that you've been following clues I don't know about. Understand?'

'Yes, sir, understood loud and clear.'

They started walking back towards the path when Driver grabbed Cormac's arm and stopped. 'What's that noise?'

'What noise?'

Driver squinted up into the sky, looking from left to right. Finally, he pointed directly above them. 'There!'

Cormac tilted his head back and looked up. A tiny speck in the sky seemed to grow larger as they watched.

'It's a bloody drone,' cried Driver. 'Some bugger's watching us.'

As he spoke, the drone plunged down towards them, hovering just a few feet above before it sped off, vanishing behind the trees.

'D'you want me to try to catch it?' asked Cormac.

Driver gave Cormac a pitying look. 'You've got a

Superman outfit on under those clothes, have you?' he asked, his voice laden with sarcasm.

'There's no need to be like that. I was only—'

'Get real. You've got no chance,' said Driver. 'That damned thing is probably moving at over forty miles an hour, and you're on foot. It could have gone off in any direction behind those trees, and you wouldn't have a clue. Chances are the bloody thing will have landed, been loaded into a car, and driven away by now. We can only guess who is behind it and why they're watching us.'

Cormac acknowledged this truth. 'Maybe someone wanted to make sure we figured out what the message is telling us.'

'And now it's been close enough for them to see our faces, they know precisely who has figured it out, don't they?' said Driver, eyeing Cormac.

'Yes, sir, I've got a nasty feeling you could be right about that.'

'And have you figured it out? I bloody hope so, because there's a limit to how many bodies Martha McGowan can fit inside her mortuary. At this rate, they'll be piling up outside before long.'

'Look, I didn't ask anyone to kill two people. If they wanted to send me a message, I would have been quite happy with a note on a piece of paper.'

'I'm not saying you asked for anyone to be murdered, but how many more deaths are there going to be if you don't figure out what the hell's going on?'

'About that,' said Cormac. 'You said you could help.'

'It's difficult to see your way in the dark,' said Driver.

'Sorry?'

'How can I help you when you won't tell me anything?'

'Oh, right. Yeah, well, I think I need to share one or two things with you.'

Driver considered for a moment. 'Does Aconna know what she's doing?'

'She's doing a missing person search, and while that's running, she's going to see what she can find out about the big house.'

'And you're happy for her to work unsupervised?'

'Yes, I am. I think she's more than capable.'

Driver rubbed his hands together.

'Well, then, in that case, I suggest we collect your car, and then we can talk over breakfast on the way back.'

'So, how did you meet Heather?' asked Driver.

'I can't remember exactly,' said Cormac. 'I know I was working a case and our paths crossed for whatever reason, and we got talking.'

'How did she convince you she was a police detective?'

'She told me she was a detective, so I chanced my arm and asked her if she could find something out for me. I can't recall what it was now, and I really didn't expect her to help, but a couple of days later she got in touch and told me what I wanted to know. After that, I asked a couple more times, and each time she came up with the goods. So, why wouldn't I think she was who she said she was?'

Driver nodded thoughtfully. 'If she came up with information only the police had, that makes me think she must have already had someone on the inside.'

'You mean I was sharing her? Oh, great,' said Cormac. 'That just makes me feel even worse.'

'Yes, well, I suggest you put your feelings to one side,' said Driver sternly. 'Two corpses are a little more important than your bruised ego, don't you think?'

'Yeah, sorry, of course they are,' said Cormac.

'So, what makes you believe the woman you knew as Heather Collins ran off with a drug dealer called Rocco Flint?'

'I won't tell you how, but I managed to obtain some CCTV footage from Gatwick Airport that showed a guy following us through check-in and onto the plane.'

'With over 200 passengers on a flight like that, there must have been plenty of men following you onto the plane,' said Driver.

'Yeah, but he was the only one who caught her eye half a dozen times. I didn't notice it at the time, but watching the CCTV, it's obvious they knew each other. The thing is, I remember seeing the same guy in our hotel on two or three occasions before she disappeared, but I'm sure I didn't see him again after that.'

'How did you know the guy was Rocco Flint?'

'I didn't back then; he was just some guy following us. But when I joined the Midlands drug squad, I had access to their intelligence. One day, I was searching through their database, and his face came up on screen. He was listed as Rocco Flint and was believed to be a major UK drug dealer.'

'So what? You think Heather is his girlfriend? Or is she a junkie?'

'I never once saw any evidence to suggest she took drugs,' said Cormac. 'And, trust me, there were no needle marks anywhere on her body.'

'Yes, well, I'll take your word for that,' said Driver. 'So, is she his girlfriend, or is she another dealer?'

'Could be either, I suppose,' said Cormac. 'Whichever it is, it makes me look a fool.'

'I don't see why she picked you,' said Driver. 'I can understand her impersonating a police detective and conning another detective to get information, especially if she found a drug squad detective, but you were freelance. What did she hope to gain by using you? Did you have a client she wanted to reach?'

'I had no clients with money and no one connected with drugs or any other sort of crime,' said Cormac. 'Believe me, I've gone over it again and again, and I can't see how she could have gained anything through me.'

'Of course, there's always the possibility she just liked you for being you,' suggested Driver.

'Yeah, right,' said Cormac. 'If you'd told me that five years ago, I might have believed it, but now I'm a bit too long in the tooth to believe fairy stories happen in real life.'

'It's as plausible as any other reason I can think of,' said Driver.

'No way,' said Cormac. 'She used me, and she would have had a reason, even if we can't see it.'

'Okay,' said Driver. 'So now bring me up to date. Why have you come back here?'

'I got a tip-off.'

'What sort of tip-off?'

'Someone told me Rocco Flint was based in this area.'

'And that was enough for you to make a career u-turn?'

'After all the crap I went through up there, and the prospect of more to come, what did I have to lose?'

'You think that by coming back here, you're going to find Heather?'

Cormac shrugged. 'Maybe.'

'I thought you were over her.'

'I don't want her back, if that's what you think.'

'So what do you want? Revenge?'

'I wouldn't mind screwing things up for Rocco Flint.'

Driver rolled his eyes. 'Do you realise how immature that sounds?'

Cormac said nothing, so Driver continued. 'This someone who gave you the tip-off, do they have a name, or can I guess?'

'It was Marky.'

'Oh, terrific,' said Driver. 'And you thought it was a good idea to keep this all to yourself?'

'I didn't see how it could be relevant,' said Cormac.

'Your phone number was in the victim's contact list, and it was the only bloody number! You're claiming to be an experienced detective, and you didn't think that was relevant?'

Cormac looked suitably sheepish. 'I admit I made a stupid mistake. Of course, I can see it now, but—'

'What about this second body? Am I going to find you're connected to that one as well?'

'I don't know.'

'What do you mean, you don't know?'

'When you see the state of his face, you'll understand. He's unrecognisable.'

'You mean it's possible, then?'

'Anything's possible,' said Cormac.

Driver rubbed his face with both hands.

'Bloody hell, Cormac. What are you getting us into?'

'I get it if you want to kick me off the case, sir. And I understand you have to tell Superintendent Eagan, and—'

'Kick you off the case? Why on earth would I boot out

the only person who might have a sliver of insight into what's going on?'

'You mean you're not going to—'

'No, I am not going to,' said Driver. 'But you listen, and you listen good. God knows why, but I'm putting my neck on the line for you. So, if I find you've concealed so much as a silent fart from me in the future, you'll be out the door so fast you'll wish you'd stayed up in the Midlands being used for target practice. Is that clear?'

'Yes, sir. Clear as a bell.'

'Right, now I have an appointment with a corpse and my favourite pathologist. You need to get back to the office and make sure Aconna really knows what she's doing. I'll brief you on the post-mortem when I get back.'

CHAPTER 8

* * *

CORMAC SLUNK away from breakfast feeling distinctly chastened and drove back much more slowly than he normally would. Driver had hit the nail on the head when he said he had been a fool to think he knew what he was getting into. He definitely hadn't factored in the possibility of Marky's murder, and if he was linked to the second victim, that would make two dead bodies connected to him in the space of forty-eight hours.

But now that he didn't have Driver breathing down his neck, he was able to think. Driver had said he believed the burner phone left with Marky's body had been planted there to frame him. But by whom? Was it Rocco Flint? If that was the case, did it mean Heather was involved? And if the second body was connected, why was it pointing to the big house? Or had he got that wrong?

He parked his car and made his way up to the incident room. He resolved to focus on the facts and stop speculating if he was going to make any sense of this mess. He wouldn't be much help to Charlie Aconna if he couldn't keep a clear head.

'Morning, Charlie. Any luck with missing persons?'

'I've got two possibilities. One is 52 years old; the other is 43, but they both have dark hair, so unless our victim dyed his hair...'

Cormac pursed his lips. 'Maybe when we get the post-mortem report, we'll know a bit more. And hopefully, the pathologist might give us a rough idea of what he looked like before the crows got to him.'

'I had better luck with your big house,' said Aconna. She walked across to the area map she had pinned up on the wall and pointed to a small red circle she had drawn on it. 'It's called Milburn Manor. Formerly the ancestral home of the Milburn family, it fell into disrepair until forty years ago when the current owner bought it and restored it to its former glory.'

'And the current owner is?'

'Lord Damon Tilthorne.'

'Isn't he the—'

'The Home Secretary, yes,' finished Aconna. 'He lives there when he's not being a politician.'

'He's not short of a few quid, then,' said Cormac.

'He's part of the Tilthorne banking family, and he has massive amounts of shares. He was on the board but stepped down when he became Home Secretary.'

'I expect he still makes a mint from his shares,' said Cormac.

'Over ten million last year,' said Aconna.

Cormac joined her in front of the map. 'So the scarecrow was found here,' he pointed to Barley Brow, 'and the house is there.'

'It's a fraction over two miles as the crow flies, if you'll excuse the inappropriate crow reference,' said Aconna.

'So, the question we need to ask is, why was the scarecrow pointing at the house?'

'It's where the killer lives?' suggested Aconna.

'Why would you murder someone and then pose the body so it pointed to your own house?'

'It's not a great theory, is it?' said Aconna. 'But do we know for sure that he was pointing to the big house?'

'I can't guarantee it, but DCI Driver thinks it's our best guess, and I agree with him,' said Cormac. 'There was no other significant landmark that could be seen with the naked eye.'

'Do you think there's any significance in him being posed like a scarecrow?'

'Maybe,' said Cormac. 'It's always something we could consider if we ever find out who he is.'

They stood before the map, both lost in their thoughts, until Cormac came to a decision. 'We can't do much more until we get the forensic and post-mortem results,' he said. 'So, how about we go to the canteen and grab a coffee? There's some stuff you need to know.'

'Is it about the case?' asked Aconna.

Cormac nodded. 'Yes, it is. It turns out I seem to be central to what's going on here.'

Aconna's eyes widened. 'Really? How does that work?'

'It's a bit involved,' said Cormac. 'Let's get that coffee, and I'll tell you about it.'

* * *

It was 11:30 when Driver returned from the post-mortem.

'We've identified the house, but we're getting nowhere with missing persons,' said Cormac.

'You can forget missing persons,' said Driver. 'I can tell you exactly who our scarecrow is.'

'Really?'

'You might think the murderer had arranged for the crows to peck his eyes out to make it impossible to identify him, but you'd be wrong. I think it was done out of spite, just to spoil his good looks.'

'What makes you say that?' said Cormac.

'If you really wanted to make it difficult for us to iden-tify the guy, you'd chop his fingers off, wouldn't you?'

'You mean his prints are on file?'

Driver smiled and nodded. 'He had a conviction for drug dealing way back when he was a teenager.'

'That's a bit of luck,' said Cormac. 'Who is he?'

'His name is Jonathon Tilthorne, 46 years old, 6 feet 2 inches tall, blond hair, blue eyes, 177 lbs. That's twelve and a half stone in old money.'

'Did you say his name was Tilthorne, sir?' asked Aconna.

'Yes, that's right.'

'Well, that's a coincidence, because the big house he was pointing at is owned by Lord Damon Tilthorne, the Home Secretary. Are they related?'

'They are indeed,' said Driver. 'Jonathon Tilthorne is the Home Secretary's son.'

'Does that mean he was the heir to Milburn Manor and the Tilthorne estate?' asked Cormac.

'Can't say without seeing the will,' said Driver. 'But it wouldn't surprise me.'

'Perhaps there is no connection with Marky's death,

then,' said Cormac. 'Maybe the will is the motive for his death.'

'I don't think we can rule anything out yet,' said Driver.

Aconna had been tapping away at her keyboard, but now she stopped, sat back, and stared at the monitor. 'You're right about him being good-looking, sir,' she said.

'What are you looking at, Facebook?' asked Driver, stepping across to peer over her shoulder.

'No. He doesn't seem to have any social media accounts,' said Aconna.

'That's unusual these days,' said Cormac. Curiosity got the better of him, and he wanted a look too.

'This photo is from one of those hoity-toity, upper-class, glossy magazines,' said Aconna. 'It was taken ten years ago.'

'So no social media and no recent photos,' said Driver. 'And he doesn't look as if he chose to be in that photo, does he?'

'He looks as if he'd rather be anywhere but,' said Aconna.

'So, why is he keeping such a low profile?' mused Driver.

'I think I can hazard a guess at that,' said Cormac.

Driver turned to look at him. 'You look as if you've seen a ghost.'

'Not quite,' said Cormac. 'You said he had a conviction for dealing when he was a kid, right?'

'Yes, when he was sixteen.'

'Seems to me that he never stopped dealing then,' said Cormac. 'He just got very, very good at not getting caught.'

'Are you going to tell us what you know?' asked Driver.

'Sure,' said Cormac. 'Unless I'm very much mistaken, you're looking at a photograph of a drug dealer called Rocco Flint.'

'Are you sure?'

'It's been five years since I saw him, and that's an old photograph, but that's definitely the guy who was following me and Heather when we went to Thailand.'

'And you think she ran off with him?' said Driver. 'That doesn't say much for her, does it?'

'Maybe it wasn't that simple,' said Cormac. 'He might have had some sort of hold over her.'

'There's no point in debating that now, is there?' said Driver. 'We need to get over to Milburn Manor and tell Lord Tilthorne that his son has been murdered.'

'Excuse me, sir.' A uniformed constable had appeared at the door. 'Sergeant Gleeson said to tell you there's a man down in the custody suite saying he needs to speak to DS Cormac urgently.'

'I'm a bit busy at the moment,' said Cormac impatiently. 'Tell him I'll be down later.'

'He said to tell you drug squad officers are on their way over to pick him up, so if you want to speak to him, it's now or never, because once they take him—'

Cormac sighed and looked at Driver, who nodded his assent. 'Okay, okay. I've got the message. I'm coming now.'

Cormac followed the constable down the two flights of stairs to the ground floor, then through several sets of doors until they reached the custody suite. Sergeant Robbie Gleeson looked up from his desk and grunted a greeting.

'Who wants to speak to me?' asked Cormac.

Gleeson ignored Cormac, pointed to the doors leading to the cells, and addressed the constable. 'Take DS Cormac through to the prisoner in cell number five.'

'I hope this is important,' said Cormac, 'because we've got two murd—'

'I have no idea if it's important,' snapped Gleeson. 'He's

probably a time-waster, but he says he's got information that you'll want to hear and he'll only speak to you.'

'Did he say what it's about?'

'If he wanted to tell me what he knows, he wouldn't be demanding to speak to you, would he?'

'How long have I got?'

'Before the high and mighty drug squad arrives to take him away?' Gleeson looked at the huge clock on the wall opposite him. 'You've got five minutes, maybe ten, if you're lucky.'

Cormac followed the PC through the doors and waited while he unlocked the door to cell number five, pushed the door open, and then stepped back to allow Cormac to enter.

Sitting on the uncomfortable-looking bench that doubled as a bed, a man turned his hollow-cheeked face in their direction. Dark circles underlined his dull green eyes as he squinted at them, his left leg bouncing nervously.

'Sniffer?' said Cormac. 'You're a long way from home. What the hell are you doing here?'

'Look, you gotta get me outta here, right?'

'Whoa, slow down,' said Cormac. 'I was told you had something to tell me.'

'You get me outta here, and I will.'

'I can't just get you out of here. It doesn't work like that.'

'But you must, right?'

'Why must I?'

'Cos if you don't, they're gonna fix me.'

'You're not making a lot of sense here, Sniffer. What are you on?'

'I'm not on nuffink, but they're gonna fix me, and I'm scared shitless, right?'

'Fix you? Who's going to fix you?'

'Rocco Flint, that's who.'

'Look, that's not going to happen. I know for a fact Rocco Flint is dead. I saw his body for myself.'

Sniffer's expression changed from terrified to confused. 'You're trying to mess with my head, right?'

'Sorry?'

'Rocco can't be dead, man,' insisted Sniffer.

'But he is. There was a post-mortem this morning,' said Cormac.

'That's bollocks, right? I mean, you can't kill Rocco. There's too many of them.'

'What do you mean, too many of them? It sounds to me like your head's already messed up. He's just one man, Sniffer. There's just one of him, and he's dead.'

'And you're saying I'm off my head?' said Sniffer. 'You're the one talking total bullshit, right?'

'What are you talking about?'

'Rocco Flint isn't a man, it's an org—'

Cormac had his back to the door and had Sniffer's full attention, but suddenly Sniffer stopped speaking, and now he only had eyes for whatever he could see over Cormac's shoulder. His eyes suddenly widened, what little colour he had drained from his face, and his leg started to bounce even faster. He looked accusingly at Cormac.

Cormac turned to see a man in jeans and a white T-shirt. The lanyard around his neck indicated he was with the police. The drug squad had arrived.

'Right, mate, we'll take it from here,' the man said to Cormac.

Cormac turned back to Sniffer, who was staring at him in apparent disbelief. 'You set me up, right?' he asked. 'You bastard.'

'What do you mean, I set you up?' said Cormac. 'I didn't

bring you in here, did I? I didn't even know you were in the area.'

'They've got to you as well, right?'

Another man had now arrived, and the two of them pushed past Cormac and grabbed their prisoner. 'Sorry to spoil your cosy chat, but I believe he's our prisoner now.'

'Hang on a minute,' said Cormac. 'I haven't finished talking to him.'

'I think you'll find you have, pal,' said the first man. He nodded to his mate, and they hoisted Sniffer to his feet and marched him out of the cell.

'Don't let them take me!' screamed Sniffer.

'Wait!' shouted Cormac.

'Sorry, pal, no time. The engine's running outside, and our lunch will be waiting when we get back.'

They dragged the struggling Sniffer out through the custody suite, with Cormac desperately trying to intervene.

Gleeson was gesticulating from his desk. 'Hey. Just a minute. You need to sign for him before you can take—'

'We already signed in. You can sign us out. We're the drug squad; we haven't got time to mess about.'

Gleeson swore at them, his face turning several shades of red until it was bordering on purple, but they just laughed as they hauled their prisoner through the back doors. Sniffer made a valiant effort to plant his feet against the door frame, but he didn't have the strength to put up enough of a fight to slow them for even a moment.

A car was waiting outside the doors with a third officer at the wheel, engine running, ready to go. The prisoner was bundled unceremoniously into the back of the car.

'Help me!' he screamed at Cormac. 'They're gonna kill me!'

One of the drug squad officers swore at Sniffer, then

turned to Cormac. 'Listen to him. It's unbelievable the crap these guys come out with. Any old bollocks rather than face up to the fact he was caught dealing dope.'

He slid into the seat next to Sniffer and reached for the door.

'I know where Heather is, right?' screamed Sniffer. 'Don't trust her. She's—'

But his words were cut off as the door slammed shut and the car sped away.

Cormac couldn't quite believe what he had just heard. Did Sniffer really know where Heather was, or was he just spouting nonsense to try and save himself? He would have to find out where they were taking Sniffer. He went back to Gleeson's desk.

'Where have they taken him?'

'How the hell do I know?'

'They must have brought paperwork,' said Cormac. 'Come on, it won't kill you to tell me where they've come from.'

Gleeson sighed and rifled through the paperwork on his desk.

'Dortmund Road,' he said. 'It's in Southampton.'

'Right. Thank you,' said Cormac. 'That wasn't so hard, was it?'

Gleeson stared balefully, but Cormac wasn't in the mood for yet another clash, so he turned and walked away.

'What was that all about?' asked Driver when Cormac got back.

'I'm not sure. It was a bit weird. The guy asking for me is called Sniffer. He was an occasional informant of mine up in the Midlands.'

'Is every Midlands drug dealer following you down here?' asked Driver.

'Sniffer isn't a dealer. He's just into coke in a very big way, hence the name.'

'So, what did he have to say? Anything that's going to help solve these murders?'

"Two drug squad guys rushed in and carted him off before I could find out what he was on about.'

'But he must have said something.'

'Well, yeah, he did. He said Rocco Flint isn't a man's name; it's the name of an organisation.'

Driver frowned. 'What? I thought you said Jonathon Tilthorne was Rocco Flint.'

'Yeah, well, as I said, Sniffer likes his coke, and if he can't get his hands on that, he'll take whatever he can get. And the way he was twitching, he must have been on something.'

Driver rolled his eyes. 'Reliable witness material, then,' he said.

'He also claimed the drug squad guys were going to kill him if I didn't stop them taking him away.'

'Sounds like drug-fuelled paranoia to me,' said Driver.

'And then, as they got him in the car and were about to drive away, he said, "I know where Heather is".'

Driver's head snapped round to face Cormac. 'And does he?'

'I don't know. They drove him away before he could say any more.'

'How reliable is this guy?' asked Driver.

Cormac shrugged. 'You wouldn't risk your life on his say-so.'

'So, what do you think? Is there anything to it, or is it just a last-ditch attempt to get your attention?'

'Well, it got my attention right enough,' said Cormac. 'But those drug squad buggers wouldn't stop.'

'I told you; they think they're a cut above the rest of us,' said Driver. 'Do you know where they took him?'

'Dortmund Road in Southampton. I'm going to see if I can arrange a visit.'

'Centralising all the area drug squads in Dortmund Road was one of the better decisions made at headquarters,' said Driver. 'Putting all the bad apples in the same barrel stops them contaminating the rest of us.'

'I've finished that search for you, sir,' said Aconna.

Cormac raised an eyebrow at Driver.

'While you were downstairs with your drug addict mate, young Charlie here was doing a little research into Lord Tilthorne. It doesn't hurt to have a bit of background information before we interview someone, whoever they are.' He turned to Aconna. 'Fire away then, Charlie.'

An embarrassed smile tugged at the corners of Aconna's mouth, but inside she was immensely pleased by Driver's use of her first name. He had even apologised for getting her surname wrong earlier. Perhaps he wasn't so bad after all.

'Lord Damon Tilthorne,' she read from her notes. 'Born 1956, Chairman of the Tilthorne banking group until 2018 when he stepped down. This was to allow him to become Foreign Secretary without anyone being able to accuse him of any conflict of interest.'

'As if a politician would look after his own interests,' said Driver.

'He was appointed Home Secretary in 2022, a post he still occupies,' continued Aconna. 'He still retains his banking shares, which earn him in excess of ten million a year on top of his ministerial salary. He married Jane Bolton-Flint in September 1978. Their son Jonathon was born in March 1979.'

'Up the duff when they married then,' said Driver.

'They had a daughter, Rosemary Jane, in December 1980. Lord Damon and Lady Jane divorced in 1993.'

'Do we know why they divorced?' asked Driver.

'I didn't get that far,' said Aconna. 'If you think it's important, I can find out.'

'No rush,' said Driver. 'I doubt it's relevant to her son's death after all this time. We need to know where she lives, though. She has to be informed about his death, and we'll need to question her. I'm assuming she's still in touch with her son and daughter?'

Aconna winced. 'I didn't find that out either. Sorry, sir.'

'Don't worry; you've done well with the time you had,' said Driver. 'But now, see if you can find anything more on the Tilthornes, especially Jonathon and the daughter, Rosemary Jane.'

'Yes, sir. I'll get onto it now.'

Driver turned to Cormac. 'I suppose you and I had better go and break the bad news to Lord Damon.'

* * *

* * *

Even though Milburn Manor was fifteen miles from Windover, they had to navigate what seemed like endless miles of narrow country lanes, so it took well over half an hour to get there. A wide gravel drive led to a pair of imposing wrought-iron gates that must have stood eight feet tall and were firmly closed.

Cormac pulled up by a large sign that read, 'Access denied without security clearance.'

Cormac sighed. 'I suppose I should have guessed that a cabinet minister as important as the Home Secretary would have security,' he said.

'It's the modern world for you,' Driver replied. 'I suppose we should be grateful we don't get lumbered with babysitting him.'

'So, where is this security who can grant us access?' asked Cormac.

As he spoke, a well-built man in a dark suit appeared

beyond the gate. Square-jawed and broad-shouldered, he stood well over six feet tall.

'It must be the James Bond lookalike,' said Driver. He handed Cormac his warrant card. 'Tell him it's important we speak to Tilthorne. You know the drill. And be careful; it looks as if he's armed.'

Cormac took the warrant card, held it alongside his own, stepped out of the car, and walked slowly and deliberately towards the gate, the bulge in the big man's jacket more than enough to convince him to take care. As he neared the gate, he held out the two warrant cards.

The man looked Cormac up and down, then gestured with his head. 'Can I help you?'

'DS Cormac and DCI Driver from Windover police. We need to speak to Lord Tilthorne.'

'No chance of that happening today, mate.'

'But it's important. It's about hi—'

'It doesn't matter what it's about. Even if you were the Prime Minister, I'd still tell you to piss off.' The man turned and walked away.

Cormac grabbed the gates and rattled them. 'Don't tell me to piss off, you arrogant prick,' he shouted. 'This is important.'

The man stopped in his tracks, then turned and marched back to the gate, fists clenching, a big smile on his face. Even though the gates were between them, there was enough menace about him to make Cormac take an involuntary step back.

The guard snarled through the gate. 'Look, hard man, any time you want to back those words with some action, I'll be happy to kick your arse all over the county. I'd love to do it right now, but I'm going to spare you because a sad day like this isn't a day for violence. Now, piss off, and think yourself lucky I'm on my best behaviour.'

'A sad day like what?' asked Cormac.

'Lord Tilthorne is in mourning. He found out early this morning that he's lost his son. Surely even you lot can leave a man alone for something like that.' With that, he turned and walked off.

Cormac stared after the man until he disappeared into a portakabin that seemed to serve as a makeshift office. Then he turned and walked back to his car.

'He won't let us in,' he told Driver.

'Why not?'

'Apparently, the Home Secretary is mourning the death of his son and will not be disturbed by anyone. Even the Prime Minister would be turned away.'

'But he can't ... Wait a minute. How the bloody hell does he know?'

Cormac shrugged. 'I don't know, but he does.'

'Who told him?'

'Well, don't look at me,' said Cormac. 'Your guess is as good as mine.'

'If I find out someone's been shouting their mouth off, I'll—'

'How many people knew?' asked Cormac. 'You, me, Aconna, and Dr McGowan, right? But the guy said Tilthorne had been told early this morning. The only one of us who might have known early enough to have tipped him off is Martha McGowan. You've known her longer than I have; is she capable of being that unprofessional?'

'I've never known her to be anything but totally professional,' said Driver.

'Then we have a mystery on our hands,' said Cormac.

Driver's phone was ringing. As he took the call, Cormac started the car and headed back towards Windover. Less than a minute later, Driver ended his call and pocketed his phone.

'That's all we need,' he muttered.

'Sir?'

'That was Superintendent Eagan. He wants to see us in his office when we get back. And I don't think we've been invited for tea and a cosy chat.'

They drove on in silence until Cormac spoke. 'Don't look now, but I think we're being followed.'

The driver tried to see behind them in the wing mirror, but it was adjusted for the person in the driver's seat. 'Is it a car?'

'Dark green Land Rover. Discovery, I think. It's staying about a hundred yards behind us.'

'Did you see where it came from?'

'Not sure. It must have been waiting in one of the side lanes and clocked us when we went past.'

'Can you see the driver? Man or woman?'

'Can't tell; it's too far back.'

'Can you see the registration plate?'

'It's covered in mud.'

'Oh, is it now?' said the driver. 'You realise it's an offence to have an obscured number plate?'

'Do you think we should do something about that?'

'As officers of the law, we'd be within our rights to stop a vehicle with an obscured registration number.'

'And you really want to do that?' asked Cormac. 'We'll look a pair of twats if I'm wrong.'

'Why would we? The number plate is still illegal.'

'Yeah, but think of the paperwork. Haven't we got enough on our plates?'

'We don't have to nick anyone. It's just an excuse to get a

closer look. If it seems innocent, you can let them off with a lecture.'

'How come I get to give the lecture? It's your idea.'

Driver smiled. 'One of the first things you learn in management is the art of delegation.'

'Do you want to stop it now?'

'Give it a couple more miles,' said Driver. 'If it's still following us, we'll pull it over before we hit the main road.'

Five minutes later, Cormac slowed right down, hit the hazard lights, and moved to the centre of what was already a narrow lane. Driver wound down his window and stuck his arm out, holding his warrant card.

The woman driver of the car following was slow to react and was forced to stop right behind Cormac's car. Cormac was immediately at her door, swinging it open and showing his warrant card.

The woman was small, in her mid-forties, with long dark hair and brown eyes. Perched high in the Land Rover, she had a large expanse of bare leg on show from beneath a very short skirt.

'Switch off the engine and step from the car, please, madam,' said Cormac.

As soon as he mentioned the word 'police,' she seemed to gain confidence.

'I beg your pardon.'

'You heard him,' said Driver, throwing open the passenger door of her car. 'Engine off, and step outside.'

'Is this a hold-up?' asked the woman nervously as she complied with the instruction. 'I can let you have money if that's what you want.'

'We're police officers, not kidnappers,' said Cormac. 'We want to know why you're following us.'

'What do you mean, following you?'

'You've been behind us for miles,' said Driver. 'We want to know why.'

'Because there's no alternative, of course,' said the woman. 'What would you have me do, drive over the verge to pass you? Have you seriously stopped me just for that? Haven't you got better things to do?'

'We've stopped you because your front registration number plate is obscured,' said Driver. 'It's an offence.'

'Is it?' She walked round to the front of her car and looked at the number plate. 'It's just a bit of mud,' she said. 'It's hardly a surprise out here in the country, is it? There's mud everywhere.'

'Surprise or not,' said Driver, 'it's still an offence.'

'Well, I'll wash it off when I get back home.'

'You need to do it before that,' said Driver. 'Can I see your driving licence?'

The woman glared at him, huffed a sigh, stomped back to the driver's side of the car, leaned in and grabbed her handbag from the passenger seat. She rifled through the bag until she found the licence and handed it to Driver, who passed it on to Cormac.

Cormac compared the licence photograph to her face. 'So, it's Mrs Anita Bogd—'

'Bogdani,' she corrected.

'That's an unusual name.'

She smiled. 'Some people say I'm an unusual woman.'

If she was hoping to charm Cormac, she failed. He was totally unimpressed. 'Do they really?'

The woman huffed impatiently. 'My husband is Albanian, so I have an Albanian surname, okay? I mean, it's not as if it's rocket science.'

'Live locally, do you, Mrs Bogdani?'

'If you can read, you can see from my licence that I

don't,' she said. 'But my husband says we're going to, so here I am, hunting for the right house. Funny enough, I've just been looking at one down the road, and if you look in the back seat, you can see I have details for several more in this area. If you contact my estate agent, he'll tell you he was just showing me around one. I've got one of his cards in the car.'

As she went to the car to retrieve the estate agent's business card, Cormac returned to his own car to make a note of the licence details.

The woman came back and handed the business card to Driver. 'What's he doing with my driving licence?'

'Just making a note of the details,' said Driver. 'We'll have to notify your local police so they can check you've cleaned your number plate.'

As Cormac returned, he looked at Driver, who shrugged and nodded.

'Well, thank you for your cooperation, Mrs Bogdani,' said Cormac, handing her driving licence back. 'You can be on your way now, but you should clean that number plate first.'

Once again, she stomped to the front of the car. This time she aimed a kick at the number plate. 'There,' she said. 'Is that good enough for you?'

Cormac walked to the front of the car. A small heap of dried mud lay on the road beneath the number plate, which was still grubby, but now legible.

'That's much better, thank you,' he said.

'I can go now, can I?'

'Yes, thank you,' said Cormac. 'I'll pull over so you can get past.'

Cormac and Driver sat in their car and watched as the dark green Land Rover Discovery inched past and then eased away down the road.

'Was she for real?' asked Driver.

'She's a piece of work, that's what she is,' said Cormac.

'But was she following us?'

'I think she was,' said Cormac.

'Well, even if she was, she isn't now,' said Driver. 'You weren't just pretending when you took the licence?'

'Oh, no,' said Cormac. 'I've got her details, and the car reg number too.'

'Good. It'll give Aconna something to do.'

* * *

When they got back to the incident room, Aconna was waiting for them.

'I've had to go back a long way to find a photograph with the whole family together,' she said. 'But I did manage to find this one.' She clicked an image, and it bloomed into life on the screen. 'It was taken when he first took over as Chairman at Tilthorne Banking. Someone did a background piece trying to portray him as the happy family man.'

Driver and Cormac crowded behind her to look at the screen. The photo showed Lord and Lady Tilthorne, their two children, and a Labrador retriever. The caption read, 'Lord Damon and Lady Jane Tilthorne, their children Jonathon and Rosemary Jane, and their dog Rocco.'

'Well, he looks happy enough,' said Driver. 'But then I suppose he would if he'd just become Chairman.'

'Don't you think it looks like a fixed smile, sir?' asked Aconna. 'It's almost as if it was glued on.'

'It's clear Lady Jane hadn't read the "happy family" script,' remarked Cormac.

'You're telling me,' said Driver. 'The boy, Jonathon, doesn't look impressed, either.'

'Perhaps that was his natural expression,' Cormac suggested. 'He didn't look as if he wanted to be in that wedding photo we saw.'

'The only one who looks happy and relaxed is the young girl,' said Driver. 'And the dog; he looks happy enough.'

'I'm glad it's not just me, then,' said Aconna. 'That's exactly what I think.'

'Have you got anything on the two children?' asked Driver.

'Not much,' said Aconna. 'Their early childhoods were very private. They both went to private schools, obviously, and both seemed to be doing well, but they have always kept really low profiles until, in 1996, Jonathon received a suspended sentence for drug dealing.'

'Do we know why it was only a suspended sentence?' asked Driver.

'Previous good behaviour,' said Aconna. 'Reading between the lines, I'd say his father's influence played a large part in it. And then, after that, Jonathon comes into some money and sets up a small florist shop in London and lives in the flat above.'

'What's the betting Daddy paid for that to try and keep him out of trouble?' said Cormac.

'What about Rosemary Jane?' asked Driver.

'Surprisingly quiet for a teenager until, in 1998, she seems to withdraw from life outside the home and never leaves again.'

'What do you mean, she never leaves again?' asked Driver.

'She appears in the census,' said Aconna. 'And according to the electoral register, she lives at the house, but outside of that, she doesn't seem to exist. She has no driving licence, no bank account, no mobile phone, and no social media accounts. It's as if she's become totally dependent on her father and Milburn Manor.'

'Maybe she's had some sort of accident and needs constant care,' suggested Cormac.

'I can't find any record of anything like that,' said Aconna.

'Yeah, but private healthcare can probably pay for a lot of privacy when you earn well over ten million a year,' said Cormac.

'It's definitely a bit weird,' said Driver. 'What about the wife, Lady Jane?'

'You were right about her being pregnant when they married,' said Aconna.

'Simple arithmetic, that's all,' said Driver.

'And get this: she was sixteen when they married.'

'Bloody hell,' said Driver. 'Was he—'

'Having sex with a minor?' said Aconna. 'My adding up suggests he almost certainly was.'

'Shotgun wedding then,' said Cormac. 'It could even have been statutory rape, although I suppose that would have been difficult to keep quiet.'

'I don't know,' said Driver. 'I sometimes think you can keep anything quiet if you throw enough money at it. Do you know anything about the divorce?'

'It's all a bit vague, but she got a very nice settlement,' said Aconna. 'A château in France, several million in the bank, an annual allowance, and a generous amount of Tilthorne Banking shares.'

'I take it the allowance was to pay for the children's upbringing?' said Driver.

'No, sir. They stayed with their father.'

'Really?' said Cormac.

'You said the divorce was vague,' said Driver. 'Vague in what way?'

'She cited him for adultery. As I understand it, back then the other person had to be named, but she agreed not to name anyone.'

'In exchange for a massive settlement?' said Cormac. 'I bet she signed a non-disclosure deal, then. Whoever he was seeing must have been someone with a lot to lose.'

'There is one other thing that seems rather odd,' said Aconna. 'I don't know if it means anything but apart from the original happy family photograph when he first went into politics I can't find any others. It's as if the divorce signalled the end of the public face of the Tilthorne family.'

'Maybe the kids didn't choose to stay with their father, but had to,' said Cormac. 'That wouldn't exactly create a harmonious family vibe, would it?'

'You've done very well, Aconna,' said Driver. 'But I wonder, is any of this relevant to Jonathon Tilthorne's death?'

'We won't begin to know that until we speak to Lord Tilthorne,' said Cormac.

'Sir?' called a voice. 'Superintendent Eagan's on the phone. He's looking for you. What shall I tell him?'

'Bugger! I'd forgotten about him,' muttered Driver. He then called back to the voice, 'Tell him we've just got back and we're on our way up to see him now.'

'Right, come on, Cormac. Let's go and face the music.'

Cormac pulled the estate agent's business card and a piece of paper from his pocket and handed them to Aconna. 'Can you check this woman out for us? We thought she was following us, so we pulled her over. Of course, she says she wasn't following us, but it won't hurt to check her out.'

'What's the card for? Are you house-hunting?'

'She says she was out there being shown a house,' said Cormac. 'Call the estate agent and see if she was telling the truth.'

'Sure. I'll do it now,' said Aconna.

'Seeing as you're not sure about Jonathon Milthorne and Rocco Flint, let's keep it to ourselves for now,' said Driver as they walked up the stairs to Eagan's office. 'He doesn't need to know everything just yet.'

CHAPTER 10

* * *

'I won't beat about the bush,' said Eagan. 'I've had the Assistant Chief Constable bending my ear this morning. He wants to know why there's been no progress in the two murder investigations. He's wondering if perhaps he needs to appoint someone from outside to take the lead.'

'This isn't a straightforward inquiry, sir,' said Driver.

'That may be so, but I have to say I felt a bit of a fool. The ACC seemed to know more than I did. I know it's your murder team, Driver, but I told you I need to be kept in the loop, and this is exactly why.'

'Can I ask how the Assistant Chief Constable knows more than you, sir?' asked Cormac.

'As I just said, DCI Driver is not keeping me informed.'

'Yes, I accept I've been remiss over that,' said Driver. 'But I think what Cormac is getting at is that I haven't spoken to the ACC either, so how does he know about the cases?'

'What are you suggesting?' asked Eagan.

'I'm not suggesting anything,' said Driver. 'I'm just wondering how he knows so much.'

For a few seconds, Eagan seemed stumped for an answer. 'It's his job to know what's going on.'

'Yes, but he can only know what he's told or what he reads in reports,' said Cormac. 'What DCI Driver is saying is that no one in our team has informed him of anything, and you just said you don't know anything, so how come the ACC knows so much?'

'Perhaps he was bluffing to test you,' suggested Driver.

'He said the second victim is the son of a prominent politician.'

'That's right,' said Driver. 'None other than Lord Tilthorne, the Home Secretary.'

'The ACC doesn't want the press to get hold of the story.'

'Oh, is that right?' said Driver. 'And how are we supposed to stop that when there's obviously a leak somewhere?'

'A leak? What sort of leak?'

Driver shrugged. 'That's what we want to know. The thing is, we only found out who the victim was at the post-mortem, and we've just brought that news back with us, yet it seems both the victim's father and the ACC knew before we did.'

'The ACC knows the Home Secretary. I expect that's how he knows,' said Eagan.

'Fine,' said Driver. 'But if that's the case, how did the Home Secretary know his son was dead before we had even identified him?'

'Well, someone must have told him, of course,' said Eagan. 'It's not rocket science, is it?'

'I think you're missing DCI Driver's point,' said Cormac.

'I mean, obviously someone told him, but if no one within the police and forensic teams actually knew who the victim was, who told him?'

It was as if a blindfold had been removed from Eagan's eyes, and he was seeing the light for the first time.

'Wait a minute. This is the Home Secretary you're talking about. When it comes to the police, he's as high as it gets. Are you seriously suggesting...' He looked at Cormac. 'Is this the conspiracy you told me about?'

'I think it's a bit soon to jump to that conclusion,' said Cormac. 'You said yourself you thought it was all a bit pie in the sky, and if you recall, I couldn't name any names because I didn't know any.'

'Changing your mind about it now, are you, Cormac? Backing out?'

'Not at all,' said Cormac. 'There's definitely something going on here, but so far we've found nothing to definitely connect my case with this one.'

Now Eagan turned to Driver. 'What does he mean, "there's something going on"?'

'We think the two murders may well be connected,' said Driver.

'Connected in what way?'

'There appears to be a drug connection. The first victim, Marcus Whitmore, was a known user and small-time dealer from the Midlands. The second victim has a past conviction for drug dealing.'

'By the second victim, you mean the Home Secretary's son, I take it?'

'Jonathon Tilthorne, yes,' said Driver.

Eagan's face fell. 'How much in the past is this conviction?'

'Thirty years ago,' said Driver. 'When he was a teenager.'

'You know what it will mean if there is a proven drug connection?'

'But these are murders,' said Driver. 'Murders are our jurisdiction.'

'Yes, but if there's a proven drug link, we'll have to call in the bloody drug squad and tell them what we know.'

'But they won't give a damn about our murder investigation. They'll expect us to step back while they mess around trying to prove the drug connection. They'll either blow our case apart or they'll get lucky and claim all the credit.'

'Yes, I know that,' said Eagan.

'You don't really want them to claim the glory after we've done all the work, do you, sir?' asked Driver.

'Of course I don't want that; it's a question of protocol,' said Eagan.

'You said if there was "a proven drug connection",' said Cormac. 'So we would need to be absolutely sure, right?'

'What are you suggesting?' asked Eagan.

'Without concrete proof, there's always an element of doubt, isn't there?' said Cormac. 'Marky Whitmore had no drugs on him, and who knows, perhaps he came down here to go straight. Whatever the case, there's no firm, proven drug connection. No drugs were found with Jonathon Tilthorne's body, and his drug conviction was thirty years ago. I don't think that's solid proof he's involved with drugs, do you?'

Eagan suddenly perked up. 'You know, you're right,' he agreed. 'And you're sure there's no reason to suggest he still deals drugs?'

'None that we've found,' said Driver. 'So far.'

'Well, in that case, I think we have no need to waste the

drug squad's time. If we learn anything to the contrary that convinces us it's all about drugs, then, of course, we'll have to reconsider.'

'So we can carry on, then?' asked Driver.

'Yes, but for God's sake, Driver, keep me informed, will you? If you want me to watch your backs on this, I need to know what's going on. All right?'

'Right, sir,' said Driver. 'I'll keep you firmly in the loop. Now, if there's nothing else?'

'Just a minute,' said Eagan. 'You said the first victim, Whitmore, was from the Midlands.'

'Did I?'

'Yes, you did. "User and small-time dealer from the Midlands" are the words you used.'

'That's right,' said Driver. 'So, what about it?'

Eagan turned his attention to Cormac.

'That's a bit of a coincidence, isn't it?'

'Sir?'

'Friend of yours, was he?'

Cormac sighed. Why did everyone think Marky Whitmore was his mate?

'I'd come across him once or twice.'

'What happened? Did he follow you here?'

'I don't know why he was here,' said Cormac.

'Am I missing something here?' asked Eagan. 'Only I don't seem to recall seeing much information about this chap.'

'We're thinking things weren't working out for him up there, so he moved down here to make a new start,' said Driver. 'And maybe he trod on someone's toes, and that's why he's dead.'

'How was he identified?'

'I recognised his face,' said Cormac.

'So, you did know him.'

'You know I was in the drug squad up there, and we just said he was a dealer. When you're in the drug squad, you come across dealers; it goes with the territory.'

'Why do I think there's something you're not telling me?' asked Eagan.

'That's all there is to te—' began Driver.

'It's okay, sir,' said Cormac. 'I think Superintendent Eagan should know.'

'Know what?' asked Eagan.

'We found a burner phone under Marky's body,' said Cormac. 'My number was the only contact stored on the phone.'

Eagan turned angrily to Driver. 'This is disgraceful! Why wasn't I told? You're both casting aspersions about the Home Secretary and the ACC, and you're—'

'This is exactly why I didn't tell you,' said Driver, calmly. 'I knew you'd jump to the wrong conclusion.'

'But you can't have DS Cormac working on this case when—'

'I don't think there's an issue,' said Driver.

'You don't think there's an issue? Well, I beg to differ. I think there's a bloody huge issue.'

'Well, I don't,' said Driver. 'And there are two reasons why: First, there's no evidence to suggest the victim and Cormac were ever in communication—'

'But he's just said his number was on the victim's phone, for God's sake!'

'Sir, if you'll just let me finish,' said Driver, patiently. 'Yes, Cormac's number is on the burner phone found under the victim's body, but there's no evidence the phone belonged to the victim.'

'Yes, but—'

'The phone isn't registered, and we have no idea who bought it or where it was bought. There are no fingerprints on the phone, nor a shred of DNA from the victim.'

'I don't think I follow,' said Eagan.

'I'm saying the phone was planted by whoever killed Whitmore,' said Driver.

'But why?'

Driver was obviously reluctant to say, so Cormac took over. 'Either they want to implicate me in the murder, or the murder is a message, and they want to make sure I know it's for me. Or it could be both reasons.'

'A message? What sort of message?'

'I wish I knew,' said Cormac.

Eagan stared at Cormac, then turned to Driver.

'Is this right?'

'It's a theory,' said Driver. 'And so far, it looks possible, although we still have no idea what the message is supposed to be.'

'Jonathon Tilthorne's body was pointing towards Milburn Manor,' said Cormac. 'So, if the murders are linked, as we suspect, perhaps that's the message.'

'Are you sure it was pointing at Milburn Manor?' asked Eagan.

'We're as sure as we can be,' replied Driver. 'It was deliberately set up to point eastwards, and the only landmark visible from the hill in that direction is Milburn Manor.'

'But that's the Home Secretary's home,' said Eagan. 'You can't just charge in there because you "think" someone is telling you to look there.'

'Yes, we realise that,' said Driver. 'It's why we're conducting discreet searches to see what we can find out.'

'For God's sake, be careful, and make sure you are being discreet,' warned Eagan. 'I can only save you from so much trouble, and a man like the Home Secretary will make it very difficult if he gets wind that we're investigating him.'

'Right, we'll be extra careful, sir.'

Driver and Cormac made their way from Eagan's office and down the stairs to their incident room.

'Did you catch that bit at the end about saving us from trouble?' asked Driver.

'It wasn't convincing, was it?' replied Cormac.

'I guarantee, if the shit does hit the fan, the only person he'll be trying to save is himself.'

'He perked up at the idea there was a conspiracy, though, didn't he?' said Cormac.

'Oh, yes, he'll take the glory for that,' said Driver. 'Just as long as he can keep his hands clean in the process.'

As soon as they entered the incident room, Aconna left her desk, carrying a sheet of paper. 'I've been digging a bit further into the divorce,' she said. 'I can't find a trace of another woman, so his Lordship must have been very discreet about his affair. I even tried the red-top newspapers but can't find a mention anywhere.'

'And yet he can't have been that discreet if his wife found out,' said Driver.

'That's why I think there has to be an NDA involved,' said Cormac. 'He must have offered it the minute she found out to ensure she kept her mouth shut.'

'It makes you wonder who the other woman was,' said Driver.

'Maybe it wasn't a woman,' suggested Cormac. 'He wouldn't want news of an affair with a man to come out after he'd made such a big deal of being a family man, would he?'

'Either way, I can't see how it helps with our murder investigation,' said Driver. 'If I thought blackmail was involved in his son's murder, it would be worth pursuing, but we've seen nothing to indicate that.'

'What if that's why Lord Tilthorne hasn't approached us?' suggested Cormac. 'What if it was a "pay up or we'll kill your son", scenario? Maybe he was playing for time, thinking he could handle it, and he waited too long.'

'So why not come to us now?' asked Driver.

'Perhaps the kidnappers have got the daughter as well, and he's been told not to go to the police,' said Cormac.

'So you're saying the kidnappers have warned Lord Tilthorne not to involve the police?' said Driver.

Cormac nodded. 'It's just a theory.'

'And they killed Jonathon Tilthorne because his father didn't pay the ransom?'

'Right,' said Cormac.

'How does that theory fit in with someone arranging Jonathon Tilthorne's body to point to Milburn Manor? If they still have his daughter, why would they tell him to keep the police out of it and then, at the same time, tell us to go to the house? I can't quite get my head around how that works.'

Cormac looked sheepish. 'Yeah, when you put it like that, it doesn't make a lot of sense, does it?'

Aconna had watched the exchange with amused interest. 'There was one other thing I found out. According to the records, the children didn't want to live with their mother and chose to stay with their father. That's quite unusual, isn't it?'

'It's usually the other way around,' said Driver. 'But maybe it was part of the NDA deal.'

'They would have been teenagers by then, so maybe the children decided to stay with the money and the big house,' said Aconna.

'Can you look into that woman who was following us?' asked Cormac.

'I already did,' said Aconna. 'Her details check out; the car is hers, and it's all above board: tax, insurance, MOT, etc.'

'Oh, right,' Cormac sounded disappointed. 'Was she looking at houses?'

'The estate agent confirms that she was. He also told me she's interested in several others in this area.'

'So she's kosher,' said Driver.

'That depends on how you look at it,' said Aconna. 'The car and the house hunting check out, but then we get to the interesting bit.'

Driver smiled indulgently. 'Go on then. You're looking pleased with yourself. What have you found?'

'Anita Bogdani is 38 years old and is married to a 40 year old Albanian named Nikolla Bogdani. They currently live in Leicester.'

Driver looked at Cormac. 'Isn't that where you came from in the Midlands?'

'That's East Midlands. I was in the West Midlands,' said Cormac.

'Nikolla Bogdani has no criminal record, but he does have criminal acquaintances and is flagged as a person of interest to drug squads everywhere,' Aconna finished.

Driver scratched his head. 'So, why would a possible Albanian drug dealer's wife be following us?' he mused.

'You think she was following us?' asked Cormac.

'Don't you?'

'Well, yeah, but I thought that from the moment I saw her in my rear-view mirror.'

'Well, now I agree with you,' said Driver. 'Not that I ever doubted you.'

'So, does that mean the estate agent is covering for her?' asked Cormac.

'What if she really is house hunting?' said Aconna. 'Let's face it, it's a handy cover story, isn't it?'

'It's a bit of a coincidence that she just happens to be looking at a house around the corner from Milburn Manor and leaves at the precise moment we're leaving,' said Driver. 'No, I can't see it. She was following us, and the estate agent story is just a cover.'

'But why would the estate agent do that?' asked Aconna.

Cormac rubbed his finger and thumb together. 'Money talks,' he said. 'Either she's paid him, or she really is buying, and he's in line for a substantial commission. There are nothing but huge, very expensive houses out that way.'

'Now, that's an interesting idea,' said Driver. 'What if Bogdani is a genuine, established drug dealer, and he's looking to move down here and expand his business? Maybe that's what all this is about.'

'You think this is a turf war?' said Cormac.

'It could be, couldn't it?' said Driver. 'Let's think about this. We believe Rocco Flint is an alias for Jonathon Tilthorne, or the outside possibility is that it's the name of a drug-dealing organisation. Am I right?'

'Except Jonathon is dead now,' said Aconna.

'Yes,' said Driver. 'But do we think he could manage large-scale drug distribution on his own?'

'Unlikely,' said Cormac. 'He'd need eyes in the back of his head. And he would be no match for a gang.'

'Right,' said Driver. 'So either he's the head, or if it's a group, he's a shareholder. But either way, we think we're looking at an organisation, possibly an army. I believe it's based in this area.'

'But Jonathon lives in the flat above his shop in London,' said Aconna.

'And yet he was found strung up at the top of a hill not far from Milburn Manor,' said Driver. 'So, does he really live in that flat, or does he want everyone to think he lives in that flat?'

'I'll check it out,' said Aconna.

'Call the shop and see if he actually works there, or if the staff run it for him,' said Cormac. 'They should know if he lives above the shop.'

Half an hour later, Aconna called Driver and Cormac over. 'That was a bit awkward. I called the shop and said I was trying to contact Jonathon. They said he rarely makes an appearance in the shop, and although he owns the flat above, he's not there very often. They haven't seen him for a couple of weeks.'

'What was awkward about that?' asked Cormac.

'They clearly don't know he's dead. I didn't know if I should tell them.'

'So his father hasn't contacted them?'

'It doesn't look that way,' said Aconna. 'Should I have told them?'

'Don't worry about that,' said Driver. 'I'll get someone from the Met to handle it.'

CHAPTER 11

* * *

IT WAS 8:30 P.M., and as usual, The Red Cow had provided an excellent evening meal. Hunger satisfied, Cormac was delighted to find someone had left a newspaper on the table next to his. Having discovered an untouched crossword, he moved to one of the two comfortable armchairs by the fireplace. The fire wasn't lit, but that didn't matter to Cormac, who simply wanted a comfortable seat to spend the next half hour or so quietly solving the puzzle while he enjoyed a pint before returning to the motel. He had just solved the first clue when a sharp female voice interrupted him.

'Is anyone sitting there?'

The owner of the voice stood barely 5 feet tall, but her choice of a bright orange sweater, pale blue jeans, white trainers, and a large powder blue shoulder bag made her hard to miss. Cormac guessed she was in her early thirties. Her pale skin, freckles, and high cheekbones contrasted with her shoulder-length ginger hair, which Cormac considered a perfect match with her sweater, complemented by a powder blue hairband and earrings. Large, round spectacles with powder blue frames highlighted a pair of dark grey eyes, the colour of which Cormac was sure he had never seen before.

He looked around the half-empty pub, then at the empty armchair next to his. He was tempted to say he was saving the seat for someone, but chivalry got the better of him, and instead he said, 'No, there's no one sitting there. Help yourself.'

'Oh, thanks,' she said, placing her pint carefully down on the table between them. Then she plonked herself down in the armchair.

Cormac grunted and returned to his crossword.

'It's nice here, isn't it?'

'Sorry?' said Cormac.

'This pub. It's nice. And the food's very good, don't you think?'

'Yeah, it's okay,' said Cormac, adding pointedly, 'On a night like this, it's the perfect place for me to sit with a pint and lose myself in a crossword.' Having dropped the hint, he returned to his clue, but she either missed his intention or chose to ignore it.

'Did I see you at the motel just up the road?' she asked.

'Yes,' he said warily. 'I'm staying there.'

'That's a coincidence,' she said. 'So am I.'

For a moment, he wondered if she was one of the prostitutes Driver had warned him about. But then he decided no; there was definitely something about her approach that was making his radar twitch, but it wasn't that.

She seemed to have run out of words, so Cormac took the chance to return to his crossword again. He even managed to fill in the next clue, but in his peripheral vision, he could see she was staring at him.

'Detective Sergeant Cormac, isn't it?' she asked.

Cormac was surprised she knew his name but kept his eyes on the crossword. Finally, he put the crossword and pen down on his side table and turned to face her. The intensity of her gaze made those eyes seem a darker grey.

'Who are you?' he asked.

'My name is Melinda Yates.'

Cormac thought for a few seconds. 'No, sorry, that name doesn't ring any bells. Should I know you? Have we met before?'

'No, we've never met before.'

'Well, Ms Yates, what is it you want?'

'I prefer Mrs Yates, but then I am divorced, so perhaps you're correct technically, and I should use Ms.'

'Mrs or Ms, it makes no odds to me,' said Cormac. 'Why are you here?'

'I'm a journalist.'

Cormac rolled his eyes and groaned. 'Oh, I see, a journalist. Of course, I should have known.'

'What? Did you think your luck was in?'

'Do you really think I would have been able to concentrate on my crossword if I thought that?' said Cormac.

'Should I take that as a compliment?'

Cormac shrugged. 'You can take it however you like. The point is, if you think I'm going to give you a story, you're wasting your time. There's a perfectly good press office at Windover police station. They'll brief you if you are interested in a particular case.'

'Yes, I know all about the press office, thank you, but it's you I want to talk to.'

'And I've just told you you're wasting your time. I'm not interested in discussing cases with the press.'

'What if I wanted to discuss Heather Collins? Would you be interested then?'

Cormac was stunned. 'What do you know about Heather?'

'We can talk about her later—'

'No. I want to talk about her now.'

'How about you scratch my back, and then maybe I'll scratch yours?'

'I can't discuss ongoing cases.'

'I'm not actually interested in whatever case you're working on, but I'm working on a story about the Home Secretary, so we might be able to help each other.'

'What makes you think we're interested in the Home Secretary?'

'Because I know you were at his house the other day. Why were you there? Was it about his son's death?'

'How do you know about that?'

'I'm a journalist.'

'Yeah, but—'

'I saw you there, okay? I also saw you stop a woman who was following you on the way back. Her name is Anita Bogdani, right?'

Cormac was struggling to understand.

'How do you know all this?' he asked. 'And what's it got to do with Heather?'

Melinda sat up straight. 'Oh, my God. You really don't know anything, do you?'

'What's that supposed to mean?'

'Oh, wow,' she said. 'I was hoping you might be able to help me, but it looks as if it's going to be the other way around.'

'What the hell does that mean?'

'Honestly, we have got so much to talk about, but we can't do it here.'

'Why not?'

'Too many people,' she said. 'Someone might hear and report back.'

'What do you mean, report back?'

Melinda looked towards the bar and then back to Cormac. 'See that guy sitting at the bar? He works security at Milburn Manor.'

Cormac hadn't noticed before, but it was the Bond lookalike from behind the gate.

'You're right, he does,' said Cormac.

'Safer if we go back to the motel, then,' said Melinda. 'Your room or mine?'

Cormac frowned.

'Look, I just want to talk,' said Melinda.

'I dunno.'

'Well, you choose somewhere, then.'

'Why don't you come to Windover police station? I'll get my boss to join us.'

Melinda rolled her eyes.

'Ha, ha, ha. Very funny.'

'What?'

'You're kidding, right?'

'Why not?'

'I'm not going anywhere near Windover police station, and I'm certainly not talking to your boss. I'll talk to you, or no one. Believe me, if Tilthorne is on your radar, you need to hear what I know.'

'Don't you want to help the police?'

'No, not really. But I do want to do a big story exposing the Home Secretary for the hypocritical bastard that he is.

Helping to put him away will be a bonus, but I'm doing this for me and my story, not because I want to help you lot.'

'Why is it so important to you? It almost sounds as if it's personal.'

'Yes, well, perhaps it is.'

'Why?' asked Cormac. 'What's he done to you?'

'If you want to find that out, you need to finish your pint and come with me.'

Cormac swallowed the last of his beer and followed her from the bar. As soon as they were outside, she grabbed his arm and snuggled up close.

'Hey, hang on a minute!' said Cormac. 'I thought you said—'

'It's okay, just play along and trust me,' she said. 'And don't get your hopes up; this is just for show in case the muscleman at the bar decides to follow us.'

'Why would he follow us?'

'Actually, it's you he's following, not me,' said Melinda.

'What makes you think he's following me?'

'Because I saw him earlier at the motel, and now he's here.'

'Why would he follow me?'

'You've been caught on camera at the gates, and they're worried about what you might know.'

'Some hard man sitting at a bar doesn't intimidate me,' said Cormac.

'Really? Well, perhaps he should.'

'I'm a police detective sergeant. They're not going to do anything to me without bringing a whole heap of grief down on their heads.'

'I wouldn't be so sure about that, if I were you.'

'What about you?' asked Cormac. 'How do you know they're not following you?'

'Because I watched him follow you here from the motel, and he's been discreetly watching you all the time he's been in here. He was so focused on following you to the pub that he was quite unaware I was following him.'

'It seems to me they'd be after you, as you seem to know so much.'

'Yeah, you'd think so,' said Melinda. 'But the thing is they haven't a clue what I know because they haven't come across me. Yet.'

'You make it sound like they're dangerous.'

'Trust me, Detective Sergeant, you don't know the half of it.'

CHAPTER 12

'THAT WAS my friend from the Met on the phone,' said Driver next morning. 'They've been to the shop and notified the staff. Apparently, there are two women who manage the shop between them. Jonathon Tilthorne looks in about once a fortnight, but he doesn't actually do any work; it's all down to them.'

'How do they feel about that?' asked Cormac.

'He tells them they're so good they don't need his help, and they're quite happy with that.'

'Does the shop make so much money that he can afford to pay them and make a living himself?'

'My mate at the Met thinks not.'

'In that case, unless he's got some sort of trust fund, you have to question how he manages to live,' said Cormac, 'and what he gets up to all day.'

'I can tell you what he doesn't do,' said Driver. 'He doesn't spend his time in the flat above the shop. In fact, he doesn't spend any time in the flat.'

'How does that work?' asked Cormac.

'According to what I've just been told, there's hardly any

furniture in the place, no food in the cupboards, the fridge is empty, and there's nothing to suggest anyone lives there. A pile of old junk mail on the side in the kitchen and a few bits behind the front door suggest someone goes in now and then to collect any post and clear the junk mail from the door, but that's it.'

Cormac thought for a minute, then nodded his head. 'Of course. That ties in with Jonathon calling in at the shop every two weeks. He probably can't risk going to the flat without going into the shop, and that's when he collects the post. What about utilities?'

'Council tax, water, and electric bills are all connected, paid on a monthly direct debit, and all up to date. Same with the shop downstairs.'

'So, on the surface, it looks as if Jonathon lives in the flat and has a working business.'

'But if it was a front, the question we have to ask is, what was he really up to, and where was he doing it?'

'It sounds like the sort of cover a big-time drug dealer might find useful,' said Aconna.

Cormac said nothing. His phone had pinged, and he was staring at the message.

See attached. Now do you believe me? M.

He clicked to open the attached photograph, and his stomach seemed to fall through the floor. It had obviously been taken at long range, but even so, it was good enough to identify two figures standing before a huge house. The man was Jonathon Tilthorne. Standing beside him was Heather Collins, the face Cormac had once loved and then lost.

Slowly, he became aware that Driver and Aconna were staring at him.

'I'm sorry, Cormac,' said Driver. 'Are we keeping you

from something more important than this investigation? Or are you feeling unwell?'

Ashen-faced, Cormac looked up at Driver. 'I'm sorry, sir. It's, er, it's nothing.'

'Why don't I believe that?' asked Driver. 'Come to think of it, why do you look like you haven't slept?'

Cormac rubbed his face. He couldn't hide it anymore. It was time to tell the truth. 'I had a visitor last night. Her name is Melinda Yates.'

'Oh, I see,' said Driver.

'No, it's not what you think,' said Cormac. 'She's a journalist.'

Driver groaned. 'I hate bloody reporters. I hope you told her where to go.'

'I was going to,' said Cormac, 'but she knew stuff I couldn't ignore.'

'Such as?'

'She knew we'd been to Milburn Manor and that we'd been turned away. She also knew we'd stopped a woman following us, and she knew that woman was called Anita Bogdani. And remember the hard man on gate duty at the Manor? Well, Melinda had watched him follow me from the motel to the pub, and she had watched him watching me all the time I was there.'

'I suppose she wants you to give her the story about Jonathon Tilthorne,' said Driver.

'Yeah, she'd like our help, but there's a bit more to it than that,' said Cormac. 'Whatever we think we've stumbled across here, Melinda thinks we're just nibbling around the edges.'

'What's that supposed to mean?' demanded Driver.

'She knows stuff about Lord Tilthorne, and about Jonathon Tilthorne, and about the daughter, Rosemary.'

'And you believe her? These journalists will offer all sorts of supposed evidence if they think they can get inside a murder case.'

'Last night, she told me stuff I didn't want to hear, and I didn't want to believe.'

'What stuff?'

Cormac hesitated.

'Come on, man, spit it out,' insisted Driver.

Cormac took a deep breath. 'Melinda told me how Heather had impersonated a DI for a couple of years. She also knew I had been Heather's boyfriend and that we had been in Thailand when she dumped me.'

'I'd be curious to know how she knew all that, but it's nothing you didn't already know, is it?' said Driver.

'Yeah, but here's the thing,' said Cormac. 'Melinda claims to know Heather's real identity. According to Melinda, she's Lord Tilthorne's daughter, Rosemary Jane Tilthorne.'

For the briefest moment, Driver was too stunned to speak, but only for a moment. 'Christ Almighty! Is this true?' He glared accusingly at Cormac. 'You knew she was behind this all along, didn't you?'

'No, sir. I admit I had my suspicions she might have something to do with it when the burner phone had my number on it, but you said yourself it didn't prove anything. And I certainly had no idea who she really was.'

'How do you know this Melinda, or whatever her name is, is telling the truth?' asked Aconna.

'As I said, I didn't want to believe it, and I told Melinda I wouldn't believe it unless she could provide proof.' Cormac held up his phone. 'That message I was just sent was from Melinda.' He placed the phone on his desk, with the photograph on show. 'There's your proof.'

Driver and Aconna leaned across the desk to see the photograph.

Cormac looked away, shame burning inside him. 'Heather used me, sir. Right from the start, feeding me enough scraps of information to hook me and make me think she cared.'

'But why would she manipulate you?' asked Aconna. 'You weren't even in the police back then, were you? So, what did she have to gain?'

Cormac shook his head. 'I wish I knew...'

'Maybe it wasn't manipulation,' said Aconna. 'Perhaps she genuinely liked you.'

'There's no point in speculating about her motives for using you,' said Driver. 'If Heather is really Rosemary Tilthorne, then she is no longer a missing person.'

'According to Melinda, Rosemary isn't just a liar,' said Cormac. 'Melinda thinks she's the person at the top of the tree. She launders money through a nest of shell companies registered in the Cayman Islands.' He fiddled with his phone until he found another photograph. This one was of an unremarkable-looking company logo. He showed it to Driver and Aconna. 'One of those companies is called Rose-croft Investments (UK) Limited. On the surface, it looks legitimate because her father's name is on the paperwork.'

'Good God,' said Driver. 'Is he part of it?'

'Melinda thinks he's not part of the organisation, but having his name on the paperwork is Rosemary's leverage over him.'

'So she's blackmailing her own father?' asked Aconna incredulously.

'It looks that way,' said Cormac. 'Melinda believes he has to cover for her because if she goes down, she takes him with her.'

'Well, whatever the consequences might be for Lord Damon,' said Driver, 'if Rosemary Tilthorne is running everything, she has just become the focus of our investigation.'

'What about the Albanians?' asked Aconna.

'Good question,' said Driver. 'Is Rosemary running everything, or now that her brother has been murdered, is she running scared because the Albanians are moving in?' He chewed on the idea for a moment. 'If she's on her own, she's hardly in a position to fight them, so we have to consider the possibility she'll skip the country.'

'She could have already gone,' said Cormac.

'All the more reason for us to move fast,' said Driver. 'So, Aconna, I want you to find everything you can on any business associated with the name 'Tilthorne.' I'll volunteer DC Gordon to give you some help. You're looking at Companies House, charities, property trusts, anything you can think of. Do you think you can do that?'

Aconna smiled. 'It'll be a pleasure, sir.'

'Cormac,' said Driver. 'Print a copy of that photograph and then come with me. There's a very posh accountant's office not far from here with a head office in Mayfair. I'll be very surprised if they're not in bed with Lord Tilthorne, so I think it's time we paid them a courtesy call, don't you?'

"That sounds like a great idea, sir.'

* * *

CHAPTER 13

* * *

CORMAC WAS no expert on high-end London accountants, but he thought the building housing the Windover offices of Hollis, Hollis and Malcolm, Chartered Accountants, was exactly what anyone would expect of a company that could afford a head office in Mayfair.

On the edge of town, the building was a huge converted barn clad in western cedar. The three partners' names were picked out in gold across a pair of enormous frosted glass doors beneath a massive solid oak porch.

'Just a tad opulent,' observed Driver as Cormac rang the bell. They waited as a shadowy figure approached on the other side of the glass. Finally, the door opened to reveal a man in his fifties wearing a smart dark blue suit.

'Good morning, gents. How can I help you?' said the man.

'Seriously?' said Driver. 'A uniformed doorman? In Windover?'

'I'm the chauffeur,' said the man. 'They have a doorman in London, but I only open doors when I'm not driving.'

Driver looked at Cormac. 'How the other half live, eh?'

'It's all right for some,' agreed Cormac.

'So, what can I do for you?' asked the doorman/chauffeur.

'DS Cormac and DCI Driver,' said Cormac, producing his warrant card. 'We need to speak to one of the senior partners.'

The man blanched at the sight of the warrant cards. 'You'll need to check in with Cynthia at reception,' he said. 'She'll sort you out.' He stepped back, allowed them inside a cavernous hallway, and pointed towards a reception desk, clearly relieved to hand the responsibility on to someone else.

Driver and Cormac made their way towards the aforementioned Cynthia, who gave them a look to match the frostiness of the glass doors. As they reached the desk, Cormac saw her name matched the look she had given them. 'Cynthia Frost' was the legend inscribed in gold upon a sleek oak plinth.

'Good morning,' said Driver. 'I'm DCI Driver and this is my colleague, DS Cormac. We'd like to speak to one of your senior partners.'

'Which one?' Her accent was cut glass. Of course it was, thought Cormac.

'I assume they all know the business, so it doesn't actually matter which one,' said Driver.

'I'm sorry, that won't be possible,' said Cynthia. 'Mr. Hollis and Mr. Malcolm aren't here.'

'What about the other Mr. Hollis?' said Cormac.

'I'm sorry?'

'It says Hollis, Hollis and Malcolm,' said Cormac. 'So,

are there two Mr. Hollises, or did the engraver make a mistake?'

'Of course he didn't make a mistake,' snapped Cynthia.

'Good,' said Cormac. 'In that case, we'll speak to the second Mr. Hollis, please.'

'He might be in a meeting.'

'Surely you would know if he was in a meeting if all visitors are subject to interrogation by you,' said Driver.

'What I mean is, he might be on a conference call.'

Driver gave her an icy smile. 'Well, tell him the police are here, and we might come back with a warrant and turn this place upside down if he doesn't end his meeting in the next five minutes.'

Cynthia's lips narrowed to a slit and her eyes blazed. 'How dare you! I've never been spoken to like that before.'

'I find that hard to believe for someone as obstructive as you,' said Driver. He turned to Cormac. 'Sergeant, make a note of this lady's name if she continues to waste our time.'

'You can't—'

'We're conducting a murder investigation,' said Driver wearily. 'Now, you might think you're doing your boss a favour, but we're beginning to wonder why you feel that's necessary and that perhaps your boss has something to hide.'

'That's ridiculous.'

'Yes, I dare say it is in your opinion,' said Driver. 'But we'd like to decide for ourselves, and we can't do that until we speak to him.'

Cynthia sighed and flapped her arms, but eventually, she picked up a phone from her desk.

'Hello, Suzie. I've got two police officers here. They'd like to speak to Mr. Hollis.' She paused for a moment to listen, then placed the receiver back down on her desk. 'Barry,' she called out to the doorman. 'Escort these two gentlemen up to the third floor. Suzie is expecting them.'

Barry led Driver and Cormac to a lift, ushered them inside, pressed the button for the third floor. 'She's a miserable, stuck-up cow, that Cynthia,' he said as the lift began it's ascent. Neither Driver nor Cormac argued the point.

Suzie Winter, the secretary waiting for them, was quite the opposite of Cynthia. She greeted them with a warm smile and showed them into a meeting room that smelled of coffee and furniture polish. 'Help yourselves to coffee. Martin will be with you in about five minutes. He's just winding up his conference call.'

Almost exactly five minutes later, Martin Hollis walked into the room. In his sixties, with greying hair and steely blue eyes, he managed a confident smile as he shook their hands.

'Now then, how can I help?' he asked.

Driver produced the photograph Cormac had printed out.

'Do you recognise either of these people?'

Hollis glanced at the photograph, shrugged, and shook his head. 'No, sorry, I'm afraid I don't.'

'You might recognise this,' said Cormac, showing the company logo photograph on his phone.

Hollis's confidence seemed to waver, just a little.

'Obviously I can't comment on clients,' he said. 'That would be unethical.'

'We're not asking you to comment,' said Driver. 'We're asking you to confirm that you act for Rosecroft Investments (UK) Ltd.'

Hollis stared at Driver without comment.

'Come now, Mr. Hollis,' said Driver. 'It's a very simple yes or no question. Or would you prefer we come back later with a production order? Frankly, we have better things to do with our day, but it's your choice.'

There was a faint muscle twitch in Hollis's cheek. 'We're a big company providing compliance services to a number of entities. I'm sure you don't expect me to recall all of them?'

'I'm not asking about all of them,' said Driver patiently. 'Just this one, Rosecroft Investments. I understand there are links to other companies, all registered in the Cayman Islands.'

Hollis folded his arms. 'We do not set up offshore structures.'

'We realise you'd steer clear of that,' said Cormac. 'But we have reason to believe you introduce clients to other people who do the setups. Then you prepare papers at this end and get them signed off so everything looks kosher and no one is any the wiser unless they start looking closely.'

'The problem for you,' added Driver, 'is that right now we are starting to look closely, very closely.'

Hollis licked his lips but said nothing.

'You see, we've come across someone called R.J. Tilthorne, and R.J. Tilthorne seems to be closely associated with Rosecroft Investments and several other companies. In fact, we believe R.J. Tilthorne is the person at the top. Does that name ring any bells for you?'

'I seem to recall that name. I can't say where from exactly, but if they're running things, as you say, then they must have the authority to do so.'

'Authority from whom?' asked Cormac.

'I have no idea. You'd have to ask them,' said Hollis.

'Do you know Lord Damon Tilthorne?' asked Driver.

'Yes, I do. We belong to the same club.'

'Don't you think there might be a connection between

Lord Tilthorne and R.J. Tilthorne? I mean, it's a bit of a coincidence, don't you think?' said Driver. 'After all, it's not a common name, is it?'

Hollis didn't offer an opinion.

'Now here's what we think,' said Driver. 'We believe Miss Rosemary Jane Tilthorne, Lord Tilthorne's daughter, is directing a group of companies to launder drug money into clean money. Anyone asking awkward questions gets shown Lord Tilthorne's name on headed notepaper, and possibly even the highly respected accountant's name, Hollis, Hollis and Malcolm.

'Now we're not saying the Home Secretary is involved; he may even be totally unaware of what his daughter is doing, but his name, allied to yours, is going to open a lot of doors, don't you agree, Mr. Hollis?'

Hollis stared at the floor. 'I couldn't possibly comment.'

'Yeah, we thought you'd say that,' said Cormac.

'The thing is we're not asking you for an opinion or a comment,' said Driver softly. 'What we're asking is where your anti-money laundering file is.'

Hollis tried to look confused. 'I don't know wh—'

'You know exactly what we mean,' said Driver. 'You're supposed to carry out enhanced due diligence. There should be a big fat file that proves you've double-checked your client's credentials and that you're satisfied they're honest and trustworthy.'

'He's the Home Secretary, for God's sake. Of course he's bloody trustworthy!' snapped Hollis.

'Why? Because he goes to the same club as you? And what about his daughter? Is she trustworthy just because her name is Tilthorne?'

'I didn't know she was his daughter.'

'Oh, come on, Mr. Hollis,' said Cormac. 'Do you really think we're that stupid?'

'Let me explain the situation to you,' said Driver. 'This has all come to light during our investigations into not one, but two murders. Now, when the Sunday papers run the story, with pictures of one victim roasted and a second victim crucified, everyone who was helping in the background, no matter if they realised what was going on, or not, is going to be asked why they stood back and watched.'

'They will also be facing charges,' said Cormac. 'I don't think that's going to do much for your swanky image, do you?'

Hollis's composure vanished. 'What do you want from me?'

'The anti-money laundering file will do for now,' said Driver.

'I'll need a couple of days.'

Driver shook his head. 'To find one file? No chance. You've got half an hour.'

Hollis headed for the door, muttering under his breath.

'Oh, and could you ask Suzie if we could have some more hot coffee while we wait?' asked Driver.

'You're going to wait?'

'Of course we're going to wait, Mr. Hollis. As my sergeant said, do you really think we're stupid?'

* * *

IN THE THREE hours Driver and Cormac had been gone, Aconna had been very busy. A new cork-board had been found, and various labels were pinned to it. She was now busily linking her discoveries with red and blue strings.

Cormac stared at the board with a mixture of disbelief and admiration. 'How did you manage to put this all together so fast?'

Aconna smiled. 'I was told to focus on the name Tilthorne, so I did,' she said.

'Yeah, but we haven't been gone that long,' said Cormac. 'I mean, how do you know how to do all this, and how have you done it so quickly?'

'To be honest, I didn't expect to get this far, but DC Gordon has been very helpful. Anyway, it turns out your friend Heather—'

Cormac frowned. 'She's not my friend.'

'Sorry,' said Aconna. 'What I mean is Rosemary Jane Tilthorne may not be quite as clever as she thinks, or maybe she's overconfident. Whatever, she didn't do the best job of hiding her tracks.'

'Well, I have to say I'm impressed with how it looks,' said Driver. 'But what does it all mean? Talk us through it.'

'Where she did try to hide the trail, she used all the usual tricks: registered office at reputable accountants; directors who live six to a letterbox in Georgetown; the PSC field "unable to determine".'

'Whoa, hold on a minute,' said Cormac. 'You're talking way over my head here. If I'm going to follow this, you're going to have to imagine I know nothing. And I still can't understand how you know so much.'

Aconna's smile became a wide grin. 'Ah, well, I have to admit I'm not exactly new to this stuff. You see, when your dad teaches forensic accounting, you can't help but pick some of it up. I even thought about following in his footsteps at one time, but I couldn't bear the thought of spending all my time in an office chasing numbers.'

She turned to the corkboard and began pointing out the connections. 'So this is what I've found so far. The blue string links everything connected to Rosecroft; that's the florist shop in London, a Midlands security contractor, and a trust that owns a cluster of farm buildings outside Templeton. The red strings are not owned by Rosecroft but are still linked to the Tilthorne name.'

'So that's the farm buildings and a logistics yard near the edge of town,' said Driver. He squinted and pointed at the board. 'What's that?'

'Three flats,' said Aconna. 'I don't know who lives in them. I haven't got that far yet.'

Driver and Cormac said nothing.

'She's using layers to hide some stuff,' explained Aconna.

'But as I said, she's overconfident or careless. For example, those farm buildings outside Templeton were bought by Rose-croft last year. They paid cash, but despite what many people think, that's not a guaranteed way of staying anonymous.'

'What do we know about the logistics yard?' asked Driver.

'It's owned by Rosecroft but leased by a company called R. Flint International Logistics Ltd.'

Cormac looked at Driver.

'Rocco Flint?' asked Driver.

Cormac shrugged. 'It's not very subtle, but perhaps they think they're so clever no one would ever be looking for a connection. It's definitely a good way of moving drugs around. Lots of vehicles coming and going, all over the UK and into Europe.'

'Lots of hiding places in a vehicle with a big load,' said Driver.

'Even if they just used a small stash here and there, with enough vehicles they could move a huge amount of drugs,' said Cormac.

'And if they had a network of logistics hubs, they could dilute the risk even further,' said Aconna.

'Or increase the volume,' said Driver. 'Is that what they're doing?'

'That's my guess,' said Aconna. 'They've bought three similar properties in the last six months. All three are in rural locations but with easy access to the motorway network.'

'Don't tell me they paid cash for those,' said Cormac.

Aconna shook her head. 'Too risky. Anyone who keeps splashing millions in cash is asking for trouble. No, they borrowed the money.'

'Someone didn't do their due diligence, then,' said Cormac.

'The lender isn't a bank,' said Aconna. 'It's called Tillex Capital, which just happens to be one of their Cayman Islands outfits.'

Driver laughed. 'You mean she's lending to herself? Bloody hell, you couldn't make it up!'

He had been holding a slim folder, but now he placed it on the desk. 'Right, this is a copy of the anti-money laundering file we managed to pry from Martin Hollis. He's done his best to redact various bits, but I think we have enough to be going on with until we hit him with an official production order.'

He flipped the file open, placed the top sheet of paper on the desk, and read from it: 'The named "beneficial controller" of everything Tilthorne is none other than R.J. Tilthorne. There is also a note granting general power of attorney for family affairs signed by Lord Damon Tilthorne.'

'So she has effective control of everything,' said Aconna.

'It gets even better,' said Driver, placing a second sheet of paper on the desk. 'To whom it may concern,' he read. 'My daughter, Rosemary Jane Tilthorne, is hereby authorised to speak on my behalf regarding all Tilthorne family finances and trusts.'

'Clever,' said Cormac. 'Any awkward questions, and that piece of paper effectively shuts them down. I mean, who is going to question the Home Secretary's daughter when she can prove he's granted her permission to run the family finances? Can I see that, sir?'

Driver slid the paper across to Cormac, who picked it up and studied it. 'This was signed donkey's years ago,' he said.

'It doesn't matter how old it is; it's still kosher unless someone can produce another document that supersedes it,' said Driver.

'That's not what I'm getting at,' said Cormac. 'She would have still been at school when this was signed. In fact, this would have been around the time the Tilthornes got divorced.'

'Why her and not Jonathon?' asked Aconna. 'I thought it was always the oldest boy who took precedence in these things.'

'Don't forget he got nicked for drugs,' said Driver. 'Perhaps his father didn't trust him after that.'

'Hang on a minute,' said Aconna. She walked over to her desk, shuffled papers for a few seconds, then called across to them. 'Sorry, sir, but the drugs bust came after that.'

'Well, maybe his father knew he was a wrong 'un who couldn't be trusted before the drugs bust,' said Driver.

'You've got to admit it does seem a bit odd, though,' said Cormac. 'I mean, she would have been what, thirteen? Fourteen at most. Who signs over the family finances to a kid like that? Would she even be old enough to legally have that responsibility?'

'That may not have been an issue if she didn't try to use the authority until she was older,' said Driver.

'Even so, it's not normal,' said Cormac. 'Don't forget we're talking about a prominent politician with a background in banking, not some numpty who doesn't know his arse from his elbow.'

'What are you suggesting?' said Driver.

'That she must have had some sort of hold over him even back then.'

'Such as?'

'I dread to think,' said Cormac. 'But I wouldn't put it past her to blackmail her own father.'

'The obvious reason doesn't bear thinking about,' said Aconna. 'But it might explain the divorce and why the ex-wife had to sign an NDA.'

'Frankly, nothing would surprise me with this woman,' said Driver. 'But let's not get sidetracked by that now. I'm sure we'll get a chance to learn more about their relationship at a later date. Right now, we need to maintain our focus on why two people were murdered and who is behind it.'

'So, what are we saying?' said Cormac. 'Rosemary runs the business, Jonathon handles the goods, or at least he did until he became a scarecrow, and their father has to cover for them to avoid a scandal that would ruin him?'

'It's looking that way,' agreed Driver. 'But whatever the setup is, we know Lord Tilthorne knew about his son's death before we could tell him, which means someone is keeping him informed.'

'Well, if it's one of ours, it has to be Martha McGowan or the ACC,' said Cormac.

'It would have to be both of them,' said Driver. 'Martha is the only person who could have told the ACC or Tilthorne directly, and I don't believe she would have told either.'

'Yeah, but someone—'

'If we're right in thinking the Albanians are making a takeover bid, then the Tilthornes must know they're coming,' said Driver. 'So what if Rosemary knew Jonathon had been murdered, and she broke the news to his Lordship?'

'How would she know?' asked Aconna.

'The Albanians told her,' said Cormac.

'Why would they do that?'

'To up the ante and hope to scare the crap out of her,' said Cormac. He turned to Driver. 'Are you suggesting she's at Milburn Manor?'

'Why not?' said Driver.

'Why would she come here?'

'If Charlie's right about the financial web, and Rosemary is the boss, I think it's a distinct possibility she's been here all the time.'

Aconna felt a little burst of pride to hear Driver use her Christian name again. Did this mean he was beginning to accept her?

The door popped open. A head appeared, followed by a uniformed arm waving a large brown envelope. 'Delivery for DS Cormac.'

'Who is it from?' asked Cormac.

'No idea. Courier delivery to the front desk. Don't worry, it's been scanned.'

Cormac stepped across the room and took the envelope. It was A4 size and felt quite thick. He carried it over, placed it carefully on his desk, and took a step back. Driver and Aconna waited expectantly.

'Are you expecting a bomb?' asked Driver.

'Sorry?'

'They already X-rayed it to make sure it's safe,' said Driver. 'And you won't find out what's inside by staring at it.'

'Yeah, right, of course.' He looked around for something to open the envelope.

'Here,' said Aconna, handing him a pair of scissors.

Cormac slit the top of the envelope open, looked inside, and then emptied the contents onto the desk. There were sheets of A4 copies, folded in half. Cormac unfolded them. A sticky note was stuck to the front. *Just in case you needed any more proof I wasn't making it up. M.*

'Is "M" who I think?' asked Driver.

Cormac peeled off the label and looked at the top sheet. 'Melinda Yates? Yes, it must be.'

'Are they bank statements?' said Aconna.

'If that's personal stuff, we don't need to see—' said Driver.

'They're not my statements,' said Cormac. 'This top one is for Tillex Capital. Here's another one for Rosecroft Investments.' He sifted through the papers, placing them across the desk. 'We've got a copy of an internal memo here about "R.J.T" approving transfers. And here's an email where a concern raised by a compliance officer had been "addressed to my satisfaction per contact with Lord Tilthorne".'

Driver read the email for himself. 'Christ! This doesn't look good for the Lord of the Manor, does it?'

'That must be one powerful hold she has over him,' said Aconna. 'Or does this mean he's complicit in what's going on?'

'If the boss is right and Heather's at the Manor, he might not have much choice,' said Cormac. 'And if she isn't there, maybe the heavy at the gate is her leverage man, and he makes sure the old man doesn't step out of line.'

'Right,' said Driver. 'Charlie, as you obviously have a gift for this stuff, I'd like you to keep digging, especially into this haulage business. I want to know who pays the utility bills and business rates, and get Gordon to find out if there have been any complaints to the local council from neighbours.'

'Any particular sort of complaints?' asked Aconna.

'We're looking for complaints about vehicles coming and

going at odd hours, especially the early hours of the morning.'

'Right, sir.'

Driver turned to Cormac. 'You and I are going to visit a logistics yard.'

'That sounds like fun,' said Cormac. 'Are we arresting anyone?'

'I think first off we'll pay them a flying visit just to get a feel for the place. We'll say we were just passing by and wondered if any of their drivers had seen anything.'

'Seen what? When?' asked Cormac.

'I don't know yet,' said Driver. 'I'll think of something on the way there.'

* * *

* * *

'Did I detect a further softening of your attitude towards Aconna?' asked Cormac as he drove them towards the edge of town.

'What makes you think that?' asked Driver.

'You called her Charlie, again.'

Driver smiled. 'Did I? I don't recall.'

'Yeah, right, of course you don't,' said Cormac. 'So, you agree she's actually quite good at her job, then?'

'There would have to be something wrong with me if I wasn't impressed with the work she's done on the financials,' conceded Driver. 'Anyway, enough about Aconna; how do we know your girlfriend journo won't publish her story and blow our investigation?'

Cormac sighed. 'Look, she's not my girlfriend; she's just a journalist I met called Melinda.'

'Okay, whatever, how do we know Melinda won't publish?'

'We don't,' said Cormac. 'But I don't think she'll do that if we work with her.'

'I don't like the idea of working with the press,' said Driver. 'Apart from anything else, how do we know we can trust her?'

'I understand where you're coming from, sir, but she didn't have to send us all those photocopies, did she?'

'You realise she probably obtained those illegally, and we can't use them as evidence?'

'Yeah, I get that,' said Cormac. 'But the way Charlie's going through the financials, I can't see that we will need them. And what about the photo Melinda sent me?'

'It's an old journalist's tactic to give you something with an emotional attachment to win your confidence,' said Driver.

'I can't argue with that sentiment, but I think there's more to it than that,' said Cormac. 'I don't know why, but she really wants to see the Tilthornes behind bars. I believe she wants us to arrest them before she publishes her story so they don't have a chance to escape.'

'I'm not in the habit of dancing to anyone else's tune,' said Driver.

'Even if it's a shortcut to solving the case?'

Driver was silent for a couple of minutes. Cormac thought he was thinking, so he stayed quiet too.

Eventually, Driver sighed. 'All right, I'll think about it, but before I give this the green light, I need to meet her myself. Then, and only then, will I make a decision.'

'I'll speak to her and see if she's willing to meet you,' said Cormac.

'If she wants us to work together, she doesn't have a choice about a meeting,' said Driver. 'It's non-negotiable.'

CHAPTER 15

* * *

THE YARD they were looking for was a collection of four large warehouses surrounded by a chain-link fence that must have been 8 feet high. Tucked away down a scruffy side road, it was conveniently less than half a mile from the nearest 'A' road, which, in turn, was less than three miles from the nearest motorway.

A barely legible sign that had clearly never been introduced to a pressure washer clung to the front of the first warehouse above an enormous roller door, *R. Flint International Logistics Ltd.*

On the forecourt sat two artics. One had Eastern European number plates and was fully loaded, engine idling as the driver checked his load. The other was almost empty, curtains drawn back to facilitate unloading. As they watched, a fork truck scooped a pallet from the back and trundled towards a second warehouse.

'I can see why they chose this place,' said Driver. 'Talk about convenient for the motorway.'

'And at the same time, it's nicely tucked away where prying eyes can't see what goes on,' said Cormac.

'Park well clear of the gates,' said Driver. 'We don't want some idiot in an HGV to "accidentally" hit our car.'

They parked alongside the fence, about twenty yards past the gates, and made their way towards a portacabin they could see inside the first warehouse.

'That must be the office,' said Driver. 'I'll do the talking; you take a discreet look around. We want to be in and out again without raising their suspicions.'

'Got it,' said Cormac. 'In, out, and away.'

Cormac followed Driver as he marched straight into the office, where a bored-looking man wearing a blue fleece with the word, *supervisor*, embroidered across the top pocket nervously watched his approach.

'You're early,' said the man sitting behind a desk that was a mess of used mugs and paperwork.

'Am I?' asked Driver.

'You're from Health and Safety, aren't you? I was told you weren't coming back until Friday.'

'Oh, yes, that's right,' improvised Driver. 'But don't worry; we're not trying to catch you out. We were just passing, so we thought we'd drop in to see if you needed any more time to get up to scratch.'

'No, I think I'm okay,' said the man. 'The reason everything was in such a state when you came before was that the bloke covering for my holiday is a lazy sod who doesn't listen and doesn't follow instructions. But I'm back now, and I've got everything as it should be. I try to run an efficient yard, you know?'

Driver looked pointedly at the desk and raised an eyebrow. 'Really?'

'I've had a busy morning,' said the man. 'So many trucks

in and out that I haven't had time to catch my breath. I was just about to tidy up.'

'Good. I'm glad to hear it,' said Driver, who then launched into an improvised spiel about oil-spill clean-up kits and first-aid kits.

As Driver droned on, Cormac wandered back to the warehouse, where a large noticeboard had caught his attention. He was disappointed to find that most of the notices were ancient Health & Safety information sheets, with a couple of flyers for takeaways and a list of cheap places to stay locally.

A delivery schedule had been pinned on top of what Cormac presumed were similar schedules from previous weeks, and a sheet labelled Holiday Rota, showed there must be six or seven warehouse employees. He didn't recognise any of the names but took a discreet photograph on his phone.

To one side, someone had pinned a Site Contact List. He took a quick photo before he read it, then did a double take at one name just as Driver was being escorted out by the supervisor.

'Who is this?' he asked the man, pointing to a line that read, *Site Liaison: European Drivers - A. Bogdani.*

'She's a volunteer adviser for drivers who come from Eastern Europe. Not all of them speak very good English, so she's there if they need anything.'

'Where's she from?' asked Cormac. 'That looks like a Croatian name or something like that.'

'She's English. Says she's got a foreign husband— Albanian or something. That's how come she speaks the lingo.'

'And you say she volunteers?'

'Yeah, just came in one day, about a month ago. Said she was moving down from the Midlands and wanted to help.'

'That was good of her,' said Driver.

'She's one of those do-gooders who think they have to give something back, whatever that means,' said the supervisor. 'I don't get it myself, but I suppose it takes all sorts. To be fair, she's been a lot of help, she's good looking, smiles a lot, and the drivers like her. And just so you know, she understands the H & E rules, so there's no safety issue.'

'That's what we like to hear,' said Driver. 'Well, it looks as if you're going to be ready when we come back for the inspection, so we'll get out of your hair and let you get on with your work.'

'We'll pass with flying colours,' the man assured them as they headed back to their car.

Cormac waited until they were heading back into Windover before he spoke. 'Anita Bogdani volunteering there? How does that work?'

'European Driver Liaison, my arse,' said Driver. 'She's there to spy on the Tilthorne's operation.'

'But how did she get in?' asked Cormac. 'If the Tilthornes know the Albanians are moving in, I can't believe they don't know which Albanians are involved. So why would they let one of them inside the yard and allow her to speak to their drivers? Or are they getting in bed together?'

'It can't be that,' said Driver. 'That guy just told us she started a month ago, yet Jonathon Tilthorne has only just been murdered.'

'You're right, it doesn't add up, does it? Not unless Rosemary's stepping back, but then if that's the case, why aren't the Albanians running the place?'

'There's another possibility,' said Driver. 'What if

Tilthorne doesn't actually know Bogdani's wife has infil-trated their drug delivery network?'

'Rosemary is as sharp as a knife,' said Cormac. 'She'd know the name.'

'Yes, but if this was Jonathon's side of the business, would Rosemary ever have come here? Don't forget we're talking about a volunteer, not someone who would appear on a payroll.'

'You think she would trust him to run this place? He doesn't seem to have been the sharpest knife in the box, does he?'

'No, he wasn't very bright, but he was probably just a figurehead, like with the flower shop in London,' said Driver. 'This place can't be just about moving drugs, can it? You can see for yourself there must be a legitimate haulage business operating here as a cover for the drug smuggling. My guess is that it's being run by a third party who, quite possibly, has no idea they're smuggling drugs in and out of Europe for the Tilthornes.'

'And all the while, Anita is turning the heads of the very drivers who do the smuggling,' said Cormac.

'So the husband, Nikolla, is taking out the people at the top of the organisation, while his wife is infiltrating the drivers who move the drugs.'

'It's a sound strategy when you think about it,' said Cormac. 'And if you're Rosemary now, what are you going to do? Stay and fight, or head for the hills?'

'She can't fight them, can she?' said Driver.

'I wouldn't put it past her to set up her father as bait,' said Cormac. 'Imagine if anything happened to the Home Secretary. There would be all hell to pay, and you can bet your bottom dollar Rosemary would have proof that Bogdani was responsible.'

'Bloody hell, do you think she would?' asked Driver. 'That would be an act of terrorism. If that's even a remote possibility, we should warn him, or at least tell Eagan.'

* * *

Back at the station, Aconna had more information for them. 'The three farm buildings outside Templeton had planning permission granted six months ago to redevelop them for industrial use. They're now storage units.'

'Storage for what?' asked Driver.

'Just storage. There's nothing specified,' said Aconna. 'But Gordon has discovered there have been several complaints to the local council about bright lights and comings and goings late at night and into the early hours.'

'Really?' said Driver. 'Now what reason could they have for working overnight?'

'Maybe that's when they move the drugs,' said Cormac. 'Gather it all together from the lorries during the day, then move it to a safer place at night. Maybe that's the drug distribution centre.'

'Yes, that's what I'm thinking,' said Driver. 'But would they be careless enough to attract attention like that?' He turned to Aconna. 'Do we know if anyone at the council has checked out the complaints?'

'They're being a bit vague about that,' said Aconna. 'I'm guessing the answer is 'no,' but they don't want to admit they're not doing their jobs.'

'Right,' said Driver. 'You two carry on with your work. I'm going to kick some backsides at the council. If they haven't checked these places out, perhaps we can deputise for them.'

An hour later, Driver was back. 'According to the council, there's never anyone on site when they go to check these places out.'

'Do you want to raid them?' asked Cormac.

'I think we need to be a bit more subtle than that,' said Driver. 'At the moment, we're guessing it's a drug distribution centre. Once we know for sure, then, technically, we should call in the drug squad. But we don't want them trampling all over our murder inquiry, so let's keep it to ourselves for now. Once we solve our murders, we can tell them where we think the drugs can be found.'

'I've been running the names from the contact list and holiday rota on that notice board,' said Cormac.

'Don't tell me, all the employees are small-time crooks,' said Driver.

'On the contrary,' said Cormac. 'Not one of the people who work there has a record.'

'That's a surprise,' said Driver.

'Maybe it is a legit haulage business after all,' said Cormac.

'I already suggested that,' said Driver. 'But even so, someone working there must be handling the drugs.'

'But perhaps it's the drivers and not the staff,' said Cormac. 'When it comes to the drivers who pass through that place, it's a different story regarding records. One has form for smuggling counterfeit cigarettes, another has an old drug conviction, and another one has been flagged as having connections with people smugglers.'

'All likely candidates for drug running, then,' said Driver.

'Exactly, and those are just the drivers who were on that list. How many others come in from abroad who aren't on the list?'

Aconna hurried over to them. 'Sorry to interrupt, but I

thought you should know about this. I ran a geolocation search on Anita Bogdani's mobile phone. There's a mast on the Milburn Manor estate. Guess whose phone pinged right next to it on the day you suspected she was following you?'

'So we were right,' said Cormac. 'She was following us.'

'Or was she spying on the Tilthornes and came across us by accident?' suggested Driver.

'That suggests she didn't know who we were,' said Cormac.

'If she was watching the gate, she might have seen you flashing the warrant cards. Either way, if they are audacious enough to get that close to the Tilthornes, I reckon the Albanians are about to make their move. And if Jonathon's murder hasn't been enough to put the wind up Rosemary, I hate to think what they're going to do next!'

'I'm wondering what Rosemary's next move is going to be,' said Cormac. 'She's obviously not planning to run, or she would have been gone by now.'

'You think she's going to fight them?' asked Aconna.

'If Jonathon's death hasn't scared her away, what other reason could she have for staying?'

'Surely with the leverage she seems to have over her father, he'll protect her,' said Aconna. 'After all, he is the Home Secretary.'

'We have to consider our responsibilities here,' said Driver. 'As Charlie has just pointed out, we're talking about the Home Secretary. We can't just sit back and allow a bunch of crooks to launch an assault on his home.'

'You think we should go and tell him?' asked Cormac.

'No, but I am going to have to tell Eagan. He will tell the ACC, and then the ACC can tell Tilthorne, as they seem to be such good mates.'

'You think the shit's going to hit the fan, don't you, sir?' asked Cormac.

'Oh yes. It's going to hit the fan big time.'

'Shall I come with you?'

'No, I think I'd better handle this,' said Driver.

'What do you want us to do?'

'Carry on as you are, and see if you can find anything that actually links Jonathon Tilthorne's death to the Albanians. They must have got the materials to crucify him from somewhere. Let's see if we can get lucky and find it was somewhere local.'

He gave them both a grim smile and set off for Superintendent Eagan's office.

CHAPTER 16

* * *

IT WASN'T long before Aconna sidled up alongside Cormac's desk with a handful of papers.

'Don't tell me you've made a discovery that will solve the case,' he said with a wry smile.

'I wish,' she replied. 'To be honest, I'm not quite sure what I've found. It doesn't make sense.'

'Come on then,' said Cormac. 'Show me what you've got.'

'I've been phoning around the local businesses that sell fencing materials, asking about recent purchases.'

'Right, yes, that's what Driver asked you to do.'

'So, I spoke to a very helpful guy at Woodbarn Fencing Supplies.' She placed a sheet of paper on his desk with a handwritten list. 'He told me a company called MGC Ltd bought half a dozen untreated fence posts, twenty metres of 25mm hemp rope, and a coil of 2.5mm galvanised fence wire.'

Cormac looked at the list. 'That's far more than was used—'

'Yes, but they're minimum purchase quantities,' Aconna explained. 'You couldn't buy less from them if you wanted to.'

'When were they paid for?'

'A week ago.'

'Right. Now that's the sort of coincidence that makes this MGC Ltd very interesting,' said Cormac. 'But why doesn't it make sense?'

'When I heard the name MGC, I thought it rang a bell. Then I remembered I came across it yesterday, so I went back through all the Tilthorne business stuff. MGC stands for Milburn Grounds Contracting. Without over-complicating it, MGC is part of the Tilthorne company network I was looking at yesterday. It's a very small subsidiary, but it's definitely in their portfolio. The interesting thing is that it was set up three years ago, but this was their first purchase.'

'Who are the directors?' asked Cormac.

'R.J. Tilthorne, J. Tilthorne, and someone called C. Prentice—I don't know who he is yet.'

Cormac scratched his head. 'I think I can see why you're confused, Charlie.'

'The business address is listed as North Gate, Milburn Manor.'

'What's that, a business unit?'

'As far as I can tell, it's the main entrance to the Manor,' said Aconna. 'It's also the delivery address Woodbarn was given for those materials. I'm told it was signed for by someone with the surname Prentice.'

'I think I might know who Mr. Prentice is,' said Cormac. 'There's a portacabin security office close to the main gate. The thug who claims to be security hangs out there.'

Cormac stared at the list. Everything was there to create the scarecrow: the posts, the rope, and the wire.

'If you're right, it looks as if a company part-owned by Jonathon Tilthorne ordered the materials used to create his own crucifixion.'

'It's not just me, then?' said Aconna. 'You're thinking it too!'

'The delivery date fits well,' said Cormac. 'And it appears the materials could have been ordered specifically for that purpose.'

'There's more, too,' said Aconna. 'MGC has one of those business fuel cards. It was used at 19:38 at the Riverside service station on the very day the body was found in the car boot.'

'Please tell me there's CCTV.'

Aconna grinned. 'Oh yes,' she said. 'I called the manager and asked, in my best voice, if he still had the footage and if he would be willing to help us, and he said yes to both.'

'So, what are we waiting for?' said Cormac.

'What about DCI Driver? He'll wonder where we are if we don't come back.'

'I'll leave him a note,' said Cormac.

The manager of the Riverside Service Station couldn't have been more pleased to see Charlie Aconna. There was no denying she was an attractive young woman, but so were many others. It left Cormac wondering what exactly her 'best voice' must sound like!

'I've got the footage for that evening all set up and ready to go,' he said.

Sure enough, when they started watching, the time-

stamp on the footage read 19:30. They observed the forecourt until, at 19:33, a green Land Rover Discovery crawled
into view and stopped. A man jumped out, walked around
to the back of the car, and reappeared carrying a 5-litre jerry
can. He pumped petrol into the car and then filled up the
can. He replaced the pump, took the jerry can to the back of
the car, and then disappeared from view as he walked into
the forecourt shop.

'Whoever that is, he's not the Milburn security gorilla,'
said Cormac.

'But he's on his own so he must have signed for the fuel,'
said Aconna.

'Right,' said Cormac. 'As you seem to have the manager
eating out of your hand, perhaps you could ask him for a
copy of the signature and see if they've got a headshot from
the camera above the till.'

'What do you mean he's eating out of my hand?' Aconna
asked indignantly.

'Oh, come on, Charlie. He nearly wet himself when you
walked in. I'm wondering what's in that best voice of yours.'

'Ha! Wouldn't you like to know?' said Aconna.

'Just see what you can get from him,' said Cormac. 'I'll
wait in the car so I don't distract him.'

Five minutes later, Aconna slipped into the passenger
seat, looking immensely pleased with herself.

'Well?' asked Cormac.

'The signature says Prentice,' said Aconna. 'I've got a
photo of it on my phone. I've also got a photo of him—full-
on face, staring straight into the camera.'

'Awesome,' said Cormac. 'Perhaps now we're actually
getting somewhere with these murders.'

'Don't you think we were, then?' Aconna asked.

'Frankly, up until this afternoon, all we had done was

prove Lord Tilthorne was dodgy, that Heather was actually Rosemary Tilthorne, that she has some sort of hold over her father, and that the Albanians are on the warpath.'

Aconna bristled. 'What about all that work I did on the accounts?'

'That's what I mean when I say up until this afternoon. Without your work, we might never have discovered MGC. That's the link that might just lead us to a conclusion, and it's on you. I'm saying well done, Charlie.'

'Oh, right. I see. Thank you.'

* * *

An hour later, Aconna turned from her computer. 'This is odd,' she said. 'I've just found Carl Prentice through the DVLA website. His address is listed as Northgate, Milburn Manor.'

'That's got to be him, then,' said Cormac.

'Yes, but his photo isn't a match for the man at the petrol station.'

'What? Let me see.' Cormac hurried to her side and peered at her monitor.

'Here you are,' she said, placing her phone on the desk in front of the monitor. 'I suppose there's a vague resemblance if you screw your eyes up and squint really hard.'

'No, you're right,' said Cormac. 'I can vouch for the DVLA photo being the security guy at Milburn Manor, but there's no way that's the same guy on your phone.' He stared at the face on her mobile phone. 'So, who the hell is this?'

'Perhaps he's a brother,' suggested Aconna. 'He did use the name Prentice when he signed.'

'Yeah, but anyone could do that,' said Cormac. 'It doesn't make them Carl Prentice, though, does it?'

Driver had returned to the office. 'What's going on?' he asked.

'How did you get on?' asked Cormac. 'Are they going to warn him?'

'Eagan isn't keen,' said Driver. 'He says he'll discuss it with the ACC, but the ACC will be reluctant to act on what he thinks is no more than speculation. He says we'll need concrete proof before the ACC will do any more.'

'Seriously?' said Cormac. 'What are they frightened of?'

'Damned if I know,' said Driver. 'You would think they should tell him there's a potential risk, even if it's just as a precaution. But no, Eagan says we need more proof. Perhaps if someone started taking potshots—'

'If he wants more proof, I think Charlie might have found it,' said Cormac.

'Go on,' said Driver, eagerly.

Cormac stepped back a pace. 'Go on, Charlie, you tell him.'

'Right, so I found a Tilthorne company called MGC, and MGC recently bought these items.' She placed the list in front of Driver. 'They were paid for and delivered in time for Jonathon Tilthorne to become a scarecrow.'

'Delivered where?' asked Driver.

'Milburn Manor.'

Driver turned a puzzled face to Cormac. 'How does that work? Are they murdering their own?'

Cormac shrugged. 'I know. It doesn't seem to add up, does it?'

'And it was definitely delivered to Milburn Manor?' asked Driver.

'The delivery address is North Gate, Milburn Manor,' said Aconna. 'It's the main entrance and the business address of MGC Ltd. It was signed for by someone called Prentice.'

'He's the security guy we met,' added Cormac.

Driver rubbed his face and looked at Cormac. 'Any suggestions as to what this means?'

'I'm scratching my head too, sir. It doesn't quite fit with our Albanian murderers theory, does it?'

Aconna moved her phone, and the photograph popped up on the screen.

Driver pointed to the photo. 'Who's this bloke?'

'This man is a complication,' said Aconna. 'He bought petrol in a Tilthorne vehicle early on the same night the body was found in the burning car. He also filled a jerry can before paying with an MGC fuel card, then signed with the same name: Prentice.'

'Please tell me he's a brother or something.'

'We haven't identified him yet,' said Cormac. 'But I can tell you he's not a brother. Carl Prentice doesn't have any siblings, and his cousins are all female.'

'If he's using the name Prentice,' said Driver, 'I suppose there is a remote possibility it's simply a coincidence they have the same surname...'

'It's always possible,' said Cormac.

'There's only one way to find out,' said Driver. 'In the morning, we'll go to Milburn Manor and ask Carl Prentice if he'd like to come and help us with our inquiries.'

'Are we going to tell Eagan?' asked Cormac.

'We have no choice,' said Driver. 'I'd like to keep it vague and spare him the details, but I can't get a search warrant without going through him first.'

'We'd better make sure what we put before him is convincing then,' said Cormac.

* * *

* * *

* * *

'You're sure about this, are you?' asked Eagan. 'You're seriously asking me to let you apply for a warrant to search the Home Secretary's property?'

Driver met him evenly. 'We only want to look at Milburn Grounds Contracting Ltd. We believe that only involves the security office and two outbuildings close to the main gate, so we don't need to go near the main residence.'

'I'm really not happy about this, Driver,' said Eagan.

'I understand that, sir, but two men are dead, and we can't ignore where the evidence is leading us. We've got evidence that a jerry can of fuel was purchased by the Milburn Manor security guard on the same night the first body was burned. Then we have evidence that fence posts, rope, and wire were delivered to the gate days before Jonathon Milburn was crucified. I don't see what more we need to secure your permission for a search warrant.'

Eagan studied the evidence Cormac had laid out before him on his desk. It included copies of an order docket from Woodbarn Fencing Supplies, a copy of a delivery note signed 'Prentice,' and a couple of still photos taken from the service station CCTV showing the vehicle and the face of the man who paid for the fuel.

There was even a photocopy of Dr. McGowan's post-mortem report. The part confirming the ligature marks matching a 25 mm hemp rope recovered from the body had been highlighted in fluorescent yellow, as had a further sentence stating that an arm had been fixed with 2.5 mm galvanised wire also recovered from the body.

Eagan sighed heavily and then looked up at Driver and Cormac. 'You do realise an estate the size of Milburn is bound to have fences that need maintaining?'

'Of course,' said Driver. 'But it's the timing and the minimum quantities ordered that made us suspicious. And then there's the petrol...'

Eagan placed his palms flat on the desk. He'd made his decision. 'Right, now listen up and make sure you understand exactly what I am saying. I've had the ACC on the phone again. He's extremely concerned about this whole affair. He has made it very clear you are not to make a pantomime out of this and that you are to exercise extreme discretion around Lord Tilthorne. In other words, you keep well away from him. The same goes for Lady Tilthorne if you're thinking of speaking to her.'

'That was a possible avenue of enquiry,' said Driver.

'Well, you can forget it,' said Eagan. 'The ACC has promised me that any waves we make for him will have become a raging storm by the time they get to us. Is that clear?'

'Crystal clear,' said Driver. 'As I already said, we don't plan to go anywhere near Lord Tilthorne or the Manor itself. At this stage, we're only interested in MGC Ltd.'

Eagan switched his gaze to Cormac. 'If, as you seem to be suggesting, Jonathon Tilthorne's murder was arranged in-house, why was the body pointing to the Manor?'

'That's one of the questions we'd like them to answer, sir,' said Cormac noncommittally.

Eagan continued to stare at Cormac. 'It's unlike you not to have a theory, isn't it?'

'I can only say that if they wanted to confuse us, they appear to have succeeded so far.'

Eagan leaned forward to emphasise his point. 'I hope you're not intending to let any of this slip to your journalist girlfriend.'

'I don't have a journalist girlfriend, sir,' said Cormac through gritted teeth. 'If you're referring to Melinda Yates, she came to me with information. I thought it was relevant to our investigation, so I brought it to the attention of DCI Driver. That is the full extent of my relationship with her. Sir.'

Eagan stared at Cormac some more, then exhaled loudly before turning his attention back to Driver.

'Right, Driver, I will go to the duty judge myself if it helps, but if this goes pear-shaped—'

'It won't, sir,' said Driver. 'You have my word.'

'I bloody well hope you're right,' said Eagan. 'And, if you want me to back you in taking this any further after your search, I want something more convincing than fence posts, rope, and petrol. I want evidence that someone at Milburn gave the order to have these people murdered.'

'A confession?' said Cormac as they walked back to their office. 'He doesn't want much, does he?'

'With the ACC being so chummy with Tilthorne, Eagan finds himself caught between a rock and a hard place,' said Driver.

'It's not like you to defend him.'

'I'm not defending him; I'm just saying he's trapped. He can't win whatever happens.'

'He'll win if we bring the Home Secretary down,' said Cormac.

'Let's not get carried away and go off half-cocked,' said

Driver. 'We need proof before we can even think about that, and we haven't proved anything yet.'

'Okay, so what now?' asked Cormac.

'I think you and Aconna should both go home and get some rest.'

* * *

THE NEXT DAY, Driver and Cormac decided to take a circuitous route to Milburn Manor, which would allow them to call at Woodbarn Fencing Supplies on the way.

'We're trying to identify the man who placed this order,' Cormac explained to the man behind the counter. 'I don't suppose you have CCTV?'

The man behind the counter laughed. 'CCTV? You must be joking. This place is still in the Dark Ages. We've only started using a computer system six months ago.'

'Oh, right,' said Cormac. 'Did you serve him?'

The man looked at the order number. 'It's got an 'S' on the end,' he said. 'That means young Simon took the order.'

'Is he here?'

'He's out the back on his break. Hang on, I'll give him a shout.'

The man opened a door behind the counter and yelled out, 'Simon? The police are here to see you.'

About thirty seconds later, a terrified-looking boy

pushed the door ajar and peered in. Cormac guessed the boy was 16 or 17 years old and, by the look on his face, had probably never encountered the police before.

'It's okay, Simon,' called Cormac. 'You're not in trouble. We're just trying to identify someone you served a few days ago.'

The boy breathed an audible sigh of relief and pushed his way through the door. 'I'm not sure I'll remember,' he said as he approached the counter. 'They all look the same to me.'

Cormac placed the photocopy of the order down on the counter so Simon could read it. 'This order,' he said. 'Do you remember it?'

Simon looked at the order for a moment. 'Yeah, I remember. I made him angry.'

'How did you make him angry?' asked Driver.

'He had his back to the counter when I said hello, but he ignored me. I could see he was wearing this earpiece, and I could see it wasn't an earbud, so thinking it was a hearing aid, I raised my voice. He got a bit nasty about it. Said he didn't like me shouting at him.'

'Can you describe him?' asked Cormac.

'He had a thick jacket and a hat.'

Cormac heard Driver tutting, so he thought he'd help the boy out. He fished his phone from his pocket and found the photograph of Carl Prentice. 'Is this the man?'

Simon looked at the photograph and shook his head. 'No. That bloke looks like James Bond with a buzz cut. The guy who came in here had longer hair, and his face was different.'

'But he signed for the order, right?' asked Cormac. 'With the name Prentice?'

Simon looked at the order again. 'Yeah, I think that's what it says.'

'Has he been in here before?' asked Cormac. 'Or has anyone else been in from Milburn Grounds Contracting?'

The older man was hanging around behind the counter. 'Simon's quite new, so he won't know,' he said. 'But I can't recall seeing anyone from that company before. If they were regular customers, they would have an account, but they don't. That's why they had to pay up front.'

'And you're sure they've never been in here before?' asked Driver.

'I've been working here for ten years, and I know all our customers. This MGC, or whatever they're called, is new to us.'

While he was talking, Cormac had been on his phone finding the other photograph. Now he showed it to Simon. 'What about this guy? Is this him?'

Simon studied the photo. 'Yeah, I think that's him.'

'Thanks, Simon,' said Cormac. 'You've been very helpful.'

'So, what have we got here?' said Driver when they were back in the car. 'Why does a man sign his name as Prentice if it's not his name?'

'Because he's not supposed to be here,' said Cormac.

'That's my guess,' said Driver.

'Or perhaps he wants it to look like Prentice placed the order,' suggested Cormac.

'Now that's an interesting idea,' said Driver. 'And if you're right, does Prentice even know our mystery man is signing his name here, there, and everywhere? Tell you what; when we question him, I think we should make out we believe he signed for this fencing stuff and the petrol, and see what he says.'

It was just before midday as they pulled up outside the North Gate to Milburn Manor. The sky was filled with heavy clouds as they eased themselves from the car and waited at the gate. Less than thirty seconds later, Carl Prentice strolled towards the gate.

'Why's he wearing shades?' muttered Driver.

'Because he's a twat,' said Cormac. 'He thinks it makes him look hard, but it just proves how much of a twat he is.'

Prentice broke into a broad grin as he recognised Cormac. 'If it isn't Detective Sergeant Cormac again,' he said. 'If you're looking for Lord Tilthorne, you've had a wasted journey just like last time. He's not here.'

'Are you Carl Prentice?' asked Driver.

Prentice turned a glare in Driver's direction.

'Yeah, why? Who's asking?'

Driver produced his warrant card. 'DCI Driver. For your information, we're not here to see Lord Tilthorne, so it doesn't matter if he's not here. We'd actually like a word with you.'

'Me? What do you want with me?'

'We understand you're a director of a company called Milburn Grounds Contracting Ltd.'

'Yeah? So what? There's no law against being a company director, is there?'

'Not usually,' said Driver. 'But it depends what the company does.'

As he spoke, a marked police car, and a white van pulled into the driveway and stopped.

'What's going on?' demanded Prentice.

'Oh, did I forget to say,' said Driver as he produced the search warrant from his pocket and showed it to Prentice. 'We have a warrant to search your portacabin, your accommodation, and any outbuildings nearby. All the buildings we intend to search are marked on the attached map.'

'What? You can't do that?'

'Actually, Carl, that piece of paper says we can,' said Cormac. 'Now, be a good lad and open the gates so our people can come in and do their jobs.'

'I can't—'

'I suggest you do,' said Driver. 'At the moment, we're happy to speak to you here, but we can just as easily take you back to Windover police station. It's your choice.'

Muttering assorted curses under his breath, Prentice reluctantly went back to the portacabin to open the gates.

'That's odd,' said Cormac. 'I'm sure when we were here the other day, there was someone else sitting inside, ready to operate the gates.'

'Perhaps it's their day off,' said Driver.

As the gates began to open with an electrical purring noise, they walked through to the cabin. When the gates had opened wide enough, the marked car and van drove in and disgorged a small swarm of police officers and forensic technicians.

Driver turned to the assembled team. 'Right, you all know what you're doing and where you're going. If you find anything of interest, I want it bagged and tagged. Anything of extraordinary interest should be reported to DC Aconna. Understood?'

There was a rumble of assent, and they all set to work. Charlie Aconna beamed happily as she began her tasks.

Driver led Cormac into the portacabin.

'This is a bit archaic, isn't it?' asked Cormac.

'What is?' spat Prentice.

'Why can't you open the gates from outside?'

'Because that way anyone could climb over and open the gates, of course.'

'Yeah, but all that walking,' said Cormac. 'Wouldn't you be better off with someone in here to open the gates when you give the signal?'

'There usually is,' said Prentice. 'But he's not here today.'

'Day off?' asked Driver.

'Not exactly,' said Prentice. 'I haven't seen him for several days.'

Driver tutted. 'I don't know; you just can't get reliable staff these days, can you, Carl?'

'Look, what's this about?' said Prentice. 'My boss is going to want to know what's going on with your lot swarming all over the place.'

'I thought you said he wasn't here.'

'Well, yeah, that's right, but there are staff in the house. Word can still get back to him.'

'Or did you mean someone else?' suggested Driver. 'Rosemary, perhaps?'

Prentice stayed rock solid. 'Who?'

'Never mind; we can come back to that later,' said Driver. He nodded to Cormac, who was carrying a slim folder. Cormac took a sheet of paper from the folder and placed it in front of Prentice. 'We'd like to know why you placed this order.'

Prentice stared at the photocopy of the order placed at Woodbarn Fencing Supplies. 'Not me,' he said. 'I don't even know where that place is.'

'But it's your name and your signature,' said Cormac.

'Oh, no, mate. You're not going to stitch me up like that. It might be my name, but that is not my signature.'

'What about this one, then?' said Cormac, producing the copy from the service station.

'This is bollocks,' said Prentice. 'I'll say it again. That is not my signature.'

Cormac produced a photograph of the car, its front registration plate clear to see. 'This is your car, right?'

'It's not mine. It belongs to the estate.'

'But you drive it, though.'

'I'm not the only one who drives it. It's like a runaround. We all use it.'

'Did you drive it to the service station when this photograph was taken?'

'I dunno. When was it taken?'

'On Sunday, 28th April, the same night a young man called Marcus Whitmore, aka Marky, was burnt to a crisp in a car at the old gasworks.'

'Oh yeah. I heard about that,' said Prentice. 'That's quite a way to go.'

'I take it you're going to deny signing for a tank full of petrol for the car and a jerry can full for the car barbecue,' said Cormac.

'I think you'll find I was off duty that weekend,' said Prentice. 'His Lordship was here on vacation. He had his official security team look after the gate so I could have a weekend off.'

'That's good of him,' said Driver.

'Yeah, he's considerate like that,' said Prentice.

'Just to be clear, then,' said Driver. 'You're denying you signed for the petrol and for the fencing goods.'

'Yes, I am. It's not my signature. I can prove it; look…' He fiddled a wallet from a jacket hanging on the back of a chair and fumbled a driving licence from it, which he handed to Driver. 'There. That's my signature.'

Driver took the licence and compared it to the two copied signatures. Then, with a sigh, he handed it to Cormac. Cormac could see why Driver had sighed; there was no way the signatures matched.

'Let's go back to the fencing,' said Driver. 'Do you deny MGC ordered those materials?'

'No, I'm not denying we ordered them. I'm saying I wasn't the person who went to place the order, just as I wasn't the guy who filled the car up that day.'

'Why did you order them?' asked Cormac.

'Milburn is a big estate. There are lots of fences to maintain. We can't do that without materials.'

'And have you used those materials?'

'No, not yet, because the bloody odd-job man hasn't come back to do the job.'

'But these are minimum order quantities,' said Cormac. 'You wouldn't repair much fencing with that lot.'

'We don't do major repairs; we just do temporary fixes. We use contractors for the big jobs.'

'Exactly how many people are on the MGC payroll?' asked Driver.

'Sorry?'

'How many people do you actually employ?'

'We don't. The company is just a front to avoid paying VAT. We have several small companies like that so we don't have to buy everything through the main estate business.'

'You expect us to believe the Home Secretary is avoiding paying VAT?'

'I'm not sure he knows,' said Prentice. 'The estate management and the accountants set it all up.'

'Are you telling me the whole setup is simply a tax avoidance scam?'

'It's only one little company,' said Prentice. 'And we've only just started using it.'

'Just one little company,' said Driver. 'And you believe that, do you?'

'Look, I'm just security,' said Prentice. 'They asked me if they could use my name as a director, and I couldn't see the harm, so I said yes.'

Driver sighed impatiently. 'Show him the photo of the other Mr. Prentice,' he told Cormac.

Cormac found the photo. 'Who is this?' he asked as he showed it to Prentice.

'That's Mike Phillips.'

'And who is Mike Phillips?' asked Driver.

'He's the pillock who should be here when I go to the gate, and he's also the odd-job man around here. That's who went to place the order for the fencing.'

'Is he illiterate?' asked Cormac.

'Why would you even ask that?' said Prentice.

'Because he signed using your name,' said Cormac.

'Well, he can't be illiterate if he can write, can he?'

'It's not a good idea to get too clever, Carl,' said Cormac. 'My point is, why would he sign using your name?'

'I don't know, do I? You'll have to ask him.'

'And now he's missing, you say?' said Driver.

'I don't know if he's missing. All I know is he hasn't been in to work.'

'I'd like his address,' said Cormac. 'I'd like a word with Mr. Phillips.'

'Well, if you find him, tell him from me he's lost his job,' said Prentice.

'How long has he been working here?'

'About three months.'

'How well do you know him?'

'I don't really.'

'You're supposed to be the security around here,' said Cormac. 'Didn't you vet him before he started working here?'

'Well, yeah. The thing is, he's ex-para, like me.'

'And that was good enough for you, was it?'

'It was good enough for the regiment.'

'Oh, well, that's okay then,' said Cormac sarcastically. 'Never mind the security checks, eh? I mean, it's only the Home Secretary who lives here.'

'He's got his own security, hasn't he?' said Prentice. 'It goes with the job. I'm just here to look after the place while they're away. We needed an odd-job man, and Mike needed a job. I didn't know he was going to be unreliable.'

'Let's recap,' said Driver. 'You're saying that you had nothing to do with the purchase of a jerry can full of petrol on the evening of Sunday, 28th April, and nothing to do with a body found in the boot of a burning car later that same night. Is that right?'

'You already know it's not my signature,' said Prentice. 'And, as I said, I was on leave that weekend. I didn't get back until Monday morning.'

'I take it you can prove that,' said Cormac.

Prentice leered at Cormac and winked. 'I'll give you her phone number if you want.'

'Yes, I do want,' said Cormac.

Prentice reached for his phone, found the number, and handed the phone to Cormac.

'And you also deny going to Woodbarn Fencing Supplies to place an order for fence posts, rope, and wire?' asked Driver as Cormac made a note of the phone number.

'Yes, I do deny it,' said Prentice. 'Hang on. Is this to do with Jonathon's murder? You can't seriously think I had anything to do with that.'

'Why not?'

'I'm paid very well to look after the estate and the family. Why would I kill one of the golden geese?'

'If you want me to believe you, you'd better hope you can account for any of that fencing stuff that's missing,' said Driver.

'I don't do fencing, but as far as I know, it should all be there,' said Prentice.

'We're going now, but don't think this is over,' said Driver.

'Yeah, whatever,' said Prentice.

Aconna had been surprised when Driver had chosen her as part of the search team. Now she was waiting for them at the gate, eager to show she could be trusted to do a good job.

'Anything?' asked Driver.

'We've taken a roll of wire that's been opened,' she said. 'I'm guessing there's only a metre or two taken from it. But we can't find a rope anywhere, and we can't find any fence posts.'

'There should be six,' said Cormac.

'Yes, I know, but we can't find any. Mind you, it's a twelve-hundred-acre estate, and we've only looked at this tiny corner. They could be anywhere.'

'Bugger,' said Driver, vehemently. 'It's better than nothing, but it's not going to be enough to convince Eagan we should look anywhere else on the estate.'

'What about this Mike Phillips?' asked Cormac.

Driver thought for a moment. 'Let's go back. Drop me

off at the office, and then you two go and check out his address. I don't think you'll find him, but it's worth a shot.'

'Me?' said Aconna, surprised to find she was being trusted even more. 'You want me to go?'

'You can handle it, can't you?' asked Driver.

'Well, yes, I think I can, sir.'

Driver smiled. 'Of course you can,' he said. 'I wouldn't have suggested it otherwise.'

CHAPTER 18

* * *

MIKE PHILLIPS's flat was one of six crammed into what was once a large family home in the centre of Windover but was now a grubby shadow of its former self. The tone of the whole street was one of grime and decay, so it fitted in rather well.

'Here we go, seventy-eight Arundel Street,' said Aconna, looking up at the dingy, grey façade of the house, the ornate glass of the original front door panels now boarded over with sheets of plywood.

'It doesn't exactly give off a welcoming vibe, does it?' said Cormac.

'Oh, I don't know,' said Aconna. 'We could be looking at the latest trend. Out with the fancy glass and in with ratty old plywood. At least a brick can't fly through it.'

'I suppose that counts for something around here,' said Cormac.

There was a row of buttons by the door numbered from

1-6. Cormac pressed 6 and waited, but there was no response from the speaker.

'No one in?' asked Aconna.

'Looking at the state of this place, there's no guarantee the intercom works,' said Cormac. 'Then again, I wasn't really expecting to be welcomed with open arms. Let's try another bell.' He pressed button number 1, and almost immediately a creaky voice answered.

'Yes? Who is it?'

'DS Cormac and DC Aconna from Windover police station.'

'Police?'

'Yes, that's right,' said Cormac.

'You want to speak to me?'

'We're looking for Mr Phillips in flat six, but there's no answer there. We were hoping you'd let us in.'

'He's not here.'

Cormac sighed. 'Yes, we know he's not there, but we'd like to come in, please.'

'Why do you want to come in if he's not here?'

Cormac looked skyward and muttered under his breath.

'Can I try?' asked Aconna.

'Be my guest,' said Cormac, stepping back.

Aconna stepped up to the intercom. 'Hello. My name is DC Charlie Aconna. Who am I speaking to?'

'Mrs. Elliot. I own the house.'

'Hello, Mrs. Elliot. I'm pleased to meet you,' said Aconna. 'When did you last see Mr. Phillips?'

'Not for a few days.'

'Right,' said Aconna. 'The thing is, Mr. Phillips has been reported missing by his employer, and we're a bit concerned. We just want to come in and check that he hasn't had an accident or anything.'

'He's had an accident, you say?'

'I said he might have had an accident,' said Aconna. 'We just want to make sure.'

'Oh, well, if he's had an accident, you'd better come in.'

There was a loud buzz as the door unlocked. Aconna pushed it open and turned a smug face towards Cormac.

'Sometimes older people need the reassuring sound of a woman's voice.'

'Yeah, right,' said Cormac. 'I'll try to remember to bring out my feminine side next time. Come on, let's get in before she changes her mind and locks us out.'

By the time they stepped into the hall, Mrs Elliot had emerged from her flat and was waiting for them. She looked even older than she sounded and shuffled along with the help of a wooden walking stick. Cormac stepped aside and let Aconna do the talking.

It took what seemed to Cormac like a lengthy five minutes before Aconna re-established that Mrs Elliot was both the owner and caretaker of the house. Then it took another five minutes to persuade her to let them borrow a key to flat six, even though they didn't have a search warrant.

'We'll only be five minutes,' promised Aconna. 'We're not searching the flat; we're just checking to make sure Mr. Phillips isn't inside. You can come with us if you like.'

'I can't get up those stairs with my knees,' said Mrs. Elliot. 'It's the arthritis, you see. Terribly painful it is.'

'Oh, dear, I'm sorry to hear that,' said Aconna. 'You go and sit down, then. I promise I'll bring the key back in a few minutes.'

The old woman turned awkwardly and shuffled back to her flat.

'Poor old thing,' said Aconna as they made their way upstairs.

'How can she be the caretaker if she can't get around?' asked Cormac. 'No wonder the place looks like a tip.'

'You'll be old one day,' said Aconna. 'Then we'll see how you cope.'

'And that's told me,' he mumbled.

'Right, here we are,' said Aconna. 'Number six. Shall I do the honours?'

'No, let me,' said Cormac. 'He might be waiting in there with a weapon.'

'I can look after myself, you know.'

'Yes, I'm sure you can,' said Cormac. 'But I'm in charge, and I've got a thing about keeping my partners safe.'

'Yes, but—'

'Look, I had a partner get shot once,' said Cormac grimly. 'Whether you like it or not, I'm trying to make sure nothing like that happens again. Understand?'

There was something about his face that told Aconna she shouldn't argue.

'Okay,' she said quietly. 'I understand.'

Cormac smiled. 'Thank you,' he said, then carefully placed the key in the lock and turned it. Once he was sure it was unlocked, he glanced at Aconna, made himself ready, and then swung the door open.

Nothing happened, so he took a step forward and looked around. 'There's no one here,' he said and walked into the flat.

It consisted of a small living room, a tiny kitchenette, and a bedroom with an en-suite, so it took less than ten seconds to know Phillips wasn't there and hadn't been there recently.

'Right, we're in here now, so let's take a quick look around,' said Cormac.

'What are we looking for?'

'No idea,' said Cormac. 'Anything that doesn't look right.'

Searching such a tiny space took all of five minutes but they found nothing of interest.

'It's rare to come across someone who has nothing,' said Cormac.

'Not so much as a bank statement,' said Aconna. 'He doesn't even have many clothes.'

'Yeah, talk about travelling light.'

'DCI Driver said he wouldn't be here,' said Aconna. 'Perhaps he lives somewhere else, and he was here to do a job, and now he's gone again.'

'He'd be an idiot to hang around if he was responsible for Jonathon Tilthorne's death,' said Cormac.

'Do you think he is?'

Cormac shrugged. 'We know he had access to the fencing stuff, and he worked at the Manor. That gives him means and opportunity.'

'But what's his motive?'

'Looking at the state of this place, I can't see him having any sort of power, but he's ex-forces, so he's used to following orders. And if there was a price on Jonathon's head ...'

'But whose orders was he following? The Albanians?'

'As far as we know, there are only two players, so it's either the Albanians or Rosemary Jane Tilthorne, a.k.a. Heather Collins.'

'You think she would order her own brother's murder?'

'I'm beginning to think she's capable of anything,' said Cormac. 'So, yeah, why not?'

When they got back to the office, Driver had gone home, leaving a message to say he would see them in the morning.

'What should we do about Mike Phillips?' asked Aconna.

'I'll call at his flat in the morning,' said Cormac. 'If he still hasn't turned up, we'll put out an alert and maybe list him as a misper. But for now, I think we should tidy up and call it a day.'

Cormac and Aconna quickly tidied their desks, made their way down to the car park, and said their goodnights. Cormac sat in his car and watched Aconna slip into her old Mini and head off home. Then he started his own car, which coughed asthmatically before settling into a steady tick-over. He was just about to put the car in gear when his phone pinged.

Grumbling to himself, he reached for the phone on the passenger seat and looked at the screen. There was a new message from an unknown number. He often deleted anything unsolicited without reading it, and he thought about doing that now, but curiosity got the better of him, so he tapped the screen and opened it.

Why did you come here? You should walk away while you still can; you'll wish you had. H.

It didn't take a genius to work out who 'H' was, and his immediate reaction was to reply to her, but instead, he stared at the message. Eventually, the screen dimmed and became a dark mirror.

'No, thank you, Heather. I don't think so,' he muttered as he reopened the message and then deleted it.

CHAPTER 19

IT WAS JUST AFTER MIDNIGHT. After tossing and turning for an hour, Cormac had been unable to sleep, so he'd made himself a cup of tea, and had spent the last half an hour sitting in bed staring at a damp patch on the ceiling of his motel room. He had discovered that if he stared at it long enough, it began to resemble Heather's face.

He thought it was amazing what a sleep-deprived imagination could conjure up. Or was it just a subconscious desire to remember her as she had been when they were a couple? He was in the process of trying to convince himself it was nothing more than a random thought when his mobile phone began to ring. He snatched it from his bedside cabinet.

'Cormac.'

'It's Gleeson.'

'I take it you haven't called to wish me goodnight.'

'No, and I'm not going to sing you a lullaby, either. We've got another body.'

'Where?'

'The river, down by the bridge. Someone called in about

a disturbance. Uniforms responded and saw a body floating underneath. They fished him out but...'

'I'll be there in twenty minutes,' said Cormac.

'Should I let DCI Driver know?'

'Let's wait until I've had a look at the crime scene,' said Cormac. 'You could give Aconna a ring.'

'I already did,' said Gleeson. 'She'll probably be there before you.'

By the time Cormac arrived, the area was awash with blue strobe lights from numerous vehicles. Martha McGowan was already on site, examining the victim, who was laid out on the path that wound its way alongside the river. Hastily erected floodlights lit the scene like a stage, with ghost-like, white-suited forensic technicians coming and going like well-rehearsed extras in a play.

Aconna was standing a few yards away, watching the pathologist. She had her back to Cormac as he approached and stepped alongside her.

'Are you okay?' he asked.

Aconna nodded. 'A bit tired. I had barely got to sleep.'

'Welcome to the job,' said Cormac. 'What have we got?'

'I'm not sure, but I think it's the guy we were looking for this afternoon.'

'Mike Phillips?'

'Dr McGowan chased me away before I got a proper look at his face, but I'm pretty sure it's him.'

'How long has he been in the water?'

'A nine, nine, nine call was placed at 11.40 saying there

was a fight going on by the bridge. Uniforms got here within ten minutes.' She glanced at her watch. 'So, unless the two events are unconnected, he's been in there an hour or thereabouts.'

'Come on, let's see what Martha says.' Cormac took a few steps forward and then called out to McGowan. 'How close can we come, Martha?'

McGowan looked over her shoulder and smiled. 'You don't have to go to all this trouble if you want to see me after hours,' she said. 'I'd be happier sharing a drink than a dead body.'

'I'll bear that in mind for the future,' said Cormac. 'Can we have a look at his face? We think we know who he is.'

She pointed out where they should walk. 'Will that be close enough?'

Cormac and Aconna followed her directions and came as close as she would allow.

'I'm afraid he's not at his best,' said McGowan.

'Yeah, well, who is when they've been dragged out of bed at this time of night?' said Cormac.

'That's a fair point,' she said. 'But at least we're all still breathing, which is more than can be said for this poor guy. Is he who you think he is?'

Cormac took a good look at the face and then at Aconna, who nodded her head.

'Yeah, that's him,' said Cormac. 'His name is Mike Phillips. Has he been in the water long?'

McGowan considered for a couple of seconds. 'I don't think so. The water's pretty cold, which has brought his body temperature down more than it would otherwise, but going by his core temperature, I'd say maybe an hour. Perhaps a bit more, but not much. They said a fight was reported, didn't they?'

'Yes, it was called in at 11.40,' said Aconna.

McGowan looked at her watch. 'There you go then,' she said. 'That sounds about right.'

'So, there was a fight, and he ended up in the water,' said Cormac. 'Did he drown?'

McGowan gave him a withering look. 'I think you've been doing this long enough to know I can't tell you that until I do the post-mortem.'

Aconna was looking at the river.

'This river is tidal, isn't it?' she asked.

'This near to the coast? Of course it is,' said McGowan.

'And the tide's going out now,' said Aconna. 'So how come his body didn't get washed out to sea?'

'We were lucky there,' said McGowan. 'The rope must have snagged on something under the water.'

'Rope?' said Cormac. 'What rope?'

'Oh, didn't I tell you?' McGowan pointed to the victim's feet. A length of rope was tied around his left ankle, and a tail of about a yard trailed from it.

'I've only had a quick look, but there are chaff marks on both ankles and both wrists.'

'So, he was tied up?' said Cormac.

'Had been, at some stage,' said McGowan. 'But there's no rope around his wrists now, and just the one ankle.'

'Suggesting someone wasn't very good at knots,' said Aconna. 'Is that the same rope that was used—'

'On the scarecrow?' said McGowan. 'Too soon to say for sure, but at this stage, I certainly wouldn't rule it out.'

'I'm confused,' said Aconna. 'I thought Phillips was the guy who killed the scarecrow.'

'This doesn't prove otherwise,' said Cormac.

'So, how come he's dead? And who killed him?'

'I'm guessing it'll be the same person who ordered him to kill Jonathon Tilthorne.'

'But why?'

'Tidying up,' said Cormac. 'Making sure there are no loose ends.'

'What do we do now?' asked Aconna.

'I'm just going to call Driver and let him know what's happened. I'll let him decide what we should do next.'

After fielding an initial barrage of swear words, Cormac explained the situation to Driver.

Half an hour later, he joined them under the bridge.

'Did dead bodies gather at your feet when you were in the Midlands?' he asked Cormac.

'I was in the drug squad up there,' Cormac reminded him. 'We didn't investigate murders.'

Driver sighed. 'Right. So, what do we know about Mike Phillips?'

Cormac and Aconna told Driver what they knew about Phillips and how they had found nothing when they searched his flat.

'So, basically all we know is that he used to be in the Parachute Regiment, that he signs for things using Prentice's name, and he's been missing since Jonathon Tilthorne was murdered,' said Driver.

'Yeah, I'm afraid that's it,' said Cormac.

'And Martha thinks it's the same rope?' asked Driver.

'She wouldn't say a definite 'yes' without testing it, but she said it looked very similar.'

'That's fair enough,' said Driver. 'So, what do we think?'

'If Carl Prentice killed Jonathon Tilthorne, is he covering his tracks?' suggested Aconna.

'Possibly,' said Driver. 'But if we're saying the first two murders are linked, do we really think Prentice killed

Jonathon? Don't forget he has an alibi for the first murder and, as he said, why would he kill the golden goose?'

'Because Heather, or rather Rosemary, told him to,' said Cormac.

'But, even if she had Marky killed, would she order a hit on her own brother?'

'It might be unlikely, but we can't rule it out,' said Cormac.

'What about these Albanians?' said Driver. 'Wouldn't they be more likely to have murdered Jonathon? He was the competition, don't forget.'

'Yeah, but then where does Phillips fit in?' asked Cormac.

Driver sighed. 'There are too many bloody possibilities, aren't there? Let's go back to the first murder, Marcus Whitmore. Who wanted us to find him before he burned to death, and why?'

'It makes more sense if it was the Albanians,' said Cormac. 'Why would the Tilthornes want to draw attention to themselves?'

'Right,' said Driver. 'So, on that basis, are we thinking they murdered Jonathon Tilthorne and made him point to Milburn Manor?'

'It makes sense,' said Aconna. 'Is there a better way to get the police interested in the estate and what's going on inside?'

'Here's an idea,' said Driver. 'What if the Albanians are responsible for the first two murders, but they want us to believe it was the Tilthornes?'

'Why would they do that?' asked Aconna.

'Because if we arrest the Tilthornes, they can walk in and take control of the drug distribution,' said Cormac. 'We get to do their dirty work for them.'

'Perhaps they're just hoping they can sit back and watch,' said Driver.

'But does that mean they also murdered Mike Phillips?' said Cormac. 'I don't think we should rule out Carl Prentice just yet.'

'Phillips signed using his name,' said Aconna. 'That brought Prentice to our attention, which I'm sure he would have hated. How do we know he didn't want to teach Phillips a lesson about that?'

'What about this,' said Cormac. 'Phillips has only been working at Milburn Manor for three months. What if he was planted by the Albanians? It would explain why he was trying to implicate Prentice by using his signature.'

'Guess what you two are doing today?' said Driver.

'Avoiding Eagan?' suggested Cormac.

'Fortunately, he's out for the day, so that shouldn't be necessary,' said Driver.

'Trying to find a link between Phillips and the Albanians?' said Aconna.

'That's exactly what I have in mind for you,' said Driver. 'But right now, you both look like death warmed up.'

'Have you looked in a mirror, sir?' said Cormac.

'All right, so we all look like shit,' said Driver. 'And so, because of that, I think we would all benefit from taking a couple of hours to go home, freshen up, and have some breakfast. I'll see you both back in the office at 08:00.'

CHAPTER 20

* * *

MARTHA MCGOWAN's post-mortem report suggested the rope burns around Mike Phillips's wrists and ankles meant he had probably been held prisoner since Jonathon Tilthorne had been murdered.

This posed an intriguing question: if he had committed the scarecrow murder, and he was working for the Albanians, had the Tilthornes sussed him out and been holding him prior to his murder? Or had the Albanians decided he was a loose end that needed tidying up?

Driver seemed reluctant to entertain the idea that Phillips had been following Rosemary Tilthorne's orders to murder her brother. Cormac was inclined to believe otherwise. Aconna claimed to be keeping an open mind but suggested Cormac might be biased against his former girlfriend.

Whatever the truth, by 4 pm Cormac and Aconna had failed to find anything to link Phillips to the Albanians. They were dead on their feet too, so when Driver suggested they should give it another hour and then call it a day, there were no arguments.

Cormac had driven straight back to the motel, taken a long shower, walked up to the Red Cow for an early dinner and was back in his room and in bed by 9 pm. The plan, of course, was to get a decent night's sleep, but his brain had other ideas and wasn't inclined to switch off. All it would allow him to do was slumber for a few minutes at a time before reminding him that three people had died since he had come back to Windover.

And then there was the question that haunted him more than anything: was his quest to find Heather the catalyst behind it all?

Just after midnight, something dragged him from his latest doze. He shook his head and wondered why he had suddenly woken. Then he heard it; someone was tapping on the door to his room. And was that a voice? Senses on full alert, he slipped from his bed, crept silently across to the door and listened.

After a few seconds, there it was again, tap, tap, tap on the door. Then a soft voice that made his heart miss a beat: 'Noly? Noly? Come on, let me in. I know you're in there.'

The voice was as unmistakable to Cormac as it was unexpected. But it had to be her; Heather was only person who had ever called him 'Noly' in his entire life. At the sound of her voice, his head filled with memories of their short time together, but just as quickly he swept them aside. This woman wasn't the Heather he had known. This was Rosemary Jane Tilthorne, and he needed to have his wits about him.

'What do you want?' he called through the door.

'We need to talk, but we can't do it by shouting at each other through a door.'

'You expect me to let you in?'

'Come on, Noly, I'm not going to stand here all night. Either you let me in, or I go away and you'll miss the chance to end the killing.'

Cormac weighed up the risk. He didn't think he was going to be in any physical danger from her, but could he trust her not to try manipulating him? He decided that, in all probability, manipulating him was precisely what she was hoping to do. But, in the past, he had been blinded by his love for her. Things were different now.

He unlocked the door and opened it enough to take up the slack on the security chain and peered through the gap. Heather smiled back at him, and it took all his will not to smile back. As far as he could see, she appeared to be alone, so he closed the door, unclipped the chain, and let her in.

She stepped inside, let him close the door, and then took a step towards him, still offering that warm smile he knew so well. Cormac held his hands up to stop her.

'Just don't, right?' he said. 'Don't you dare come here and expect me to pretend things are what they were. It's never going to happen.'

She pouted. 'You could at least look pleased to see me, Noly.'

'To be honest, I wasn't sure,' he said. 'On balance, I thought I would be pleased but, actually, now you're here I find I'm unimpressed. No, that doesn't even come close. I feel much worse than that.'

Her smile widened, as if she were pleased to see his discomfort.

'I'm glad you think it's funny,' said Cormac. 'Really, I should arrest you. You wouldn't find that so funny, would you?'

She held his gaze. 'Arrest me on what grounds?'

'Drug dealing and suspicion of murder will do for a start,' he said.

She shook her head. 'You might have your suspicions, but we both know you need evidence to make either of those stick.'

'We know you're behind it all.'

'We can all speculate, but you don't have any actual proof, do you? Of course not, because I wouldn't be stupid enough to leave any. And even if you did manage to find any, Daddy would have me released before you could even get started.'

'Oh, yes, good old Daddy. What exactly is this hold you have over him?'

'I can't believe you haven't worked that one out yet. Let's just say Daddy and I were once very close.'

'What's that supposed to mean?'

'You're the detective; work it out.'

'Why are you here, Heather? Or should I call you Rosemary?'

'I suppose it should be Rosemary as that's my real name, but if I'm honest, I liked being Heather to your Noly.'

'Don't give me that bullshit,' said Cormac. 'You used me, right from day one.'

'I admit that was my original intention, but I made a mistake. You weren't a police detective.'

'So why keep stringing me along?'

'Because I liked you, silly.'

'Bollocks!' spat Cormac.

'It's true. Why else would I let things develop the way they did? When we were talking about getting married, I meant it.'

'Oh, please, spare me from all this crap,' said Cormac. 'You lied to me right from day one with your fake name and your fake police warrant card. You led me on about getting married and let me take you to Thailand. But, not content with treating me like a fool for months, you then buggered off and abandoned me without a word.'

'It wasn't quite like that. I loved you, Noly. I was seriously considering marrying you, but that would have meant either explaining who I really was or getting you to come over to my world.'

'You mean becoming a drug dealer? Yeah, well, that would never have happened.'

'Yes, I realised that. You were far too straight-laced to do anything remotely dangerous.'

'So that was why you just walked off and left me? You could at least have told me something. I was going out of my mind...'

'I admit I could have done better there. That was a mistake, but it was such a rush it couldn't be avoided.'

'Why?'

'Because my brother turned up and told me I was about to be assassinated and that if I was found with you, you'd be shot as well. I couldn't let that happen to the man I loved. I had no choice.'

'If you were so worried about the, "man you loved", why didn't you warn me?'

'Because you probably would have wanted to poke your nose in and try to find out who was making the threat. That's why I got Daddy to arrange for you to be compassionately repatriated. Isn't that what they call it?'

This wasn't exactly what Cormac had been expecting to hear. 'You're expecting me to believe you had me deported to save my life?'

'But you weren't deported, darling, and anyway, I had to

do something once you started asking so many questions. You could at least sound grateful!'

'Grateful? My world had just been turned upside down. I didn't know what had happened to you, I was worried sick, and then suddenly I'm being told to leave the country. Why the hell should I be grateful?'

'Because I saved you.'

'Saved me from what?'

'A horrible death at the hands of a bunch of Albanian drug dealers.'

'Yeah, right,' said Cormac. 'Why should I believe that?'

'I'm serious. They were after me, but they would have been happy to murder you just to get at me.'

Cormac considered for a moment. 'There was a time when I might have been tempted to believe you, but the thing is I've now learnt so much about you, and your brother, and how you operate the family business, that I know I can't take anything you say at face value.'

'We're not the first wealthy family to have a business portfolio, you know.'

'Yeah, but they don't all use them for laundering drug money,' said Cormac. 'Believe it or not, I wouldn't normally give a damn about your business portfolio but in this case I do give a damn because of the three murders we're investigating. One of them is your own brother, but you don't seem to be grieving much.'

'That's British upper class stiff upper lip for you, darling. It's just not the done thing. Besides, Johnny was always an accident looking for somewhere to happen.'

Cormac was appalled. 'Jesus! Can you hear yourself?' he said. 'This is your own flesh and blood you're talking about.'

'Yes, but, truth be told, he was always something of a liability; at least he ended up being useful for something.'

'That's three dead people who all seem to have links to you and Rocco Flint, yet you don't seem to give a damn!'

Her mouth twitched, and for a moment she almost looked embarrassed, but she recovered and did her best to look puzzled. 'Rocco Flint? Who is he?'

'You think you're so clever, don't you?' said Cormac. 'You might have been able to play me for a fool once before, but my eyes are wide open now. I remembered you told me about the family dog, Rocco, right? And your mother's double-barrelled name; the second part was Flint. And then someone told me Rocco Flint wasn't a person but an organisation. Yes, it took me a while, but I got there in the end.'

'That's all very well, Noly, but as I said before, it's all speculation, and if you ever find any proof, Daddy will make sure to keep me safe. And he'll probably make sure you're directing traffic for the foreseeable future, too.'

'All three murders can be linked back to Milburn Manor,' said Cormac. 'One of the victims was your brother. Another worked on your estate.'

'Should you be sharing this with me if I'm your chief suspect?'

'It would be your word against mine,' said Cormac. 'If I swear I didn't tell you anything, there's only one way you could have that information. Go ahead, be my guest; my boss would be delighted if you were to incriminate yourself like that.'

She shrugged and sighed. 'Dream on, Noly, darling.'

'Did you have Marky killed?' asked Cormac.

'Don't be silly.'

'You know who I'm talking about, though, don't you? What was he, one of your runners?'

'Small fry who got too big for his boots,' said Heather. 'He thought he could play us against the Albanians, but we didn't kill him, and we didn't take his tongue.'

'How do you know about that?' asked Cormac.

'Everyone knows about it. It's Nikolla Bogdani's way of showing everyone it doesn't pay to talk. But if you're going to employ a deterrent like that, you have to make sure everyone knows; otherwise, what's the point?'

'So, are we right to think there's a war brewing between you and Bogdani?' asked Cormac.

'Yes, but the last thing I want is a bloody war. That's why I'm here.'

Cormac yawned and looked at his watch. It was fast approaching 1 a.m. and he'd been mostly awake for over twenty-four hours.

'Get to the point, will you?' he said. 'I'd quite like to get a couple of hours' sleep before I go back to work.'

'I can help you take out the Albanians,' she said. 'That is my point. I get them off my back, and you catch your murderers.'

'Are you mad?' said Cormac. 'If you seriously think I can authorise a deal, you don't live in the real world. I just don't have that sort of authority. And what is this deal? I suppose you think we're going to let you carry on dealing drugs afterwards, is that it?'

'Of course, I don't,' said Heather. 'But I would expect something in return.'

'Like what?'

'Immunity from prosecution. In return, you get the Albanians, and, as a bonus, I stop dealing.'

Cormac looked suitably unimpressed. 'Isn't Daddy going to step in and save you?'

'I don't think he can this time, and anyway, I've had

enough. I've got more than enough money put away, and now I want out. You could join me, if you want to.'

'No, I don't think so, it's not my scene. Anyway, you know what they say; once bitten, and all that jazz.'

'You've got a couple of days to change your mind. You'll feel different once you've thought about it.'

'No I won't,' said Cormac. 'Even if I had a couple of weeks to think about it, it's just not going to happen.'

'But the deal; you can get it arranged through your boss, can't you?'

'I have no idea,' said Cormac. 'It's one or two levels above him, but all we can do is take it to them and see what they say.'

'Right. I'll wait while you call them,' said Heather.

'No,' said Cormac. 'That's not how this is going to work. You're going to tell me how you intend to arrange for the Albanians to hand themselves over, and then you're going home. I'll run it past my bosses in the morning, and if they decide to go ahead, I'll let you know and then you can make the arrangements. But I'm making no promises, because I just don't know what they're going to say, okay?'

* * *

* * *

'WHAT DO YOU MEAN, Heather came to see you last night?' demanded Driver. 'Why the hell didn't you arrest her?'

'You know as well as I do that we can't go around arresting people without solid grounds,' said Cormac. 'And she knows it, too. She wouldn't have come anywhere near me if she had thought there was any risk of that happening. And even if I had been foolish enough to do it, what would have happened? One phone call to Daddy and she would be free, and we'd all be back on the beat.'

'You could have called me.'

'Oh, yeah, of course,' said Cormac. 'What would I have said, "Just hang on a minute while I call my boss"? She would have been gone in a flash.'

Driver was almost gnashing his teeth in frustration. 'She knows how to manipulate you.'

'She thinks she does,' said Cormac. 'But that was five years ago. Now, I think we have a chance to manipulate her.'

'And how are we going to do that?'

'She wants to make a deal.'

There was a stunned silence as Driver grappled with this idea, finally broken by Aconna's phone ringing in the background.

'A deal?' spluttered Driver. 'She wants to make a bloody deal? What sort of deal?'

'She wants to set up a sting to enable us to catch the Albanians.'

'And what's in it for her?'

'We get the murderers, she gets twenty-four hours' head start,' said Cormac.

Driver raised an eyebrow. 'She seriously expects us to let her escape?'

'That's what she expects,' said Cormac. 'But that doesn't mean she has to get it.'

Driver smiled. 'Planning a little revenge, are you?'

Cormac shrugged. 'I don't know what you mean, sir,' he said, innocently.

'You realise making this sort of deal is above my pay grade,' said Driver.

'Yeah, I told her it wasn't something that can be done in five minutes.'

'Come on then,' said Driver. 'Let's go and run it past Eagan.'

'Sir?' called Aconna.

'Not now, Charlie, we're just going to—'

'There's another body,' said Aconna.

'Where?'

'Lay-by on the dual carriageway.'

Driver sighed as he turned to Cormac. 'I'm afraid your lady friend and her deal will have to wait.'

* * *

By the time they had arrived on site, the lay-by had been cordoned off and was filled with police cars and forensic vehicles, blue lights flashing maniacally. A large tipper truck was parked at one end where most of the activity was taking place.

The body had been concealed behind some bushes at the back of a lay-by and was being attended to by Dr McGowan and her team.

Driver and Cormac were standing to one side, waiting for the pathologist to offer some news. Aconna had been speaking to one of the uniformed officers who had been first on scene.

'Do we know who found the body?' asked Driver.

'Lorry driver,' said Aconna. 'Poor guy stopped to relieve himself behind the bushes.'

'He didn't—'

'No. He says he didn't even get as far as unzipping his—'

'Okay, spare me the gory details,' said Driver.

They watched in silence as Dr McGowan and a technician carefully turned the body over. Cormac took an involuntary step back as he saw the face.

Driver turned to him. 'Are you all right?'

'It's Sniffer.'

'What?'

'It's Sniffer. The guy who was in the cells and wanted to talk to me.'

'But wasn't he collected and taken to Dortmund Road?'

'Yeah, that's right. Three drug squad detectives dragged him from the cells and drove off with him. The poor bugger knew this was going to happen. He was screaming it at me, and I just stood there and watched as they stuffed him in their car and let them drive him away. Now look. I let him down!'

'This isn't your fault,' said Driver. 'Whatever has happened, you're not to blame.'

'He's dead, and I could have stopped it,' said Cormac. 'Of course it's my fault.'

'We don't know that,' said Driver. 'What can you tell us Martha?' he asked.

'My initial guess is that it's a drug overdose. There's bruising around a needle mark in his arm that suggests it's recent. Other signs are consistent with that, but as I say, this is only a guess. I can't be sure without a post-mortem.' She looked at her watch. 'I can do 4 p.m., if that helps.'

Driver sighed. 'Oh, well, if it's a suicide at least it doesn't add to our murder count.'

'Let's not go jumping to conclusions,' said McGowan.

'Sorry?' said Driver.

'I didn't say it was suicide,' said McGowan. 'There are one or two anomalies that need dealing with before I reach a verdict.'

'Such as?' asked Driver.

'I'll start with the fact I can't see any other needle marks on his arms. Of course, they could be hidden away where they're not obvious, but if that's the case, why choose his arm this time? And before you ask, I am not stripping his clothes off out here to find out. Also, I'm wondering why he would be shooting up out here in a lay-by?'

Driver looked despairingly at Cormac. 'If this is a fourth murder victim, this is beyond getting out of hand. The ACC is going to go potty. How many more are there going to be before I get fired?'

'Wait a minute,' said Cormac. 'I appreciate why you're upset, sir, but aren't you missing something?'

'What's that?' asked Driver.

'If Sniffer was in custody at Dortmund Road, how has he managed to overdose in a lay-by just outside Windover? I mean, even if they released him, how did he get back here?'

'He could have hitch-hiked,' said Driver.

'I think that's unlikely,' said Cormac. 'But even if he did, where did he get the drugs from? Gleeson said he had no money on him when he was brought in to Windover.'

'These people always seem to be able to find money to score without too much difficulty,' said Driver.

'He'd still have to find a dealer. And anyway, Sniffer's drug of choice was coke, taken up the nose, not heroin injected in a vein.'

'Are you're suggesting this is down to the drug squad?'

Cormac turned to McGowan. 'How long do you think he's been out here, Martha?'

McGowan looked down at the body and felt his clothes while she considered. 'Right now, it's hard to say with any degree of accuracy. Rigor mortis has been and gone, his clothes are damp enough to suggest he was out here when it last rained, but then they would probably get damp from the surroundings anyway. My best guess is anything from two to four days.'

Cormac turned to Driver. 'D'you think they would have released him from Dortmund Road that quickly?'

'They obviously thought he was worth coming to collect,' said Driver. 'But it's hard to believe they would go to that trouble just to take him down there and then let him come straight back here.'

'I don't think they took him anywhere near Dortmund Road,' said Cormac. 'I'd say this was his final destination.'

'Are you serious?' asked Driver.

Cormac nodded. 'Honestly, sir, Sniffer was terrified

when those guys took him away. He knew what was going to happen.'

'But we can't go round accusing drug squad officers of being bent.'

'Why not?' said Cormac. 'Can you think of any other explanation for this?'

Driver tried, but he couldn't. 'But who are they working for and why would they want to shut him up?'

'He told me he knew where Heather was, and that I shouldn't trust her,' said Cormac. 'And if she's been running drugs around here and never got caught—'

'It's likely they're on her payroll,' said Driver.

Cormac nodded. 'That's how it looks to me.'

'We're going to have to keep this quiet,' said Driver. 'We can't let the drug squad know we're on to them.'

Cormac indicated the scene around them. 'That might be difficult with this circus going on. The local press and radio will probably be onto it by now.'

'All right, so they'll know we found a body,' said Driver, 'but they don't have to know we suspect they killed him. If you're right about this, it rules out any possibility of doing a deal with her.'

'Really?' said Cormac. 'I think it gives us even more reason to strike a deal. If we do it right we could catch the Albanians, Heather, Daddy, and the bent drug squad guys.'

'We'll see what Eagan has to say,' said Driver. 'I reckon he'll agree with me.'

'He'll go for it,' said Cormac. 'He lives for catching bent coppers, and if you add in a bent Home Secretary, well, he'll be in heaven, won't he?'

'There's only one way to find out,' said Driver. 'And I think we should do it sooner rather than later.' He turned to Aconna. 'Can you stay here until forensics have finished? Get someone to give you a lift back to the station.'

'Yes, sir, of course,' said Aconna.

'Come on, Cormac,' said Driver. 'Let's see if the boss is tempted to go for the big fish or he agrees we're being taken for fools.'

* * *

'HAVE you two taken leave of your senses?' demanded Eagan when Driver and Cormac outlined their plan. 'Are you seriously suggesting we work with this woman? What on earth makes you think she can be trusted?'

'I agree,' said Driver. 'Trusting her is too risky.'

'We're not going to trust her,' said Cormac. 'We'll be going into this situation with our eyes wide open, but if I can persuade her to trust us, we could wrap this whole thing up in one go: Albanians, Heather and her cohorts, which may well include the two bent drug squad officers. We might even catch the Home Secretary in the same net.'

Eagan's eyes seemed to light up at the mention of the Home Secretary, and Cormac sensed he was weakening. 'The ACC won't like it,' he said.

'Then don't tell him, sir,' said Cormac.

'I have to tell him,' said Eagan. 'Apart from every other consideration, it would mean deploying armed officers, and

I'm not high enough up the food chain to sanction an operation like that. And the drug squad need to be involved.'

'I'm not in favour of this idea,' said Driver. 'But if you do decide to go ahead, we can't involve that lot. We believe at least two of their officers are involved in the latest death, and they could be involved in the others, too.'

'I don't think you'll be catching them anytime soon,' said Eagan. 'Apparently, two of their detectives have gone missing.'

'That doesn't necessarily mean all the bad apples have left the barrel,' said Driver. 'Rot can spread all too easily. Best to keep them out of the loop for as long as possible.'

Eagan steepled his fingers and stared at nothing in particular as he thought. 'So, how exactly would this work?'

Driver nodded to Cormac. 'Cormac's her point of contact. I'll let him explain the plan.'

'It's pretty straightforward,' said Cormac. 'Heather tells the Albanians she wants to do a deal and arranges a meet. We surround the place, wait until they're all present, then move in and grab all of them before they know what's happened.'

'And we let her walk?' asked Eagan. 'That's the bit I'm not happy about.'

'That's what I'm going to tell her will happen,' said Cormac, 'but that's not how it's going to go down. She'll go in thinking we're going to let her walk, but we'll just grab her with the rest of them.'

'This all sounds far too easy, if you ask me,' said Driver.

Eagan ignored Driver's protests and focused on Cormac. 'You mean we're going to renege on the deal?'

Cormac shrugged. 'There'll be nothing in writing. She'll understand; it's the sort of thing she does all the time. Besides, if she says that was part of the deal, I'll deny it. It'll be her word against mine. That's why I think we should make sure it's just me who arranges things with her. One to one, no-one else involved.'

Eagan turned his attention back to Driver.

'Can Cormac be trusted?' he asked. 'Aren't we talking about a woman he was going to marry?'

'It's not a question of can we trust him,' said Driver. 'I don't think we can trust her!'

'Hold on a minute,' said Cormac, indignantly. 'I am here, you know. If you've got any doubts, you can ask me to my face.'

Eagan turned to Cormac. 'Can I trust you?'

'Of course you can. Didn't I tell you I could bring you a big fish when we first met?'

Eagan studied Cormac's face for a moment, then turned to Driver. 'I don't know if I like this idea or not. The ACC won't be easily persuaded.'

'I think I've made my position clear,' said Driver. 'I'm not exactly over the moon with the idea, but as I understand it, the ACC is hopping mad that we have bodies popping up all over the shop, and there is an outside chance this may be the best, and possibly the only, way we have of stopping the murders before it escalates into a full-blown drug war. If that happens, we'll have bodies everywhere.'

Eagan's face told them that was the last thing he wanted, but Cormac thought he had an answer that would sway the argument.

'A drug war would be a disaster,' he said. 'But if we get this right, we stop the war before it starts and bring down a growing drugs operation which the drug squad have failed to even slow down.' He smiled at Eagan. 'Think what that would do for your reputation, sir.'

Eagan seemed to swell with pride. 'Now that's a good

point, Cormac. It would be hard for anyone to ignore a success like that. You didn't mention anything about the Home Secretary, though.'

'Well, yes, there's a good chance we might bring him down, too,' said Driver. 'But if you really want to do this it's probably best if you forget to mention that part to the ACC. With any luck, he won't work it out for himself until it's too late.'

'You know, when you put it like that, he might just go for it,' said Eagan.

'Are you saying that's a "yes" then, sir?' asked Cormac.

'I'll let you know later, after I've spoken to him,' said Eagan, reaching for his phone.

* * *

'What's all this about bringing Eagan a big fish?' Driver asked Cormac as they made their way back to the incident room. 'Was I right all along? Did you know right from the start that Heather was really Tilthorne's daughter, Rosemary?'

'I swear I had no idea she was his daughter,' said Cormac. 'I had a reliable tip that she was living somewhere in this area, but I had no idea where. I certainly hadn't made the connection between them; but why would I? I didn't even know the Tilthornes lived in this part of the country, never mind living at Milburn Manor.'

'But you knew he was the big fish you were after.'

'No, honestly, I didn't,' said Cormac. 'All I knew was that someone had arranged for me to be removed from Thailand and brought back home. It didn't need a rocket scientist to work out that whoever that person was, they had a fair bit of clout. I actually thought it would turn out to be some high-ranking civil servant, perhaps with ties to the Foreign Office.'

Driver didn't look convinced.

'You don't believe me, do you?' asked Cormac.

'Honestly? No, I'm not sure I do,' said Driver.

'So, how do I convince you?'

Driver sighed and frowned. 'Right this minute, I don't think you can, but if we're going to close this case, I'm just going to have to take you at face value for now and hope I'm doing the right thing, aren't I?'

* * *

It was clear the atmosphere had changed when Driver elected to take Charlie along to the post-mortem. He said it would be good experience for her, which was true enough. Cormac knew that wasn't the real reason, but he decided if Driver wanted to sulk, well, that was his problem.

Eagan called down just before 5 pm to tell him the ACC had given permission for the operation to go ahead, "as long as you keep the Home Secretary out of it." Cormac thought the idea of the Home Secretary being involved was absurd. What did they think he was going to do, ride shotgun in Heather's car?

He sent a text message to Heather asking her to set the trap for the Albanians, then hung around waiting for Driver to call with Dr McGowan's conclusions. By 6:30 pm he felt it was clear that call just wasn't going to materialise, so he tidied his desk and went back to his motel room, where he had a long shower, dressed in casual clothes and then walked to the Red Cow. By 8 pm, he had eaten his dinner and was sitting in his favourite armchair relaxing with a pint and a crossword.

'On your own again?'

Cormac looked up. Tonight, the owner of the voice had chosen a fluorescent lime green collection of accessories to contrast with her freckled white skin and ginger hair.

'Hello, Melinda.'

She plonked herself down in the armchair next to his. 'Is it okay if I join you?'

Cormac looked around the bar. At least half the tables were empty. 'Do I have a choice?'

'I'm afraid not.'

'Yeah, that's what I thought.'

He returned to his crossword, but Melinda wasn't easily put off.

'I'm sitting here thinking, we'll have to stop meeting like this,' she said. 'Or people will talk.'

Cormac glared at her. 'Two things,' he said. 'First of all, we didn't "meet" like this. You chose to park yourself next to me, uninvited, which is not the same thing. In fact, I'm beginning to think you could actually be stalking me. And second, people can say whatever they like; I really don't care because they'd be wrong. I'm just a guy trying to enjoy a quiet pint, having his peace interrupted by a woman he hardly knows.'

'What's happened to put you in such a good mood tonight?'

Cormac sighed and put his crossword down. 'You're not going to stop, are you?'

'I'm just trying to help. You look as though you need cheering up, and I'm volunteering.'

'Well, thanks for the offer, but whatever you may think

you've gleaned from my demeanour, I'm actually fine as I am.'

'You're obviously not fine, or you wouldn't be so hostile,' said Melinda. Then, after a short pause for effect, 'Oh, hang on, I get it. You're happy to be friends when you want information from me, but after that, I'm nobody, right?'

'That's not fair—'

'Damn right it's not fair. I didn't have to help you, and I don't have to keep sitting on my story.'

Cormac frowned. 'You're right,' he said. 'The truth is I've had a shitty day. But that's not your fault, and I have no right to take it out on you, and I apologise for my attitude.'

'I take it that means your case against the Home Secretary isn't going so well, then.'

Cormac knew he had to tread carefully around journalists, but as long as he stuck to the bits Melinda already knew, he figured he should be okay. He might even learn something new.

'Don't get me wrong,' he said. 'The information you gave us has moved things forward against Rosemary, but we're not convinced we've got enough to press charges against her father. We could probably ruin his career, but we found a letter signed by him handing Rosemary control of the family's financial affairs. We think he'll probably argue she was doing everything behind his back, and with his connections, he'll get away with it.'

'Do you think she is?'

'I'm pretty sure she's in charge of the money, but I find it hard to believe she's doing it behind his back. But believing it and proving it are two quite different things.'

'I've always wondered how she was able to do as she pleased with the finances,' said Melinda. 'Do you think he

handed control over to her so he could use it as his defence
should they ever get caught?'

Cormac knew they hadn't looked at it that way, but he
wasn't going to let Melinda know that.

'Hang her out to dry, you mean? It's a possibility, but
we're more inclined to think he gave her control because she
has some sort of hold over him. We just haven't figured out
what it is yet.'

'Why do you think that?'

Cormac looked around the pub as if he suspected eaves-
droppers, then lowered his voice. 'If anyone asks, I didn't tell
you this, but Heather had barely turned fourteen when he
signed control over to her, although as far as we can tell, she
didn't actually take control straight away.'

'Fourteen?' echoed Melinda. 'That's ridiculously young,
isn't it?'

'That's why we think she must have some pretty
powerful leverage.'

Melinda considered for a moment. 'That would have
been around the time her parents divorced.'

'Just after,' said Cormac.

'Is that relevant?'

Cormac shrugged. 'Frankly, your guess is as good as
mine. We haven't come up with anything so far.'

'Have you tried the ex-wife?'

'We've been forbidden to go there. Anyway, she signed
an NDA which we believe she won't be willing to breach.
He'd sue the arse off her and leave her with nothing.'

'That's a pity,' said Melinda. She looked at her watch.
'Oh, crap! Look at the time. I have to go. Sorry I disturbed
your crossword. I'll catch you next time.'

As Cormac watched her rush off, he wondered what
that had been all about. If she had intended to pick his

brains about the case, why try to do it when she had to be somewhere else? He was sure he hadn't told her anything important, or anything she didn't already know, so he couldn't see any other reason why she would have rushed off so hurriedly.

He wondered idly if it was simply that she found him attractive, but quickly dismissed that idea; he'd seen himself in the mirror before he left his room, so he knew how rough he looked. And anyway, you don't make a move on someone when you've got to be somewhere else, do you?

To be honest, it wasn't that he didn't find the idea of being with her appealing. Melinda was an attractive woman, and he couldn't deny he was intrigued by her outrageous colour choices. There again, he guessed he must be at least fifteen years older, and that was too big a gap. Wasn't it?

CHAPTER 23

* * *

I<small>T WAS</small> 8 a.m. Eagan had called Driver, Cormac and Aconna to his office for a strategy meeting.

'Right, so where are we?' asked Eagan.

'It's arranged for tonight,' said Cormac. 'The Albanians have insisted Heather comes alone—'

'They'll be armed to the bloody teeth,' said Driver. 'If she goes in alone, there's no way she's coming out alive.'

'Just between us four, I think that might not be such a bad thing,' said Eagan.

Aconna was so surprised she almost spilled her coffee. Eagan spotted her discomfort. 'I'm sorry if that suggestion upsets you, Aconna, but what you have to remember is that this woman is responsible for distributing huge amounts of drugs in this area, and it's also quite possible she is responsible for the recent spate of murders, if not directly, then through her association with drugs and drug trafficking.'

'Yes, sir,' said Aconna. 'It's just that I thought we were supposed to stop the killing, not condone it.'

Eagan bristled. 'If this operation goes right we will stop it. But, unfortunately, with operations of this nature there's always a possibility things won't go exactly to plan. As long as any collateral damage doesn't involve our own people, I can live with it.' He looked at Cormac. 'Carry on, Cormac.'

'Heather is aware of the potential risk, but she has told the Albanians she is prepared to step aside and let them have her business.'

'And they believe that, do they?' said Driver. 'I wouldn't trust her as far as I could throw her.'

'I don't think either side trusts the other,' said Cormac. 'But then neither side really wants a war, either, because it will only attract even more of our attention.'

'So, it's Hobson's choice,' said Aconna.

'Exactly,' said Cormac.

'Where and what time?' asked Driver.

'The old gasworks at midnight,' said Cormac.

'The gasworks?' said Driver. 'I don't like the sound of that. We've already recovered one body from there. Why did she choose there?'

'It's out of the way, and there's a way in and a way out. Heather figured if she suggested somewhere with just one entrance, the Albanians would be more inclined to suspect a trap. There's also plenty of cover for our guys, and it's unlikely any members of the public will be around.'

'I'm still not sure this is a good idea,' said Driver. 'How do we know she will even turn up?'

Eagan turned to Cormac. 'Well, you're the contact. How do we know she can be trusted?'

'Look, I can't guarantee anything,' said Cormac. 'But I've done everything I can to convince Heather we're going along with her deal. She's expecting to be rounded up with all the others to maintain her cover, and then she will be released later. Only she won't.'

Driver was shaking his head. 'I'm not convinced. This is all too easy,' he said. 'I'm bloody sure she's stringing you along.'

'What do you mean she's stringing me along?' said Cormac.

'I mean exactly what I said. She's stringing you along. She's done it before, and she's doing it again.'

Cormac was seething. 'Yes, all right, I was stupid enough to believe her once before, but do you really think I didn't learn from that? I've admitted I was blinded by her before, but I'm not blind now. If you really think it's such a bad idea, why not call the whole thing off?'

'Because it's not my decision,' said Driver, his voice rising angrily. 'If it was, I would never have let it get this far!'

'Right, that's enough!' roared Eagan. 'I will not have officers arguing like schoolboys in my office. What sort of an example is that for DC Aconna?'

There was a brief, stunned silence before both detectives mumbled apologies.

'That's better,' said Eagan. 'Now, DCI Driver, I understand your reservations about this operation, but it's my decision and I'm going to overrule you.'

'You're the senior officer; that's your prerogative,' said Driver.

'I must say I'm disappointed by your pessimism, Driver, but whatever you feel, I expect you to do your job, and do it well,' said Eagan. 'We badly need a result, and I believe this is too good an opportunity to miss.'

'Oh, we're going to get a result, all right,' said Driver grimly. 'I'm just not sure it'll be the one we all want.'

'Right, that's agreed, then,' said Eagan, looking expectantly at the others. 'If there's nothing else, I need to speak with the ACC to confirm the arrangements, armed officers and what have you.'

* * *

Driver, Cormac and Aconna took the hint and made their way back to their incident room.

'Superintendent Eagan is going to honour her deal, isn't he, sir?' Aconna asked Driver.

'He won't have much choice once her father gets involved.'

'But we're not seriously going to allow that to happen, are we?' asked Cormac. 'I mean, does he even need to know? Can't we keep it from him until it's too late.'

'He's the Home Secretary, Cormac,' said Driver. 'He's been giving the ACC grief about this case, so obviously, he already knows about it.'

'I don't see how,' said Cormac.

'Because his daughter's up to her neck in it,' said Driver.

'Not to mention his murdered son,' said Aconna.

'But she told me she doesn't tell him anything,' said Cormac.

Driver shook his head. 'I'm sorry, Cormac, but if you really believe that, you're still blinded by her. I'd bet my house that his daughter keeps him informed of everything, so he knows just how deep he's in the shit. How do you think she's managed to stay under the radar for so long?'

'Yeah, but—'

'Why can't you see her for what she really is?' said Driver. 'I'll tell you why. It's because underneath it all you're still besotted with her.'

'That's bullshit,' said Cormac.

'Is it?' said Driver. 'I guarantee Daddy already knows about this meeting tomorrow night, and I don't doubt he also knows all about the deal she has arranged with you.'

'No,' said Cormac. 'If it was that easy for her to get out of trouble, she wouldn't have asked for a deal.'

'You dream on if you want to, Cormac,' said Driver. 'I wouldn't be at all surprised if the ACC doesn't call Eagan tomorrow to instruct him that we have to let her go.'

'I'm not going to argue with you,' said Cormac. 'I'm going out.'

'That's probably a good idea,' said Driver.

An uneasy truce had developed between Driver and Cormac by the time they gathered for Eagan's 4 pm briefing in the canteen. Apart from Eagan, Driver, Cormac and Aconna, there were upwards of a dozen uniformed officers and six detectives from Windover, plus two lead officers from the firearms unit.

Cormac thought Eagan looked star-struck by the two firearms officers, and sure enough, the first thing he did was welcome them and hand them the floor. The lead officer, DCI Damien Donald, was introduced as the Tactical Firearms Commander (TFC) who would be in overall command of the firearms team.

'That means he sits in a bloody van well away from the action, and watches while his team of cowboys make a balls-up,' Driver told Cormac from the corner of his mouth.

Donald took to the centre of the floor as if he were the star of the show. He held his hands up as if he were quieting a round of applause from an overgenerous audience, although he had been greeted, not with applause, but mumbled opinions that were anything but complimentary.

'Arrogant twat,' muttered Driver.

From what he had seen so far, Cormac thought Driver's opinion concurred with his own. He couldn't decide if the arrogance or the macho attitude the man seemed to exude, but whatever it was, the entire room appeared to have taken an instant dislike to him.

Donald was on the floor for ten minutes. Cormac was sure he had devoted at least eight of those minutes bragging about how special and fantastic his team were, before sketchily outlining how the operation would go down, and how his colleague, PC Jacob Corbin, was the Operational Firearms Commander (OFC) and would lead the team on the ground.

'Sounds straightforward enough,' said Cormac.

'Not with that twat in charge,' said Driver.

'Do you know him?' asked Cormac.

'We shared an operation once before,' said Driver. 'Let's just say I wasn't impressed.'

Cormac was intrigued to know more, but Eagan had taken over the floor again.

'This is an operation of the utmost importance,' said Eagan. 'It's an opportunity to make a real difference. In one beautiful swoop we're going to take out a large amount of drugs, a huge chunk of dirty money, and most importantly we get to take an Albanian drug operation off the street. It's just the sort of story the press will love.'

'As long as the Albanians are dumb enough not to recognise a trap when they're walking into one,' muttered Driver.

'I'm sorry, DCI Driver, did you wish to add something?' invited Eagan.

'I think you're already aware of my feelings about this

operation,' said Driver, leaning back against the wall, arms folded.

Eagan managed a thin smile. 'Yes, your ill-perceived pessimism has been noted, but fortunately I'm the one who calls the shots and we're going ahead.' Arming himself with a pointing stick, he turned to a rough, hand-drawn map of the site. 'Right, so, to sum up, we'll have armed response officers here, here, and here,' smacking the map with his stick. 'A team will be in place at the far end of the site, ready to close the far gates once we go in. DS Cormac and DC Aconna will cover the front gate. DCI Driver will be the advance observer out on the road, watching for our targets to arrive.

'I will be with the TFC in the command vehicle, where strategically placed cameras will allow us to observe the entire site and communicate via radio. We don't know if these drug dealers will be prepared to use their weapons, so I expect everyone to wear body armour as a precaution. Any questions? No? In that case, good luck everyone.'

Aconna turned to Cormac. 'Anyone would think he didn't want to take questions.'

'Of course he doesn't,' said Cormac. 'He can't spare the time because he's too busy brown-nosing the Firearms Commander.'

'I notice he didn't mention nabbing your lady friend,' said Driver.

'Not specifically, but she'll get swept up with the rest of them,' said Cormac.

'Don't bank on it,' said Driver. 'I reckon the ACC has already warned him off. That's assuming she turns up, of course.'

'What do you mean?' said Cormac. 'Of course she'll be there.'

'I hope she is, for your sake,' said Driver. 'You're going to be in a whole world of shit otherwise.'

Cormac didn't reply but turned his gaze to the map. Ever since Heather had come to his room with her plan, he had been telling himself this was his chance to catch her and end five years of torment, but deep inside, the tiniest seeds of doubt were stirring.

With a sigh, he turned away. As he did, Driver was staring at him, as if he could see those doubts beginning to swell.

* * *

CHAPTER 24

* * *

BY NIGHTFALL, thick clouds were scudding across the sky, allowing only the occasional sliver of moonlight to illuminate the old gasworks site and the immediate surroundings. Much of the site had been cleared, with just one extensive building remaining. This used to house the offices at one end and garaging for vehicles at the other. It was the venue for the sting.

Two hours before midnight, everyone was in place. The firearms team was hiding behind the main building, and smaller back-up teams had found places to conceal themselves and were lying in wait.

Cormac and Aconna were squeezed against each other in a tiny space beneath a collapsed corrugated iron shed near the main gates. They couldn't see anything outside the gates, but had a view across the cleared area towards the building. Or they would have had a view if it weren't so dark.

'I can't decide; is it better being so dark or would it be preferable if there were no clouds?' said Aconna.

'We could have done with a clear night,' said Cormac.

'But wouldn't we be easier to spot?'

'Maybe,' said Cormac. 'But it's so dark most of the time I can barely make out where the building is.' He looked at his watch for the umpteenth time. 'Fifteen minutes to go.'

Aconna shivered. 'I can't decide if I'm excited or scared.'

'I'd prefer it if you were a little on the scared side,' said Cormac.

'Really?' said Aconna. 'Why's that?'

'There's less chance of you taking any unnecessary risks. Just remember it's the firearms team who are going in first,' said Cormac. 'As long as they do their job properly, we'll be fine.'

They were wearing lapel microphones and earpieces for communication. A slight crackle warned them a message was incoming. 'This is Driver. Two vehicles approaching. Turning onto the access lane now.'

This was followed by another crackle. 'This is Eagan. Be alert, everyone, it's showtime.' He seemed to emphasise the first syllable and extend the last.

'Did he really just say it like that, or did I imagine it?' asked Aconna.

'Yeah, I know what you mean,' said Cormac. 'He sounds an even bigger twat than usual on the radio.'

'D'you think he's wearing the snazzy suit and green mask?' asked Aconna.

'Oh, trust me, he has a collection of masks,' said Cormac. 'A different one for every occasion.'

They could hear the growing sound of engines approaching, and the area they could see was suddenly lit by headlights as a dirty white Transit van turned in through the gates, followed by a dark-coloured Land Rover Discovery.

'Vehicles inside gates,' muttered Cormac into his microphone. 'One Transit van, one Land Rover Disco.'

Next to him, Cormac felt Aconna freeze as the vehicles turned in through the gates. The small convoy rumbled past, engines burbling, tyres crunching gravel. It was only when the two sets of taillights were halfway across the clearing that Aconna let her breath out.

'Do you think that's both the Albanians and Heather?' she whispered.

'No way. If they met somewhere else beforehand, why would they come here? Bogdani's wife drives a Disco. Maybe he's borrowed it for the night. I'm guessing his henchmen are in the van.'

'They must be expecting to collect a humongous amount of drugs if they need a van that size.'

'Or perhaps there's a dozen troops in there armed to the teeth,' said Cormac.

'D'you think so?'

'We'll soon find out when Heather turns up,' said Cormac.

They watched as the taillights disappeared into the building. A couple of minutes later, the inside of the building lit up.

'Look at that. They've even brought their own lighting,' said Cormac.

'Second vehicle on the way.' It was Driver calling in from the main road. 'Turning onto the lane now. Heading your way.'

'That'll be the woman,' Eagan's voice crackled over the radio. 'Stand by.'

Cormac smiled with grim satisfaction. 'And Driver was convinced she wouldn't turn up,' he muttered.

A large SUV crept through the gates and loomed into their field of vision, the engine idling.

'Vehicle inside gates,' said Cormac over the airwaves.

'Is it her?' whispered Aconna.

Cormac squinted at the car. 'It's too bloody dark to make out the driver, or if there are any passengers,' he said. 'It looks like the Milburn Manor SUV, though.'

'Everyone stand by.' It was Eagan on the radio again, more eager this time. 'Wait for my word.'

'Listen to him,' said Cormac. 'Like a kid with a new toy. He's loving this.'

As they watched the taillights of the SUV bob across the uneven surface of the clearing, the clouds parted, bathing the clearing in moonlight. The brake lights of the SUV glared red as the vehicle stopped about ten yards from the open doors of the outbuilding.

'What's she doing?' said Aconna.

Before Cormac could answer, a figure emerged from the outbuilding and waved a greeting to the car. A second figure emerged with raised hands.

'They're showing her they're not armed,' said Cormac.

The SUV's brake lights dimmed, and the vehicle crawled forward through the doors. As if on cue, the clouds covered the moon again and darkness returned.

'Bugger,' said Cormac. 'What a time to turn the outside lights off!'

'This is the TFC,' said a voice in their ears. 'Firearms unit, move in. I repeat, firearms unit move in.'

Cormac and Aconna watched armed officers run from the back of the building, torches slashing white beams across the ground as they ran. They disappeared from view as they swarmed through the doors, shouted voices echoing through the night:

"Armed police! Don't move! Hands where we can see them!"

Then Eagan's voice over the radio. 'Secure the gates, and stand by.'

Ever since the SUV had turned in through the main gates, Driver had been working his way down the access lane. He reached the gates just as Cormac and Aconna ran across to close them.

'Something's not right about this,' he said.

'How do you mean?' asked Cormac.

'She's supposed to be a criminal mastermind and yet she's just driven into a building crawling with Albanian gangsters. Does that sound right to you?'

'She's probably got her own people in the car with her,' said Cormac.

'Trust me, there was only one person in that car,' said Driver. 'There were no passengers. Would she really risk coming here to face them on her own? I can't see it.'

Cormac didn't know what to say, but the tiny seed of doubt that had been gnawing away at his insides seemed to be turning a monster that was eating him alive. Driver was right, and he knew it.

A loud click heralded another burst from the radio. 'This is the TFC. Suspects disarmed without a shot fired. I repeat, suspects disarmed. Clear to go in.' Then Eagan's voice: 'Go, go, go!'

Cormac didn't hesitate; he ran as fast as he could.

Aconna aimed a questioning look at Driver. 'Should I go after him?'

He shook his head. 'There's no need to rush. It sounds

like Firearms have got it all under control. It's just a case of taking them all into custody now.'

'What about Cormac?'

'Yes, indeed,' he said thoughtfully. 'What about Cormac?'

Aconna wasn't sure what that was supposed to mean, but from the feeling of impending doom that was creeping up on her, she knew it heralded nothing good.

She walked across the clearing with Driver and into the building. As they reached the doors, the van housing Eagan and Donald came bouncing in from the far end and screeched to a halt by the doorway.

The firearms team had rounded up eight men, who were standing in a group, hands on their heads, watched over by armed officers. Cormac was standing alongside the armed officers.

'I don't see Bogdani amongst that lot, do you?' Driver snarled as he joined Cormac.

Cormac shook his head. 'I don't think so, no.'

'I bloody knew it,' muttered Driver, turning to where armed officers surrounded the dark SUV. Inside, a driver could just be made out, sitting with hands in the air.

'I think they're waiting for someone to give the order,' Cormac told Driver.

'Well, go on then, get her out,' shouted Driver.

A firearms officer strode forward and flung the door open. 'Come on. Out!' he shouted.

A small, wide-eyed young woman stepped from the car, arms still above her head. She trembled violently, obviously terrified.

Cormac took an involuntary step back, his mouth open in shock.

'Well, isn't that a bloody surprise?' roared Driver. He

turned to Cormac, his voice now low and menacing. 'I told you she was pissing us about and that she couldn't be trusted, didn't I? But would you listen?'

Cormac flapped his mouth, but nothing came out. He was feeling sick, and he didn't know what to say.

Driver was right in his face now. 'Or maybe you knew all along,' he hissed.

'What? No, of course I didn't,' said Cormac. 'It was my idea to set the trap, remember?'

'Was it?' said Driver. 'I seem to recall you said she had come to find you.'

'Yeah, but—'

'D'you know what I think?' hissed Driver.

Cormac really didn't want to know, but it was clear Driver was going to tell him anyway.

'I think you're working for her, and that's how she manages to stay one step ahead all the time. And I think this bloody fiasco has been organised to get us out of the way while she does some other deal somewhere else, and then makes her escape.'

Eagan had arrived, and he clapped Driver on the back. 'How about that then, chaps? Have you ever seen anything go so smoothly? Absolutely perfect from start to finish, don't you think, Driver?'

'No, I'm afraid I can't agree,' said Driver through gritted teeth. 'And if I were you, I'd tear up that press release you had prepared.'

Eagan pointed to the prisoners. 'But look at this lot. What more could you ask for?'

'The bloody Tilthorne woman,' said Driver. 'That's what I could ask for.'

'But who is that?' asked Eagan, pointing to the young woman who was being led away.

'She's a bloody decoy,' said Driver.

'So she's not—'

'No, she damned well isn't,' said Driver. 'And I have a suspicion we're going to find the other lot aren't Albanians, and even if they are, they'll turn out to not be the people we're expecting them to be.'

'But you haven't even questioned them yet.'

'No, I haven't, but just look at them,' said Driver. 'Do they look like Albanian gangsters?'

Eagan scratched his head. 'What does it all mean?'

'What it means, sir, is that we've been made to look a bunch of idiots by that woman,' said Driver. 'And I believe DS Cormac is in league with her and knew all along that this would be the outcome.'

Eagan stared at Cormac. 'Is this true?'

'Of course not,' said Cormac. 'DCI Driver is mistaken.'

'Well, you're not going to stand there and admit it, are you?' said Driver. He turned to Eagan. 'I believe DS Cormac has compromised this operation and has a lot of questions to answer. In view of this, I request he be suspended from duty with immediate effect.'

'Now let's not be too hasty, Driver,' said Eagan.

'It's okay,' said Cormac. 'I can see how this looks, and I understand why the DCI feels I'm involved, but I swear I'm innocent.'

Driver was unconvinced and turned to Eagan. 'Sir, I insist.'

Eagan looked from Driver to Cormac, and back to Driver. 'Very well,' he said reluctantly. 'DS Cormac, you will be escorted back to the station where you will wait for me to return. Is that clear?'

'Yes, sir, crystal clear.'

Eagan turned to Aconna. 'DC Aconna, please arrange

for two uniformed officers to escort DS Cormac back to the station and make sure they understand he is to be detained at the station until I say otherwise.'

Aconna looked guiltily at Cormac, who nodded his acceptance of the situation. 'It's okay, Charlie,' he said. 'Best do as the boss says.'

Aconna nodded sadly and slowly turned away.

The mood worsened after Cormac had been taken away, especially when Driver discovered the "Albanians" were just members of the Windover Drama Club, who thought they had been hired as extras in a new gangster film.

'We were hired to work as extras in a film,' said their spokesperson, Dane Strange.

'And you believed that?' asked Driver.

'Why wouldn't we?' said Strange. 'We work as extras all the time.'

'And the absence of camera and crew didn't arouse your suspicions?' raged Driver.

'We were told it was being filmed using new tech-niques,' said Strange. 'They said the cameras would be hidden and that if we couldn't see them, we would act more naturally. You need to understand filmmaking is an innova-tive industry that uses technology that develops all the time.'

'Where did the vehicles come from?'

'They were supplied along with the bags in the back.'

'And what were you told you had to do?'

'Drive into the building, get out of the van, open the

back doors and make out like we were drug dealers waiting to do a major deal.'

'What about the girl?' Driver pointed towards the young woman who had been driving the Milburn Manor vehicle. 'Is she one of your lot?'

'No, we don't know her. They said it would be more authentic if we didn't know her, although that didn't matter once your gun squad came charging in.'

'But some of you people could have been shot,' said Driver. 'Didn't you consider that?'

'Look, mate, we were told we were making a film, and we had no reason to doubt it. The raid was supposed to be carried out by actors with dummy guns. No-one said there would be live ammunition and real police.'

By the time the "extras" had been loaded into vans and taken back to Windover, Driver was apoplectic.

'You need to calm down before you have a heart attack,' said Eagan. 'We have to consider how we're going to handle this situation.'

'I take it what you mean is the buck's going to stop with me, although I was the one who had reservations about the whole thing,' said Driver.

'Well, obviously, that goes without saying,' said Eagan. 'But with your record, the worst you'll get is a slap on the wrist. After all, we all make mistakes, don't we? But what I was actually referring to is the Cormac situation.'

Driver frowned. 'Sir?'

'I accepted his transfer on your recommendation, and—'

'But there's nothing in writing to say that, is there?' said Driver.

'Well, no, but—'

'And there's nothing in writing because you want

everyone to think you can do it all on your own. Isn't that right, sir?'

'Ah, yes, about that. I was thinking maybe you could—'

'Backdate a written recommendation?' Driver shook his head. 'Sorry, sir, but I'm thinking maybe I could not. After all, as you said just a moment ago, we all make mistakes, don't we?'

For once, Eagan didn't have an answer.

'Now, then, if that's all,' said Driver. 'I've got a female drug boss to catch.'

'And how are you going to do that?' asked Eagan.

'I'm going to raid Milburn Manor and hope I get there before she leaves.'

Eagan shook his head. 'That's not going to happen, Driver. The ACC—'

'Bugger the ACC,' said Driver. 'We can't sit back and let her make a mockery of us! I don't care who her father is; what they are doing is illegal, and if he's condoning it and covering for her, that makes him a criminal, too!'

'Don't expect me to have your back if you go there without permission from the ACC,' said Eagan.

'I think I already knew that,' said Driver.

'Think of the consequences.'

'What consequences? You're already going to hang me out to dry for this fiasco rather than admit you made a mistake against my advice, so what have I got to lose?'

'But you don't have a search warrant, and no magistrate will grant one against the Home Secretary.'

'Then I'll just have to go without one,' said Driver.

'You won't even get past the gate.'

'Yes, but—'

'You will not go anywhere near Milburn Manor, DCI Driver, and that's an order!'

* * *

It was just after 7 p.m. After two days of intensive questioning, Cormac had been allowed to leave the station and return to his motel room. He remained suspended from duty pending further investigations and thus did not know how the investigation was going after the fiasco at the gasworks.

Right now, he was lounging on the bed in his motel room, contemplating his choices. Should he make his way down to The Red Cow, eat his dinner and get legless, or should he make his way to The Red Cow, forget dinner and get legless? He knew from experience that oblivion would come sooner without food, and he was currently leaning that way.

The other, and rather more important, choice was what he was going to do career-wise. Should he resign, as had been suggested, or should he stay, suffer the indignity of another investigation by Professional Standards?

If things went against him with Professional Standards,

he could find himself demoted again; only this time he would almost certainly be back working as a PC in uniform. He was innocent, of course, but then he had been innocent when his team had come under fire up in the Midlands, and look how that had ended!

There was also a worst-case scenario that couldn't be ignored. He could end up being charged with corruption and, if found guilty, this would result in a custodial sentence. The very idea of being a former police officer in prison painted a picture of the sort of living hell Cormac wasn't convinced he could survive.

The alternative that had been put to him was that if he resigned, the expensive internal investigation would end; all potential criminal charges against him would be dropped, and he could leave with his record intact.

There was an almost apologetic knock on his door. It was so quiet Cormac wasn't even sure it had been a knock, but then it happened again. Warily, he walked across to the door.

'Who is it?' he called.

'It's Charlie.'

He opened the door to find Aconna standing outside, looking rather sheepish.

'Charlie? What are you doing here?'

'I was on the way home and I thought I'd call in and see how you were holding up. You don't mind, do you?'

'Do I mind?' said Cormac. 'Why on earth would I mind? Its good to see a friendly face.'

Now Aconna managed a smile. 'I wouldn't blame you if you felt we'd all deserted you.'

Cormac stepped back. 'Come on in, if you don't mind my mess.'

Gingerly Aconna stepped into the room, then relaxed.

'It's not that bad,' she said. 'In fact, for a man's room, I think it's quite tidy.'

Cormac closed the door and tried not to be standing right on top of her, which wasn't easy considering how small the room was.

'These rooms aren't made for entertaining guests,' he said.

'I won't stop if it's awkward,' said Aconna. 'As I said, I just wanted to make sure you're okay.'

'Thanks, Charlie. I appreciate you coming, but you don't need to worry; I've been here before. I'll survive. Are you sure you should even be here? I wouldn't want you to get dragged into this and tarred with the same brush.'

Aconna fished a mobile phone from her pocket.

'They asked me to return your mobile phone.'

'They've finished with it, already?'

'Surely that's a good sign, isn't it?'

'You can never be sure with Professional Standards. Does it mean they've finished with it? Or does it mean they've cloned it and they plan to listen in to everything I say? Mind you, if that is the plan, all they're going learn is just how boring my life is.'

'I think you're being very pessimistic about this situation,' said Aconna. 'I'm sure it'll be all over in a day or two.'

'Let's hope you're right,' said Cormac.

'And for your information, I don't need anyone's permission to look in on a friend,' said Aconna.

'Sorry?'

'You said I should be careful coming here.'

'That's right. The thing is you're only just starting your career. You don't want my bad news to rub off on you.'

'I wouldn't be here if I thought you were guilty of doing

anything wrong,' she said. 'I think I would have done the same as you. Everyone would.'

'Yeah, everyone except Driver,' said Cormac. 'He had doubts about Heather right from the start and, to be fair, he did warn me not to trust her. He warned Eagan too. I made the mistake of thinking I knew better when I should have listened to his advice.'

'I still think they're treating you like shit,' said Aconna.

'It's good to know someone's on my side, but I'd keep that to yourself if I were you,' said Cormac. 'You won't gain many brownie points with opinions like that.'

There was a brief silence, then Cormac said, 'Look, I was just going to the pub. They do good food up there. Care to join me? That's if you don't mind being seen with me.'

'Of course I don't mind being seen with you, as long as you're not planning to pick my brains about the case against you.'

'That would be pointless, as I'm sure you're being kept out of that particular loop,' said Cormac. 'And anyway, that's not what I had in mind.'

Aconna frowned.

'Oh, wait,' said Cormac. 'I didn't mean... It's not a date... I just thought...'

Aconna chuckled. 'Actually, I didn't think you were asking me out on a date. I was frowning because I was intending to call in on a friend, and I don't like letting people down.'

'Oh, right,' said Cormac. 'Well, not to worry. Maybe some other time.'

'However, my friend isn't expecting me so, technically, I won't be letting her down. And I'm starving, so I'd love to join you and see just how good their food is.'

* * *

Aconna stared at the plate that had been placed in front of her and then looked up at Cormac.

'Wow! I'm not sure I can eat all this. Are they always this generous?'

'It's what they call police portions,' explained Cormac. 'The landlord is Driver's cousin. He thinks the police need looking after. Driver told him I was a colleague, so he looks after me. Looking at my plate, I'm assuming Driver hasn't yet told him I'm unlikely to be a police officer for much longer. So, we'd better get stuck in before he finds out.'

'You don't really think that's going to happen, do you?'

Cormac sighed. 'Ever heard of a guy called Hobson?'

Aconna shook her head.

'Right. Well, way back in history, he owned a load of horses that people used to hire. But he found everyone wanted to hire the best horses, which meant they were being overworked. So, rather than allow people to choose which horse they wanted, they were only allowed to choose the one in the first stable. Hobson made sure the horses were rotated in that stable so the workload was shared.'

'So there wasn't really a choice,' said Aconna.

'Which is the essence of Hobson's choice,' said Cormac.

'I always wondered where that expression originated,' said Aconna. 'I didn't realise this evening would turn out to be so educational.'

'Yeah, well, anyway, if the choice was quit, or face being behind bars with a prison full of people who hate you, what would you choose?'

'I see what you mean,' said Aconna. 'But it won't come to that. You're no more corrupt than I am.'

'That's as may be,' said Cormac. 'But it's a risky strategy

to rely on. It only works if the jury believes me, rather than the prosecution, and there's no guarantee they will.'

* * *

Half an hour later, Cormac had eaten his fill and slumped in his usual after-dinner armchair in front of the unlit fire. Aconna slouched alongside him in the second armchair.

'I should go home, but I feel so bloated I can't sit up straight,' she said. 'I've even had to loosen my belt. It's as if I've eaten a horse.'

'You didn't have to eat it all,' said Cormac.

Aconna smiled. 'Yes, I know, but I hate waste. And you were right; it was delicious.'

A new, sharper female voice sounded from behind them. 'Aha! I was on my way to your room, but I thought I'd try in here first.'

The owner of the voice stepped alongside Cormac. It was Melinda. Tonight she was wearing purple, accessorised in pale pink. Her face turned to a matching colour as she realised Cormac wasn't alone.

'Oh! You have company. I'm sorry.'

'Hello, Melinda,' said Cormac. 'This is my colleague, Charlie Aconna. Charlie, this is Melinda Yates. Melinda is—'

'You're the journalist,' said Aconna, smiling brightly. 'You helped us with the financials.'

'Yes, that's right,' said Melinda.

Aconna looked at her watch. 'Goodness, look at the time. I must be off. I'm supposed to be meeting someone.'

'You don't need to leave,' said Cormac.

'No, don't leave on my account,' said Melinda.

'It's fine,' said Aconna, collecting her bag from the floor

by her chair and getting to her feet. 'As I said, I have to be somewhere.' She turned to Cormac. 'I'll call you.' She looked at Melinda again, then back to Cormac. 'Bye, then.'

'Bye, Charlie, and thanks for calling in,' said Cormac.

Melinda watched Aconna until the door closed behind her, then she turned to Cormac with a smile on her face. 'She's nice.'

'Yeah, she is,' said Cormac.

'Can I join you?'

Cormac inclined his head towards the now vacant armchair. 'Be my guest.'

Melinda sat down, her grin growing wider. 'I'm sorry if I interrupted something.'

'You didn't interrupt anything, Melinda. DC Aconna is just a colleague,' said Cormac.

'She's very attractive.'

'But she's still just a colleague,' said Cormac.

'You admit she's attractive, then?'

'I admit I'm not blind,' said Cormac. 'But I'm her immediate boss, and I'm also old enough to be her father.'

'Only if you started early.'

'I'm forty-four, Charlie is twenty-five, so it wouldn't have been that early.'

'There are plenty of young women who like older men,' said Melinda.

Cormac sighed. 'Did you want something, Melinda? Or have you just come to annoy me?'

'I came to say thank you, and to tell you to look out for the headlines in the next day or two.'

'What's that supposed to mean? Thank me for what?'

'Let's just say that, thanks to something you said, I anticipate an imminent announcement regarding the resignation of a high-ranking member of the government.'

Cormac jolted awake. 'Who?'

'Who do you think?'

'Tilthorne? But why would he resign?'

'You said you thought his daughter had a hold over him, and that you had your suspicions what it was, right?'

'Well, yeah, but please don't tell me you've written an article about him based on my suspicions. I'm in enough bloody trouble as it is.'

'Of course I didn't write an article based on your suspicions. I'm not some sensationalist tabloid chancer. I take my job seriously, which means I investigate and make sure I have uncovered genuine facts before I write a word. Apart from anything else, it makes it impossible for anyone I write about to sue the arse off me.'

'So, how did you ... Oh, hang on; have you been to France?'

Melinda winked. 'There's nothing like hearing it from the horse's mouth, is there? I mean, of all people, you should know that.'

'Yeah, but what about her NDA? If he sues her she'll be left with nothing, won't she?'

'The NDA expired last year, and she feels she's been gagged for far too long. Now she wants the truth to come out so the world can see what, he really is.'

'Bloody hell,' said Cormac. 'So, what is the truth?'

Melinda winked. 'If you listen to the news, or read a newspaper, you'll find out like everyone else.'

On another night, in different circumstances, Cormac might have made more effort to indulge Melinda. She clearly wanted him to ask more but, frankly, he couldn't be arsed.

'Okay, fair enough,' he said. 'I'll wait.'

Melinda pouted. She was hoping for a bit more effort from him. 'So what's this trouble you're in?' she asked.

'Sorry?'

'When you thought I'd written the article based on your hearsay, you said, "I'm in enough trouble already."'

'Oh, that. It's nothing, really. Just a silly misunderstanding at work.'

'It sounds more than a silly misunderstanding to me.'

'Yeah, well, it's nothing for you to worry about,' said Cormac.

'You haven't been playing fast and loose with the lovely DC Aconna, have you? I would imagine that would be a problem if you got found out.'

'Really?' said Cormac. 'I thought you just told me you weren't a tabloid chancer.'

Melinda snorted. 'I'm not!'

'Then stop behaving like one,' said Cormac. 'Why can't you just accept that Charlie is a colleague?'

'Oh, dear, we are touchy tonight,' said Melinda. 'Look, I'm sorry if I spoke out of turn. I just thought...'

'You just thought what?'

'I thought she was your girlfriend.'

'Why would you think that?'

'Because you look so comfortable together.'

'When two people work closely together, it's not unusual for them to develop a rapport.'

'She only left in such a hurry because she thought I was your girlfriend and she was going to be playing gooseberry rather than have you all to herself.'

'What makes you think that?' asked Cormac.

'Women's intuition. A girl can tell.'

'A girl can tell?' echoed Cormac. 'Is that right? You don't

think it might have something to do with you announcing you were going to my room?'

'No, I don't think she even noticed I said that.'

Cormac shook his head. 'What's happened to doing your research and uncovering actual facts? Doesn't that matter when it concerns my private life?'

'Am I wrong?'

'You're about a million miles off the mark with me and Charlie.'

Melinda waited, but Cormac said nothing else.

'What about me being your girlfriend?' she asked.

'But you're not my girlfriend,' said Cormac. 'I don't have a girlfriend and, right now, I don't want a girlfriend.'

'You're in a shitty mood tonight, Cormac, do you know that?'

Cormac grunted. 'Yeah, well, I'm sorry about that, Melinda, but I've got a lot on my mind.'

'Do you want to talk about it?'

'No offence but, no, I don't think so. Now, if you'll excuse me, I'm going back to my room.'

She considered making a snarky remark, but whatever was on his mind, his concern was obvious.

'Okay, take care,' she said. 'If there's anything I can do, just let me know.'

CHAPTER 26

* * *

It was 6 a.m., and as Cormac emerged from a deep sleep, he struggled to figure out what was going on. It took several seconds for him to gain sufficient consciousness to remember he was living in a motel room. But what was the bloody awful noise? He sat up and cast around the room, his eyes finally coming to rest on his mobile phone.

Muttering darkly about how he couldn't be on call if he was suspended from duty, he tried to ignore the phone. Eventually, it went to voicemail, but whoever was calling had no intention of leaving a message, and within seconds it was ringing again.

He tried burying his head under the pillow, but that didn't work, so having no choice, he threw the covers back and climbed from his bed.

'Yes!' he snapped into the phone. 'Don't you know what time it is?'

'Cormac. It's Driver. If you've got a television in that room, you should switch it on right away; BBC News.'

'What? Oh, hang on, I'm hardly awake. I can't remember where I've put the remote.'

'I'll hold while you find it,' said Driver.

For some unfathomable reason, the remote control for his television was in the en-suite bathroom, and it took Cormac two or three minutes to find it. Finally, he aimed it at the television and clicked the button. Almost immediately, the face of the early morning newsreader appeared. Behind her, a photograph of the Home Secretary filled the background.

Cormac slumped back onto the bed, his mouth sagging open as he listened to the headline story unfold. Slowly, he realised his phone was still in his hand, Driver's voice doing its best to attract his attention. He raised the phone to his ear.

'You've found it, then,' said Driver.

'Yes,' said Cormac.

'Get yourself dressed,' said Driver. 'I'll pick you up in half an hour.'

'Aren't you forgetting I'm suspended?'

'We'll talk about that over breakfast.'

Cormac realised Driver had ended the call before he could reply. He glared at the phone, flung it onto the bed, and refocused on the newsreader. Then he spent the next half hour dodging between the TV and en-suite, trying to get ready and watch the news at the same time.

It appeared the former Lady Jane Tilthorne had done a real hatchet job on her former husband's reputation. Cormac had had his suspicions about the relationship between Tilthorne and his daughter, but even so, the revelation that Tilthorne had abused her from the age of twelve made him feel queasy.

It had been this shocking discovery that had led Lady

Jane to divorce her husband. At the time, he was only saved from disgrace by the nondisclosure agreement she was forced to sign. The claim that she regretted signing it now didn't sit well with Cormac. In his eyes, it just showed how money talks, no matter what it hides.

Cormac's musings were interrupted by loud knocking on the door, heralding Driver's arrival. As he approached the door, Cormac was unsure how he stood with his boss. He wasn't even sure if Driver still was his boss. If he were suspended from duty, did he even have a boss?

Driver was shuffling awkwardly on the spot as Cormac opened the door. 'Well, come on then, Cormac, let's get going,' he called over his shoulder as he turned away and strode towards his car.

Cormac followed and slid into the passenger seat. 'Why are you doing this?' he asked. 'I thought I was suspended from duty.'

Driver started the car and pulled away, managing a cough and a sideways glance at Cormac as he did.

'Ah, yes,' he said. 'About the suspension. It's, er, it's been lifted. As of now, you're back on duty.'

'But I thought you were convinced I was, now, what was it you said ... oh yes, "in league with that Tilthorne woman". That was it, wasn't it?'

'Yes, all right. I admit I did say something along those lines, but you can't deny the evidence was pointing that way.'

'It was all circumstantial evidence, at best.'

'But there was a lot of it.'

'I spent two nights in a cell,' said Cormac.

'Yes, I know, and I'm sorry. I was mistaken.'

'So, what changed your mind?'

Driver sighed. 'I was raging when everything went tits

up, mostly with myself because even though I had my doubts from the start, I let you and Eagan talk me into it. But I had no right to pin the blame on you.'

'Yeah, but if I'm being honest, I can see why you thought what you did,' said Cormac.

'But I should have seen past that,' said Driver. 'It took my wife to remind me, but I've been manipulated myself in the past, so I know how easy it is for an experienced con artist to take someone in. As my wife pointed out, I'd be a bloody hypocrite if I held it against you, so I did my best to show the evidence didn't prove anything, and that I had jumped to the wrong conclusion.'

'And that's it?' asked Cormac.

'Look, I admit I made a mistake, but I won't beg for your forgiveness for doing my job.'

Cormac stared at Driver, but his face bloomed into a grin. 'I never for one minute thought you would. I'm actually surprised you're even prepared to admit you were mistaken.'

'Yes, well don't get carried away,' said Driver. 'I'm still the DCI and you're still the DS.'

'As if I could forget!'

Cormac hadn't been paying much attention to where they were going, so he was surprised when Driver stopped the car.

'I thought we could have a spot of breakfast while I bring you up to speed,' said Driver.

A few minutes later, they were huddled either side of a table, two mugs of tea steaming before them while they waited for their breakfasts.

'Right. Fire away then,' said Cormac.

'Okay, let's start with the Albanians,' said Driver. 'You

probably saw enough of them on the night to realise they were no more Albanian than you or I.'

'Who were they?'

'Bloody actors, every one of them, and not a single criminal conviction between them. They say they were recruited as extras to appear in a low-budget film. They even had a fake contract.'

'Didn't they check it out?'

'They're young, aspiring actors who jumped at what they thought was a chance to be in a film. It never occurred to them they were being set up and, to be fair, if they thought opportunity really had come knocking, why would they question it?'

'So, that's drawn a blank then,' said Cormac.

'Not entirely. They gave us a description of the "agent" who recruited them.'

'Heather?'

'No, it was Carl Prentice.'

'Sounds as if he might be a lot more involved than we thought.'

'They said they didn't know the Heather impersonator in the car, but it turns out she was another actor, recruited from further afield, but under the same impression that she was an extra in a film.'

'Did Prentice recruit her?'

Driver nodded. 'Looks that way. The description she gave is close enough to be him.'

They stopped speaking as their breakfasts were placed in front of them, then resumed talking as they ate.

'Total fiasco then,' said Cormac. 'Heather really played me, didn't she?'

'She played all of us,' said Driver. 'But you won't be

surprised to know Eagan's trying to cover his own arse and keep it quiet.'

'Yeah, good luck with that,' said Cormac. 'Those people were acting in good faith and we barged in and frightened the crap out of them. I can't believe they're not going to sue, or at least speak to the press. I would.'

'As for the real Albanians and the drug operation, well, that's out of our hands now. It's been handed over to the drug squad so I suspect we're going to have a long wait before we get to question them about any murders.'

'What happened to Rosemary, or Heather, or whatever we're calling her now?' asked Cormac.

'No idea,' said Driver. 'She's vanished.'

'Not at Milburn Manor then, hiding behind Daddy?' asked Cormac.

'That's always a possibility, but somehow I doubt it,' said Driver.

'A possibility? You haven't been there?'

'Not officially,' said Driver. 'Eagan wouldn't allow me to apply for a search warrant. Apparently, Lord Tilthorne swore she wasn't there and, as we lacked proof of her presence, we have to take his word for it.'

'What about all the financial evidence Charlie dug up?'

'Eagan agrees it suggests Heather is laundering money, but he says it's not enough to incriminate Lord Tilthorne.'

'What does he want, a signed confession?'

Driver smiled. 'I'm not sure even that would be enough.'

'This is bollocks,' said Cormac. 'Tilthorne's hardly ever there, so how would he know if his daughter was there? And who took his word for it?'

'His best buddy, the ACC, I would imagine,' said Driver.

'I would have gone up there anyway.'

'I did,' said Driver. 'Unofficially, of course.'

'Any good?'

Driver shook his head. 'Frankly, it was humiliating and embarrassing. I didn't even get past the gate.'

'You must be able to handle a twat like Prentice.'

'I was looking forward to clashing with Prentice, but he wasn't there. The man in his place at the gate was one of the Home Secretary's official security detail. He's called DS Prat, but I think the only real prat at the gate was me. He told me, and I quote, "wooden-top DCIs don't tell MI5 officers what to do," and then when I tried to argue with him, he told me to "f off, or he would call my boss". As I wasn't supposed to be there, I couldn't risk pushing it any further, so that was it.'

'So, where was Prentice? I'm sure he must have known we'd be calling, and he would have loved telling us where to get off.'

'We did try to track him down so we could question him, but we couldn't find him anywhere. Even the MI5 Prat, claimed he hadn't set eyes on him. That was the one question he was prepared to answer politely.'

'Yeah, but that lot help no one but themselves, so that could have been bollocks anyway,' said Cormac.

'I think on this occasion he was telling the truth. He was pissed off at having to do gate duty like it was beneath his dignity. I'm sure if he knew where Prentice was, he'd have dragged him in and chained him to the gate. No, I believe he genuinely didn't know. Prentice seems to have disappeared.'

'D'you think he's run off with Heather?' asked Cormac.

'We can't ignore that possibility,' said Driver.

'What about Marky and Sniffer? Have you got any further with their murders?'

'I'm not sure we'll ever know for sure, but the evidence still suggests Marky was murdered because he talked too much. His death seems to have kick-started everything.'

'Our starter for ten,' said Cormac.

'Yes,' agreed Driver. 'But unfortunately, we don't seem to have come up with many answers.'

'What about Sniffer?'

'My best guess? Sniffer had to be eliminated because he somehow knew about the corruption inside the drug squad.'

'So you think I was right about that?' asked Cormac.

'When you consider two drug squad officers seem to have fled the country, it's the only thing that makes sense,' said Driver.

'Mike Phillips?'

'I'm afraid we're clueless about that one. I can't even begin to guess where he fits in. We're thinking Prentice murdered him, but why? It seems excessive to murder someone just for forging your signature.'

'Jonathon Tilthorne?'

'Not sure about that one. I reckon it's a toss-up between the Albanians and Rosemary Tilthorne.'

'You really think she did that to her own brother? But why would she?'

'She probably didn't do it herself. I'm thinking Prentice is likely to be her go-to guy when she has dirty work to do. As for why; we've found evidence that he was in contact with the Albanians.'

'You think he was double-crossing her?'

'Let's say I think it's a likely avenue of enquiry,' said Driver.

'What if Mike Phillips went rogue and killed Jonathon? Maybe he had something against him personally, and it had nothing to do with the drug business. Rosemary might have sent Prentice after him for revenge.'

'I think you might be clutching at straws there,' said Driver. 'I'm more inclined to think Phillips knew too much and had to be silenced.'

They had finished eating now.

'Well, thank you for breakfast. Where to now?' asked Cormac.

'Back to the office,' said Driver. 'We need to tie up some loose ends. And on the bright side, we might not have had enough evidence for a warrant before, but now Tilthorne is suspected of child abuse, that should no longer be a problem. Even the ACC can't excuse that sort of behaviour.'

* * *

'THE FIU HAVE NOTICED some interesting activity in the Tilthorne Cayman Island bank accounts, sir,' said Aconna as soon as Driver and Cormac came through the doors.

'What sort of interesting activity?' asked Driver.

'Lots of money being transferred in, and then almost immediately out again.'

'That's not unusual for money laundering, is it?' said Driver.

'I think there's a bit more to it than that,' said Aconna.

'How much are we talking? And transferred where?'

'Ten million was paid into each of five different Tilthorne accounts five days ago.'

Driver did a classic double take. 'Did you say five times ten? That's fifty million quid!'

Aconna nodded her head. 'That's right, fifty million quid, sir,' she confirmed. 'And that money was then transferred out to three different accounts set up in the name of Heather Collins.'

'That's Rosemary's alias,' said Cormac. 'That's what she called herself when I first met her.'

'Are these new accounts?' asked Driver.

'No, sir. I'm sorry, I should have spotted them before,' said Aconna. 'But I was looking for anything Tilthorne. No-one said anything about Collins.'

'No-one is blaming you, Charlie,' said Driver. 'I just want to know when they were set up?'

'Six months ago.'

'And the money has just been transferred into them now?'

'Four days ago, according to the FIU.'

'And they didn't think to let us know until now?' asked Driver.

'Does it matter?' asked Aconna.

'Well, yes it does matter. If we'd known about the money sooner, we might have suspected the fiasco at the gasworks was a set-up, and planned accordingly,' said Driver.

'Do they know where that fifty million came from, Charlie?' asked Cormac.

'The FIU say it's from an account they've been moni-toring for some time. They believe it's laundered money from a large criminal organisation.'

'Which criminal organisation?' asked Driver.

'They say there's so much subterfuge behind the setting up of the account they can't be certain, but they believe its origins are in Albania.'

'Are they seriously saying Rosemary Tilthorne was paid off with money from an Albanian gang?' asked Driver.

'That's how it looks,' said Aconna.

Cormac slammed his fist on the desk. 'Bloody hell. She's

played us. This is a business takeover that's been six months in the planning, isn't it?'

'What is?'

'This is her exit strategy! She told me she'd had enough drug dealing and wanted out. I took that with a pinch of salt when she told me, but now I can see I was mistaken.'

'Go on,' urged Driver.

'She made sure we got it all wrong. There was never going to be a drug war; she just made us think there was. The Albanians have taken over all right, but they've done it by negotiating and making a deal.'

'So you're saying they started talking about this deal six months ago?'

'I reckon it explains why she set up those bank accounts when she did,' said Cormac. 'Then, finally, when the price was agreed, Heather, or the Albanians decided, for whatever reason, that they wanted to make us look like a bunch of idiots. That's why Heather contacted me and offered us the chance to catch them all.'

'But why would they do that?' asked Driver.

'I don't know,' said Cormac. 'Perhaps she suggested it as her ultimate act of defiance?'

'I'm wondering what they were doing that night that they wanted us out of the way?' said Driver.

'Maybe they weren't doing anything,' suggested Aconna. 'Maybe the Albanians asked Heather to prove she was acting in good faith and show they could trust her.'

Driver looked sceptical.

'Charlie may have a point, sir,' said Cormac. 'That's the sort of grand gesture Heather would make. She's not one for doing things by halves.'

'And you think the fifty million was paid to her once they knew we'd been set up?' said Driver.

'The timing fits too well to be a coincidence, doesn't it?' said Cormac.

Driver studied Cormac's face for a moment. 'You transferred to Windover at just the right time, then?'

'Sorry?' said Cormac.

'She needed someone inside the police that she could manipulate, and suddenly you arrived.'

'But I didn't know she was here.'

'I thought you said you had a tip-off that she was in this area.'

'Well, yeah, but ...' Cormac's face reddened. 'Hang on a minute. Where are you going with this? I thought you said I had been cleared of all suspicion.'

'And so you have been. I'm not suggesting you were a willing accomplice, but you can't deny it looks as if you were part of her escape plan all along.'

Realisation struck Cormac like a slap across the face. He'd been played, and he could no longer hide behind his self-denial. He sagged and sighed like a deflating balloon. 'Look, it's hard enough having to accept I've been taken for an idiot by that woman, and that it started five years ago. I don't need my boss adding to that by suggesting I'm part of her bloody escape plot.'

'I'm sorry, but I think you're overreacting,' said Driver. 'You need to calm down.'

Cormac realised his fists were clenched. He eased his hands open and took a deep breath. 'Right, yes. I'm sorry, sir. It's a bit of a sore point after the last few days. How about I go and round up some coffees from the canteen?'

'I think that's an excellent idea,' said Driver.

They watched as Cormac pushed through the doors, then Aconna turned to Driver. 'You don't really think he's done anything wrong, do you, sir?'

'Remember they first met five years ago,' said Driver. 'And he was so besotted by her back then, he was even considering marrying her.'

'Yes, but that was a long time ago,' said Aconna. 'He told me he was over her years ago.'

Driver grimaced. 'But is he over her? She's a cunning woman; how do we know she didn't rekindle the flame six months ago when she came up with this plan, and that's why he transferred down here? And don't forget he told us she went to his motel room. He admitted it happened once, but how do we know that was the only time?'

'Sorry, sir, but I'm not sure I can accept that everything Cormac has told me is a lie,' said Aconna.

'Honestly I hope you're right, and I'm wrong,' said Driver. 'But remember it's our job to keep an open mind until we know for sure. I'll understand if you can't do that, but I must.'

The phone in Driver's office was ringing, so he rushed off to answer it. By the time he came back, Cormac was back with the coffees.

'That was our dear leader on the phone,' he said. 'He wants to see us in his office.'

'What now?' asked Cormac.

'I think we can drink our coffees first,' said Driver.

Normally, Superintendent Barry Eagan looked pretty immaculate. Whether in uniform or plain clothes, he always looked sharp. But not this morning. This morning he looked as though he'd grabbed a suit from the seconds rail in a charity shop, and if he'd slept at all, he must have been woken almost immediately after he had closed his eyes.

He tossed a broadsheet newspaper onto the desk as soon as Driver and Cormac walked in. 'Have you seen this?'

The headline shouted the big news;

HOME SECRETARY RESIGNS AFTER FAMILY SCANDAL REVEALED

Melinda Yates' byline stood proud beneath the story, the scandal laid bare in merciless prose.

'Er, I've not had time to read it, but we both saw it on the TV earlier,' said Driver.

Eagan stared at Cormac. 'This is the journalist you're friendly with, isn't it?'

'I know her, yes,' said Cormac, picking up the newspaper. 'It was Melinda who put us on to the Tilthorne bank accounts.'

'And now the man's career and life is ruined,' said Eagan. 'Did you tell her about this?'

'It's as much news to me as it is to you,' said Cormac, quickly scanning through the story.

'Of course Cormac didn't tell her,' said Driver. 'According to the television news, it was his wife who spilled the beans. Trust me, if we'd known about this, I'd have been all over him like a rash.'

'But he's the Home Secretary, and now he's been forced to resign,' whined Eagan.

'With respect, he should never have been appointed as Home Secretary,' said Driver. 'And he should resign. The fact is, a man like that should never have been allowed anywhere near high office, and he doesn't deserve respect from any of us. In fact, I'm asking you for permission to obtain a search warrant for Milburn Manor, and I sincerely hope this time you won't obstruct us from doing our duty.'

'What do you mean, obstruct you?'

'You know very well what I mean,' said Driver. 'You've allowed the ACC to block every attempt we've made to access that place.'

'He's a very persuasive man,' said Eagan.

'He didn't need to know,' said Driver. 'If you were a bit more concerned about doing your job instead of saving it ...'

'Actually, there's been a bit of fallout over all of this,' said Eagan.

'What sort of fallout?' asked Cormac.

'Apparently, Professional Standards were invited to look into Head Office a few weeks ago by the Chief Constable. He has believed for some time that someone was feeding information to the Home Office. They had had their suspicions as to who was responsible, but investigating Cormac gave them an unexpected opportunity to link their suspect with not just the Home Office, but directly to the Home Secretary himself.'

'It's the bloody ACC,' said Driver.

'No wonder the Tilthornes were always a step ahead,' said Cormac. 'And I got the blame for it!'

'Well, it won't happen again,' said Eagan. 'The ACC was taken into custody earlier today and is currently being questioned. Needless to say, he is suspended from duty and is probably going to be charged.'

'I hope they throw the bloody book at him,' said Driver. 'We wouldn't have stopped all the murders, but we probably could have prevented one or two if he hadn't interfered.'

'Yes, well, I'm afraid I don't come out of this very well,' said Eagan.

'I think you'll find it's called managing up,' said Driver. 'I thought you were good at that sort of thing.'

'I admit I should have argued our case more assertively, but he was the man who got me this job.'

'Oh, I see,' said Driver. 'He gave you the job so you let him walk all over you.'

'All right, Driver, remember who you're talking to; I'm still the boss around here.'

'I take it we can get a search warrant now, then?' asked Driver.

'Yes, of course you can. Get on with it.'

As they left the office, Cormac considered the story he had just read and wondered why it didn't mention how Rosemary had somehow gained enough leverage to turn the tables on her father and change from being the controlled person to becoming the controlling person. It seemed unlikely Lady Jane would be unaware of such a drastic change in the relationship dynamic between father and daughter, so why was this not included?

He concluded Melinda must be saving this part for a follow-up story. And who could blame her? It must be a real scoop and, after all, he thought, why should she get paid once when she get write a further instalment and double her money?

* * *

CHAPTER 28

Driver and Cormac were in the main drawing room at Milburn Manor. Aconna and a team of forensics technicians were searching the house for clues, but an initial extensive search had revealed no trace of Lord Tilthorne or his daughter, Rosemary. A solitary member of the security detail was currently on the receiving end of Driver's rage. Of course, it had to be DS Prat, who remembered his previous clash with Driver and was relishing the opportunity to hinder him again.

'How the hell has he got away?' demanded Driver. 'You're supposed to be MI5. Don't you arrest criminals?'

'Look, mate, we're just here to protect the man,' said Prat. 'That's our job; that's what we do. Plod work is what you guys do, right?'

'Protect him?' echoed Driver. 'How can you say you're protecting him when you don't even know where the hell he is?'

Prat managed a smug grin. 'Lord Tilthorne resigned at

6pm yesterday evening, but the Prime Minister agreed to keep it hushed up until after midnight.'

'Six?' said Cormac. 'Why did he resign at six? Did he know the story was about to break?'

'It's not my place to know what he knew, what he agreed with the PM, or why they made a deal. You'll have to ask him that question,' said Prat. 'But, as I'm sure you can imagine, a man in his position has friends everywhere, so it wouldn't surprise me if someone tipped him off.'

'So, where did he go?' demanded Driver.

Prat sighed and smiled like an indulgent parent dealing with a recalcitrant child.

'The thing you need to understand, DCI Driver, is once someone resigns, our job is finished unless we're given a direct order to the contrary. We were informed by 6:15 that the Home Secretary had resigned, and we didn't receive any contrary order, so that was it. What he does once he's no longer in our care is his business, not ours.'

'And you think it's okay for him to have been abusing his own daughter when she was just twelve years old, do you?' snarled Driver.

'I didn't know anything about that until this morning,' said Prat. 'We were just told we had to keep schtum and stay here until this morning, which we did.'

'What about his daughter, Rosemary?' asked Cormac.

'What about her?'

'Where is she?'

'How should I know? As I've told you before, she doesn't live here.'

'What about Carl Prentice, the thug that's usually on the gate? Have you seen him?'

Prat's patience was wearing thin and being replaced by belligerence. 'Last time you were here, Driver, you will recall I was doing the gate because Prentice was missing. As far as I know, he's still missing because I haven't set eyes on him since.'

'Why isn't anyone on the gate now? We drove straight in.'

'As I said, it's no longer my problem, mate.'

'I'm not your bloody mate,' hissed Driver.

'Thank God for that,' said Prat.

Cormac watched as Driver's face reddened and he drew himself up to his full height. He wondered if he should intervene or stand back and let his boss punch the MI5 officer. He was definitely asking for it. But Driver saw sense and chose to defuse the situation himself.

'I need some air,' he told Cormac, then walked from the room muttering under his breath.

'He's not a happy bunny, is he?' said Prat.

'No, he's not. We're both fed up with being frustrated at every turn, and your taunting doesn't actually help anyone, does it?' said Cormac. 'Do you really have no idea where Tilthorne's gone? I mean, seriously? I thought you guys were supposed to be the best. That's what you tell everyone.'

'All I know is that he was talking to someone about a private jet.'

'Who was he talking to? Was it Rosemary?'

'I'm not sure, but it could have been.'

'Did he book a flight, or what?'

'I don't know.'

'Come on, man, just for once, can't you help us?' insisted Cormac. 'The man and his daughter are fugitives. If they get into the air, we'll lose the chance to stop them.'

Prat shrugged and spread his arms. 'Look, I'm sorry, but that's all I heard.'

'You're not really sorry, are you?' said Cormac. 'Let's be honest, you don't give a shit about helping us.'

'He did drive out of here just before 7 pm.'

'Who, Tilthorne? And you're just telling us now? What was he driving?'

'One of the Manor's Land Rovers. Defender, I think.'

'You bastard,' said Cormac. 'You've given him the best part of a day's start over us. I've a good mind to punch your lights out myself.'

Prat grinned. 'Another time, perhaps. Right now I have few days off so I'm going home. My work here is done, and I've done all I can to help with your investigation.'

'Like letting a child abuser escape?' said Cormac.

'I've seen no behaviour like that while I've worked for him and, as I already said, I knew nothing about it until this morning.'

'Just make sure you don't run into my boss on the way out,' said Cormac.

'Is that a threat?'

'Oh, grow up,' said Cormac. 'Of course it's not a threat. You're the guys who go in for that macho, "come and have a go if you think you're hard enough," crap. We're a bit more professional than that, but we might consider doing you for obstruction.'

'You reckon? Well, good luck with that. And tell your boss it's not my fault he can't do his job properly. He'd get on better if he changed his attitude.'

'We'd all get on better if a few of you guys changed your attitudes and learned how to cooperate.'

Prat nodded, his grin widening. 'You wooden-tops are all the same, aren't you? Can't do your own jobs properly so you blame everyone else.'

'Yeah, whatever,' said Cormac. 'At least I'm not the definition of an annoying prat.'

With that, he turned away and set off to look for Driver,
eventually finding him in the garden, sitting on a bench,
staring at nothing in particular.

'Tilthorne drove out of here at 7 pm yesterday,' said
Cormac. 'Prat watched him go. Says he thinks he heard him
talking about a private jet.'

Driver nodded his head. He managed a resigned sigh,
but that was all. As Cormac settled alongside him on the
bench, Driver turned to glance at him, then turned back to
observing the infinite. Cormac bided his time.

After a minute or two, Driver let out another massive
sigh. 'Sometimes I have to ask myself, is it all worth it?
Should I carry on swimming against the tide, or should I
give up, take my pension, and spend more time with my
wife?'

'We've had better days, right?' said Cormac.

'Four bloody murders and we can only hazard a guess as
to why the victims are dead, and who murdered them.'

'But we know it was one side or the other,' said
Cormac.

'Ah, but we don't know, though, do we?' said Driver. 'All
we have is speculation. Yes, we think it must be one side or
the other, but we don't actually have anything concrete to
prove it for sure. And were there ever two sides going
against each other? The latest evidence suggests they were
in it together!'

'Yeah, when you put it like that, we've actually got
nowhere, have we?' said Cormac gloomily.

'We've got two fugitives on the run, who could tell us
everything we need to know, but one has a day's start and
the other has probably been gone even longer. And with

their money, they'll almost certainly have new identities and be halfway around the world by now.'

'But, on the other hand, isn't speculation part of the job?' said Cormac. 'Isn't trying to unravel all that stuff and make sense of it the challenge we take on every day? Yes, it can be bloody frustrating, and we might not always get it right, but think what would happen if we gave up trying?'

Driver turned and raised an eyebrow at Cormac. 'If you're going to come out with deep, meaningful speeches like that, you should understand they're wasted on me. Perhaps you should consider becoming a leader somewhere else.'

'What, me, a leader? You must be joking, sir. I make far too many cock-ups to do that. And I've just recently demonstrated I'm a piss-poor judge of character.'

'Ha! An who amongst us can say they've never made that mistake?' said Driver. 'If it's any consolation, I'm not exactly operating at genius level, am I?'

They sat in silence for a few more moments until Driver nudged Cormac with his elbow. 'I suppose I'd better dredge up the enthusiasm to try to find that car.'

'I've already passed the reg number onto traffic. They're running it through the ANPR system. They should be able to track its movements.'

'If he was heading for the nearest airfield, we've got no prospect of catching him, but well done for trying,' said Driver.

As they stood to leave, Driver's mobile phone rang. He fished it from his pocket and looked at the screen. 'It's Eagan,' he said. 'What the hell does he want now?'

He accepted the call, raised the phone to his ear, said 'Driver' into the phone and then listened. Slowly, he sank back onto the bench as the call unfolded. The only words he uttered during the three-minute call were, 'And they're quite sure?' followed a minute later by, 'Yes, quite. Thanks for letting us know.'

He lowered the phone and slipped it back in his pocket. 'That was Eagan. You can call off the ANPR search.'

'You mean Tilthorne's been found? Where is he?' asked Cormac.

'He's currently lying on a slab in the morgue.'

'What?'

'According to Eagan, at around 9 p.m. yesterday evening a man jumped from a bridge over the M3 motorway. Eyewitnesses say he seemed to wait for a convoy of heavy lorries to come along and made sure he landed right in their path.'

'Where was this?' asked Cormac.

'M3 Southbound, not far from Frimley.'

'Southbound? What was he doing heading south?'

'His car was tracked going into Blackbushe Airport at 7:45 yesterday evening and then, an hour later, it was tracked coming out again.'

'But why? From what Prat said, I thought he was catching a flight out of here. Why would he turn back and then jump off a bridge? It makes no sense.'

'Or perhaps it does,' said Driver. 'You see, another eyewitness who was walking their dog at the other end of the bridge claims he saw someone else with Tilthorne, and that they ran off after he jumped.'

'They think he was pushed? Who by? Did the witness give a description?'

'He says he didn't see the person clearly, but he heard a car start up shortly after they ran off. He glimpsed the car driving away and thinks it was a big SUV, like a Land Rover or something similar.'

'So someone drove him there in his own car, pushed him over the rail, and then drove off again?'

'That's how it looks, if the witness on the bridge is reliable,' said Driver. 'And the same car was tracked going back into Blackbushe at 9:25. The car has been found in the car park. It's being taken apart by forensics as we speak.'

'How come we're only hearing about this now?' asked Cormac.

'It took several hours to identify the body. It was hit by several lorries, so it was a right mess. Then, of course, Frimley is in Surrey, and Surrey Police didn't know about our investigation. And now they do know about it, they're reluctant to share anything with us as they see Tilthorne's death as their investigation.'

'Bloody police politics,' said Cormac. 'Shouldn't we all be on the same side?'

Driver offered him a wry smile and shook his head. 'You'd think it should work that way, but you know as well as I do it just doesn't, does it?'

'So, I guess that means we're left with Rosemary Tilthorne and Carl Prentice as our main suspects,' said Cormac.

'And my guess is they're sitting on a beach somewhere laughing their heads off.'

'Who do we have as favourite for this one, Prentice?'

'I would think he's the more likely suspect,' said Driver.

'So what are we thinking? Rosemary was at the airport waiting for him to do the deed, and then he came back and joined her for take-off?'

'You think she's cold enough to arrange for Prentice to bump off her father while she waited at the airport?'

'I wouldn't put it past her,' said Cormac. 'Or, I suppose

they could both have been there. She could have been Prentice's getaway driver.'

'Or vice, versa,' said Driver. 'A decent ANPR photo might prove if they were both in the car.' He sighed. 'But here we are guessing again, aren't we?'

'But if we know they were at Blackbushe we should be able to find out which flight they were on, and where it went.'

'That's assuming they were both on the same flight,' said Driver. 'But even if they were, they won't sit around waiting for us, will they? Rosemary Tilthorne is nobody's fool. I would imagine she's organised a series of new identities, and no doubt she plans to move a few times before they settle anywhere. I suspect they're as good as lost in the works, and we'll be left with bugger all.'

'I'll get back to the station and see what I can find out,' said Cormac.

It was 8 pm by the time Driver joined Cormac back at Windover station. The DCI seemed to have shrunk, his eyes surrounded by dark shadows.

'Look at me,' he said. 'These aren't bags under my eyes; they're more like bloody suitcases. Where are we with this private jet?'

'Night flights are restricted at Blackbushe and have to be booked in advance.'

'Yes, well, I guessed it wasn't a spur of the moment decision,' said Driver.

'Right, so there were only two private flights that took off from Blackbushe after 9:30 last night,' explained Cormac. 'One had six passengers heading for Paris. The other had two passengers with an eventual destination of Cape Verde.'

'I assume all these passengers had passports.'

'Yeah, of course,' said Cormac. 'As you'd expect, the names Tilthorne and Prentice didn't show up anywhere, and the six people who went to Paris were regular fliers, known to the airport.'

'So, they've gone to Cape Verde?'

Cormac nodded. 'That's what I was thinking, especially after a sharp-eyed customs officer thought there was something suspicious about the couple taking that flight.'

'Suspicious how?'

'He thought they appeared guilty about something, but he couldn't actually find anything that would allow him to stop them.'

'Was it the Tilthorne woman and Prentice?' asked Driver.

'Can't be sure until we see copies of the passports, but I think not.'

'The passports weren't forgeries?'

'Fake, or not, they were good enough to get through,' said Cormac.

'Just a minute!' said Driver. 'You don't think it's them do you?'

'It makes sense for them to be heading to a destination where there's no extradition treaty, the problem is the descriptions didn't fit.'

'Why not?'

'The man definitely isn't Prentice. He was described as in his sixties, average height with an average build. Prentice is about forty, tall and built like a tank. And the woman doesn't match Rosemary; wrong hair colour, and wrong eye colour.'

'Yes, but hair can be dyed and contact lenses can change the colour of someone's eyes,' said Driver.

'But she can't grow six inches taller and take twenty years off her age, can she?'

'So, where the hell are they?' said Driver.

'The only thing I can think is that they went back to Blackbushe to dump the Land Rover and had another car waiting to take them on somewhere else.'

'So, you think this whole thing with Lord Tilthorne and going to Blackbushe Airport was planned just to create a smokescreen?'

'I'm afraid so,' said Cormac. 'And it looks as though Rosemary and Prentice have vanished in the haze.'

'I don't believe this,' Driver slammed a bunched fist on the nearest desk. 'Bollocks!' he said. 'Bollocks, bollocks, and more bollocks.'

'Sorry, sir. I'm afraid we've been outsmarted.'

Driver looked stricken by disappointment, as if it was almost too much for him to bear. 'Outsmarted, Cormac? The truth is we've been made to look a bunch of idiots!'

'It's hard to argue with your assessment, sir.'

'I have to say it, but you've got to hand it to her; she's been streets ahead of us right from the start, and she still is. Her and her pet thug have literally got away with murder, haven't they?'

'Several times over, by my reckoning,' said Cormac. 'And if you're right about her organising multiple IDs, it's going to be nigh on impossible to find them now. '

Driver slumped into a chair and sighed. 'This investigation has turned from a nightmare into a bloody disaster,' he said. 'There's bound to be an inquiry as to how we got it so wrong. I'll probably be retiring a bit earlier than I had planned.'

'D'you think so? I think most of the blame for what happened is down to the ACC.'

'Even so, I'm not sure that will be enough to save my skin,' said Driver gloomily. But then he mustered a little defiance. 'Well, you know what? I don't give a damn if they haul me over the coals, or not. Right now, I've had enough. I'm going home.'

Cormac watched his boss trudge across the incident room and out through the doors, a wave of sympathy washing over him. He yawned, stretched, and then reached across to switch off his computer. He'd had enough too. If he hurried, he could get to The Red Cow for his dinner before they closed the kitchen for the night.

CHAPTER 29

* * *

Cᴏʀᴍᴀᴄ ɢᴏᴛ ʙᴀᴄᴋ to his motel at 11 pm. As he slipped his key into the lock of his room, he felt tired enough to sleep for a week, so he undressed straight away and turned the covers back on his bed.

A large, expensive-looking cream envelope lay in the centre of the bed. He stared at the envelope. On the front, someone had hand-crafted the single word Noly in Gothic script. Cormac gasped as a sudden emptiness grabbed his insides, almost as if he had been hollowed out somehow.

The source of the envelope was obvious, but how had it got there? Had Heather been inside his room? They had assumed she had fled the country, but had they got it wrong? Was she still out there, watching him, attempting to pull his strings yet again?

The initial shock had startled him, but the police officer inside him gradually took control, and he knew what he must do. He went outside to his car, returning with a pair of latex gloves. He slipped the gloves on, flexed his fingers once or twice, picked up the envelope and weighed it in his hand. Satisfied it contained no booby-trap, he carefully slit the envelope open. As he emptied the contents onto the bed, he caught a hint of perfume. He immediately knew it as the same one she used to wear when they first met.

The paper was equally as expensive as the envelope, but then he had expected nothing less. There appeared to be three sheets of paper, and as he unfolded them, a photograph slipped out from between them and landed face up. It showed himself and Heather, a happy sun-kissed couple hugging and smiling for the camera, she in a yellow bikini, he in blue shorts.

He was surprised to find the photograph triggered a vivid recollection. They had been on a beach in Thailand, and a fruit seller had come along. Cormac had bought all the fruit and then Heather had asked the seller to take a few photos. He had never been happier than he was that day, but the very next day, Heather had disappeared. For a moment, he recalled the feeling of desperate emptiness all over again.

With a visible effort, he shook himself out of his melancholy and reminded himself that the Heather he had loved was merely a fantasy conjured up by Rosemary Tilthorne.

Then, he read the letter:

* * *

Dear Noly,

I'm sure you believed I had intended to give myself up but that's your problem, you see; you think you can save everyone. The thing is, you can't save people like me because we have no desire to be saved. All I ever wanted from you was your attention, and for these last few short days, I finally got it.

Thank you for playing your part so well. I could always bend you around my little finger, and once you were in place, I was confident you would do what I wanted. And gosh, you're still so predictable you didn't let me down!

Please don't think too badly of me. Daddy had it coming for years, and as for Jonny, well, he was always a liability, and he should have known going behind my back would only end badly for him! Let's call the others collateral damage; it's such a neat, catch-all phrase when you have loose ends to tidy away.

Finally, I wouldn't waste your time looking for me; we both know you don't like what you've found, and it won't get any better, so it's best this way.

All my love,

Heather (or perhaps that should be Rosemary now you know the truth.)

xx

P.S. I was hoping to sleep with you for old times' sake, but you didn't seem pleased to see me.

He read the letter again and was neither shocked nor surprised by the revelations. He felt disappointed to see their suspicions about the murders confirmed, but then felt conflicted at being disappointed!

Next, he wondered what money she was talking about, but then realised the answer was on the third sheet of paper, which was a bank statement from a Cayman Islands account in his name with £50,000 in it.

He sat motionless on the edge of the bed, pondering the

letter and bank statement, but he couldn't stop his attention gravitating to the photograph. It was almost as if he could conjure up Heather's presence through that photo, but the more he stared at it, the more the image blurred. After a couple of minutes, he sighed, wiped his eyes, and stood up.

'Pull yourself together, you soppy bugger,' he muttered as he walked back outside to his car.

A minute later he returned with a clear evidence pouch, scooped up the letter and bank statement, took one last sniff of the faint perfume, and then slipped them into the evidence pouch.

He stared at the photograph lying on the bed and wondered if he should keep it. It had no significance to the case, and only he would know it had been inside the envelope, but after a short deliberation, he knew what he had to do.

'I'm sorry, Heather,' he said out loud, 'but you've been in my head long enough. It's time to let you go.'

He picked up the photo and slipped it into the pouch before sealing it, dating it, and signing it. Satisfied it couldn't be opened without breaking the seal, he set it to one side with his keys, ready to take to work in the morning.

DID YOU ENJOY THIS BOOK?

You can make a big difference

I hope you have enjoyed reading this book. Reviews are one of the most powerful tools in any authors arsenal when it comes to getting attention for books, and I'm no different. A full page ad in a daily newspaper would be great, but that's just a tad beyond my budget!

But I do have something equally powerful (probably more so), and that's a growing bunch of loyal readers.

Honest reviews of my books help to bring them to the attention of new readers who will, hopefully, go on to join this growing band.

If you've enjoyed this book and you can spare a few minutes, why not leave a review? It doesn't have to be War and Peace, just a few words will do!

ABOUT THE AUTHOR

Having spent most of his life trying to be the person everyone else wanted him to be, P.F. (Peter) Ford was a late starter when it came to writing. Having tried many years ago (before the advent of self-published ebooks) and been turned down by every publisher he approached, it was a case of being told 'now will you accept you can't write and get back to work'.

But then a few years ago, having been unhappy for over 50 years of his life, Peter decided he had no intention of carrying on that way. Fast forward a few years and you find a man transformed. Having found a partner (now wife) who believes dreamers should be encouraged and not denied, he first wrote (under the name Peter Ford) and published some short reports and a couple of books about the life changing benefits of positive thinking.

Now, happily settled in Wales, and no longer constrained by the idea of having to keep everyone else happy, Peter is blissfully happy being himself, sharing his life with wife Mary and their three dogs, and living his dream writing fiction.

You can follow P.F. Ford here:
https://www.pfford.com

A Date With Death

Donald & Gamble Mysteries

In Need of Closure

At Cross Purposes

Dave Slater Novellas

An Innocent Victim

A Complete Fiasco

Printed in Dunstable, United Kingdom

70295512R00173